Preserving the Evidence

Preserving the Evidence

A Hart of Texas Murder Mystery

Kaz Delaney

TULE
PUBLISHING

Dedication

For my beautiful friend Anne Gleeson, for your support and life-long friendship, and for dragging me out of my cave and reminding me there is life outside my four walls.

Acknowledgements and Author's Note

Wouldn't you know? Rosie Hart has gotten herself into hot water again! And so our next adventure begins! Once more it's been a huge buzz to bring you another story in the *Hart of Texas Murder Mysteries* series. This time we're in the throes of a lazy, hazy Texan summer and Airlie Falls is buzzing!

You know though, the dichotomy of book creation is that writing is essentially a solitary occupation, and yet at times like this when we, as authors, sit down to thank those who might have assisted along the way, we discover there's a whole army in there with us.

Leading that line-up for me, as always, are the people who ultimately make me look good. These being my amazing team at Tule. Jane Porter you are dynamo. Thank you from my heart to my editor, Kelly Hunter, who along with Tule team members Nikki Babri, Meghan Farrell and Lee Hyat are the best support an author could have. Thank you again, Helena Newton for all you do to ease my worries and also to my whip-bearing web mistress, Paula Roe.

My everlasting gratitude, as always goes to all those who helped in myriad ways—sometimes by just listening, and many times so much more. Monique McDonell, Helen Katsinis, Heather Cleary, Michelle Douglas, Annie West,

Mary Brehe, Leanne McMahon, Julie Dunne and Rachel Mallaby. Without these people, this would have been a far bumpier ride.

Shannon Curtis – you deserve your own line. Thank you for so, so much. For your time, your love and support, your wisdom, your patience, your skill and your lunches. Most of all your friendship.

Thank you too, to all my lovely Facebook friends who help me with dilemmas, share the excitement with me and often share it even further. I'm very grateful. Especially to my sister-in-law, Marianne Redman, who makes me laugh with every single post.

Thank you, Anne Gleeson. I said it all in the dedication because well – that's what BFF's do!

To my family – my patient children and grandchildren, I love you all, and that's something that will never change.

And finally, to my ever patient husband, Rob, who deserves the highest award in the land for standing by me and supporting me through my entire career. I may not have the authority to ensure you get that award, but you have certainly earned the highest award in my heart.

And finally but most importantly thank YOU – my readers. Without you, authors have no purpose.

Chapter One

TEXAS SUMMERS TAKE no prisoners; they're full-on from day one. At only seven in the morning, a sheen of perspiration already dotted the brow of my houseguest, Midge Moylan, as she wandered up the wide front steps leading to the porch. Her concentration was taken completely by the newspaper she held in her hand, and her face alternately frowned and cleared as she perused each article or heading.

"Happy?" I looked up from the list I was making of jobs that had to be done that day. *From the Hart*—my dessert stand at the Airlie Falls Craft and Farmers' Market—had taken off like there was a hungry big cat after it, and I was having trouble keeping up supplies. So I was looking for things that would freeze ahead to help bulk out all the non-freezables I would create fresh for the stall.

Deep and shady, the porch was one of my favorite places in the farmhouse home I'd inherited—well, one of two houses—from Miss Alice Auchinschloss who'd passed away early last spring. Midge took one of the padded wicker chairs at the matching round table and reached for the coffeepot that sat between us. As owner and editor of the *Airlie Falls Gazette*, our weekly newspaper, Midge was always anxious on publication day, scouring the paper from beginning to end, searching for mistakes.

She shrugged, the cotton T-shirt she wore with her soft pj bottoms slipping off her shoulder as she did. "So far, so good," she answered somewhat absently. "I'm not sure how Clay's going to take this challenge to his mayoral position, though. It's looking like election time in Airlie Falls is going to be a very different affair this time around."

"Someone's running against Clay Fencott for mayor?"

She nodded, passing the paper over for me to read. "Frederick Clausen," I read out loud. "Representing a bright and prosperous future. Promising wealth and success for Airlie Falls by bringing it into the twenty first century." I looked across at her. "What does he even mean by that? And do we *want* to be brought into the twenty-first century? I mean, we're not exactly locked in the past, but I figured it was the old-fashioned values and slower pace that drew people here—and kept them here. I know it works for me."

"It works for most people around here, Rosie—but it was a big, full-page, paid ad and I'm not financially secure enough to turn it away. Besides, who would vote against Clay?"

A heaviness settled over me as I read. In a very short time I'd come to view Clay as a father figure, and I was obviously very fond of him. His son, Jonah, was my boyfriend. We'd only been together for a few months, but we both had hopes of this building into a *forever* thing—and so far, so good. My support for Clay ran deeper than as the father of the man I loved, though. He and his wife, Fiona—Jonah's mother, who'd become one of my closest friends—had welcomed me with open arms during one the scariest times of my life, when I'd been accused of murder. And I would always owe them for that.

"He's been mayor for twenty years!" I said unnecessarily. "The town loves him. *And* Fiona. Between them they've turned Airlie Falls into a thriving community."

"I know, and that was one of the reasons I gave myself for accepting the advert. As you just said, everybody loves them, so what could it hurt? Trust me, money was a motivator, but I had to satisfy my conscience as well. Besides—it's a free country and all... Bill of Rights. First amendment. Democracy. Et cetera, et cetera."

I really felt for her; running a small-town—*very* small-town—newspaper was always going to be fraught with conflicts like this. The community members became like family, and so to report against them was very tricky. She and I had bonded over murder of all things, and when her rented accommodation needed urgent repairs I'd offered one of my spare rooms out here at the farm, and that had stretched into months—and so far we were both enjoying the setup.

"You've done the right thing, Midge," I reassured her. "I

might not personally like the content, but it had to be included."

Her eyes opened wide as she listened, and as always I was struck by the likeness we shared. Both small boned and dark haired, blue eyed, and what others had described as *having delicate features*. Being rather clumsy myself, that description never sat well with me—but, ironically, I could see how it fit Midge.

As my mind jumped around, my anxiety over the mayor situation eased and I began to giggle. "Do you think this Clausen guy has any idea what he's up against? Clay is an institution. And obviously Clausen hasn't met Fiona. He'd be one tough dude if he could face her and stick around to take her on for round two."

Midge chuckled her agreement from her side of the table.

I adored Fiona, but she had a reputation. In her late fifties, Jonah's mom was tall and stately, drop dead gorgeous, had a heart as big as Texas, and was adored by everyone who encountered her. She also had an iron-strong will that wouldn't bend in the most violent of tornadoes. And that made her a fierce opponent.

"So, what chance do we give him? Clausen, I mean."

Midge tilted her head to one side as she thought it out. "If he gets ten votes, I'd be putting money on the fact that he paid for nine of them."

The clump of boots momentarily startled us both out of our discussion. We hadn't heard Jonah's truck because he'd parked down by the road and walked up the long drive, although I suspected our laughter might have drowned it out anyway.

His boots hit the steps heavily as he made his way to us, scraping out a chair and reaching for the coffeepot before he even said hello. Tiny, who'd been lying at my feet, whimpered and crawled on her belly to greet her old master. Poor baby. If ever a dog needed a pet psychiatrist for guilt issues—it was this one. Grinning, I watched her make such a fuss of seeing Jonah, reaching to him with her huge plate-sized paws—like she was making up for defecting to me when Jonah had loaned her as a guard dog several months before when a murderer had targeted me.

"Does this mean we're officially taking each other for granted?" I asked cheekily as he poured the piping coffee into a mug. "You haven't even kissed me."

He grinned and leaned across to right his wrong and lifted a salute to Midge. "No, Rosie darlin', it means I'm officially the owner of two new healthy calves whose mothers both had difficult births and I sat up all night keeping the vet company."

"Yay!" Shrugging, I added, "Oh, okay, so not yay about having been up all night, but yay on the two new babies being born safe and well."

His answering grin was tired. "So, what were you lovely ladies gigglin' about when I arrived?"

I think we both felt the burn of embarrassment. "Your

mom and dad facing off with Fred Clausen," Midge admitted.

"How is Clay?" I asked. "Coping?"

He took a long draw of coffee and leaned back in the chair. "Y'all know Dad," he began, "he's being philosophical about it all. Reckons that if it's time for someone else to take over, then so be it. He'll bow out gracefully and give the other guy—or gal—his full support."

Typical Clay. "And Fiona?"

Now he took more time answering. "She's fine for the most part. She'd be happy for Dad to pull back a bit. Being a dedicated mayor *and* the town dentist for all these years has taken its toll."

There was a *but* coming, and I was pretty sure I knew what it would be. I'd gotten to know Fiona very well over the past months. "But she's worried Clausen isn't the right person to take the reins?"

"Got it in one," he said, lifting his cup to drain the last of his coffee. Holding it out as I offered a refill, he added, "Mom makes it her business to know everybody, and it's thrown her off course to realize there's someone in town she doesn't know. That would be bad enough—but someone she doesn't know who wants to take over as mayor? That's got her in a spin."

"So, what's the deal there?" I asked. "Can anybody just turn up and set himself or herself up as a candidate? I thought there'd be more to it than that?"

Midge nodded. "There is. I checked him out before I put the ad through. To sit on Council the person has to be a resident and have lived here for a prescribed time. It appears Clausen owns some property about ten or fifteen miles out of town. He's owned it for years."

"Just *owned* it, or lived there?"

"Well," Midge answered slowly, "that's where it gets tricky. It's a substantial property and there are several dwellings on it, and the thing is, while I couldn't irrefutably prove he *has* lived out there, I also couldn't prove he *hasn't*. There are regular utility bills in his name and he gets mail delivered there." She shrugged. "Yet—"

"Yet," I finished for her, "I bet none of us has ever seen him in town, right? And you can't find anybody who has?"

She nodded, her mouth set in a line of grim acceptance.

"Quite frankly," I said, "I have to wonder why someone would want to become mayor of Airlie Falls. We're not exactly a hub of commerce or a potential jewel in any political crown."

"No argument from me. And y'all know my mom— these are the things that are botherin' her," Jonah said. "His mayoral duties aside, Dad takes things in his stride, believing the truth will surface and worrying when there's an obvious need to worry. Whereas Mom does the worrying first and doesn't give up on the worrying until she's satisfied everything's as it should be."

Nodding, I went back to the paper lying on the table.

Fred Clausen's photo stared back at me, and I tried to imagine if I'd vote for him if I didn't have all this extra knowledge or emotional attachments to Clay and Fiona. Of course it was an impossible task—we can never *unknow* what we know.

The photo showed him to be possibly Clay's age—late fifties, early sixties. He certainly didn't have Clay's looks or presence—both of which Jonah had inherited in spades—and he also didn't have that sense of calm authority and warmth. Also things that Jonah had inherited.

No, Fred Clausen—while certainly good looking—was more polished and worldly. Slick. Clay was a stunning man to look at, but he wore those looks with humor and humility. Clausen's features were tight; his mouth was curled into a smile that had a kind of cruel quality about it that some women went crazy for. Not me. Plastic—that was what I saw. And I just hoped his ethics and his dedication to the community he'd be representing were more substantial.

Jonah tilted his coffee cup toward Midge. "Guess you'll also be writing up that mysterious body story this week."

That jolted me out of my reverie. And when we both leaned forward, he grinned. He knew we were both hooked on mysteries. It was one of the reasons Midge had become a journalist. I had no such noble rationale for my curiosity; I was purely and simply a cozy-mystery junkie. "Body?" I managed to get out first. *"And you're just telling us now."*

"Mysterious body?*"* Midge added. "Where? Who?"

Tired as he was, the cheeky grin was firmly in place. "Well, I'd say that's why it's a mystery. They don't know."

I narrowed my eyes feigning beastly intent. "Okay, cowboy. Spill." My hand darted toward him. "Or I take the coffee."

Laughing, he settled back, petting Tiny, who now had her head lying in Jonah's lap. "You two and your mysteries. They sucker you in every time." He paused and drew breath. "Okay, though I've gotta warn you, I don't know much. Eric told me—"

"Eric?" I asked. Not wanting to miss a teeny bit of this story.

"Vet," they answered in unison.

"Janet Falkes's son," Midge expanded. "Sheriff Kinnead's nephew. His mama is the sheriff's sister; the receptionist cum dispatcher down at the sheriff's department."

I nodded. I'd met Janet several times, and I really liked her. "So?"

"So," Jonah continued, "Eric heard from his mom that one of the farmers found a body out on Redrock Road."

"No ID?"

He shook his head. "That's one of the puzzling things. On the surface it looks like he died an accidental death, and yet he had no identification."

"Drifter?" I offered.

Jonah tilted the brim of his ever-present Stetson to cut the angle of the sun that was becoming more determinedly cheerful. "Apparently he'd be a very well-dressed drifter if he was," he answered.

Midge put her mug down, and I could tell she was already writing the story in her head. "You said 'one of the puzzling things'? There was more?"

"Yeah, this is probably the zinger. According to the sheriff, the body had been moved."

"Why move a body if the death was accidental?" Midge asked, though I figured it was a self-directed question.

"Someone in the wrong place? Maybe he stopped to, you know." Jonah inserted a little whistle where words should have been.

I frowned. "To pee? Then what? Someone conked him on the head and he fell into a ravaging poison ivy and it killed him?"

"Or maybe he was moved to protect someone or something? Or deflect attention from a certain area?" Jonah shrugged. "Those are the big questions."

I nodded, my mind conjuring all the reasons he might have been moved. "And why it's a mystery. If he hadn't been moved, it would simply have been deemed accidental." We all sat and pondered that for a moment until I asked, "So, how *specifically* did he die? Was he old or young?"

He answered the last question first. "Young guy. Late twenties. As for cause of death, early reckoning is some kind of bite. Or maybe it's a flora thing. There's definitely some kind of allergy associated with his death—so your crazy guess about poison ivy wasn't that far off the mark. Apparently it looked like he was severely allergic and was bitten, consumed something, or encountered something that set it off."

"Gee," Midge muttered. "Next time you say you don't know much, remind me to grab a pen and ream of paper."

I was on a different track. "Tragic," I said softly. Somehow that allergy fact had made it all a bit too real. Sure, Midge and I were caught up in the salacious details of a mystery right here on our doorstep; however, we couldn't forget this was a real person, not a character in a book. A real person who'd died a sad and probably painful death. A young life cut short. Reading my mind, Jonah reached across to cover my hands with his. "At least he wasn't alone, I guess..." I whispered.

They both looked at me. "Well," I explained, "if he was well dressed but had no ID and there's no vehicle to identify and he was moved—he wasn't alone."

"Unless," Midge said slowly, "here's another possibility: He was moved after he died. Like, as if someone found him and moved him to a different place."

Tragedy aside, it was this part of any puzzle that drew me in. "But why take the ID?"

"To slow up the identification process?" she offered. "Why?"

Jonah set his cup back on the table. "You two are making this way too complicated."

I shrugged—I didn't think so. And one look at Midge

confirmed she was with me on that. We pumped Jonah for information for a few more minutes, finally satisfied he had nothing more to offer.

I stretched, feeling my T-shirt start to cling, even at this early stage of the day. "Gosh," I continued, "what a week for sleepy little Airlie Falls! The mysterious death of that poor young man, and a late election challenge!"

Jonah grinned. "It'll be standing room only in Merline's this week."

Yep, like most small towns, the hotbed of gossip was the beauty parlor. Merline herself admitted that any time a disaster or scandal hit Airlie Falls her business tripled, so she'd be geared for a big week. And in a weird way it one of those quirks I loved about this town.

The sound of a chair scraping brought me back to the present. Midge was going up to shower and change, and I decided Jonah needed something more than just coffee if he intended to get any work done. I flicked a kiss at his forehead, laughing when Tiny cocked her head for one as well. "I'll go get you some scrambled eggs and sausage. And no," I said as he started to rise, "I don't need help. You stay here in the sun and catch a few *Z*s while I get that food."

Tiny was on her feet instantly, ready to follow me. If there was one human word she recognized it was *food*.

For once, though, Jonah stayed where he was. He didn't always comply when I issued orders, but I could see his exhaustion was really catching up. His building company always had a lot of projects he had to juggle, and on top of that, lately, all his spare time had been spent helping me get this house renovated and the overgrown yards into some kind of working order.

I was thrilled by my new vegetable gardens and the work we'd put in to breathe new life into the fruit orchards—to say nothing of my simply stunning state-of-the-art kitchen and luxurious bathrooms.

The calves that had kept him awake last night were part of his hobby farm and had nothing to do with me, but suddenly I felt the weight of guilt that he hadn't had much downtime lately. I'd have to make sure he got more of that.

PROMISING TO CALL it quits early, Jonah left and I cleaned up, and after ensuring Tiny had enough water and food, I made my way to Brenda Kinnead's place, on a big parcel of land on the edge of town. Not acreage, just enough space for a small orchard, trained berry vines, and thriving vegetable gardens. Most of which she used for the produce for her market stall. Her husband was Frank Kinnead, the sheriff who had his office right here in Airlie Falls. We'd gotten to know each other when he'd suspected me of murder earlier in the year.

At the time, Brenda had become quite famous for her jams and preserves, and demand was high but all the work was taking its toll, and when I'd been cleared of the murder, I offered to help her out.

However, as I traveled to help Brenda that morning, my mind wasn't solely on the wonders we might create. Electoral placards were dotted around town and as yet-another smiling image of Clay whizzed by my side window I felt an arrow of concern spear through me. All the times in the past weeks that I'd driven past all the campaign signs reminding people to vote for Clay, I'd barely registered them. Clay was mayor, and he would stay mayor. Who could do a better job? No other candidates had thrown their hats into the ring; it was, as apparently it had been for years, a one-horse race.

Until now.

Less than a week until the election and someone had joined the race. It was ludicrous, really. Did this guy actually expect to win? The election was timed to coincide with the market weekend because farm and ranch folk would be in town. What could you do in a week to change the thinking of a whole town?

My thoughts slowed. What could you do, indeed? Especially with a dead body to distract and confuse the issue.

I wasn't sure how reflecting on the election challenge had so smoothly taken me back to the conversation about the mysterious body, but, barely noticing the shift, it was what now took center stage.

My own words at the time drifted back. I'd marveled at the juxtaposition of two random—yet significant—events in our peaceful little town. I'd even made a joke about it, but now, in the quiet of the car and with more clarity, it suddenly seemed that maybe the two incidents weren't as random as I'd first imagined.

Adding the puzzling facts surrounding the discovery of the body triggered an uncomfortably familiar churning in my stomach. I hoped I was having a drama queen moment.

Because surely the other scenario flitting around in my head couldn't be true, could it? The scenario that was whispering crazy suggestions. Like, that maybe there was nothing random about the discovery of the body, that the timing was deliberate.

And to consider that meant there was nothing accidental about that man's death…

Chapter Two

B RENDA GREETED ME with a hug, and despite my worries I was already smiling, ready to be thrilled at how much healthier she looked than she had a few months back. Lately, I'd noticed the strain was gone from her face and she wore her grandmotherly extra pounds with pride. But today, my smile died when I took in her high color and the grim set of her mouth.

"Rosie Hart. Thank you for coming, darlin'. If ever I needed cheering up, it's today."

I guided her to a chair. "Miz Brenda! What's wrong? Are you unwell? Should I call the doctor? Call Frank?" I paused. "Are you upset about that body? I know it's shocking, but…"

Setting aside the television remote she waved me away. "It's nothing like that. I'm not sick, and it's not that body they've found that's upsettin' me. That's Frank's worry, not mine. No, this is just plain temper." My confusion grew until she handed me the piece of paper that had been sitting on the table before her. "This was poked into our mailbox sometime last night. Apparently they're all over town."

Had we gotten one? I hadn't checked. Frowning I read the single page, my blood running colder with each word. Closing my eyes proved to be a futile attempt as I tried to block out the thoughts racing through my head. Thoughts that were eerily aligned with those I'd had in the car coming over here. "Oh, Brenda… I hope I'm wrong, but I've got a gut-deep feeling this isn't going to end well."

When I again opened them she was watching me, her gaze solemn. "I hope you're wrong, Rosie, however, I fear you're not."

Frustration burned. "How can Clausen even say these things? Isn't this libel?"

Her sigh filled the room. "Not according to Hank Henderson. I called him first thing. He'd gotten one as well, and he was as hot under the collar as I am. He's gone over it carefully, but because it doesn't mention Clay by name, it's impossible to prove that all this nonsense is actually about Clay."

"Well, Hank's the lawyer and obviously I'm not," I said as I slowly reread the page, "but as I go back over it, even I can see he's right. It's very general—and yet it's not. The questions it poses have a nasty edge, although it could be argued they're just hypothesizing." I squinted and then picked out an example. "Like, *What if you had a mayor who didn't let anyone, including close relatives, involve themselves where they have no right?* And *What if you had a mayor who didn't have conflicting business interests in town that might tempt his or her decisions against what's best for the town?"*

I was so livid at this point I honestly felt I'd explode. This was plain cruel and so, so wrong. "Obviously the first example I read refers to Fiona," I continued, barely able to get words through my clenched teeth. "And the second refers to Clay's dental practice and their B&B. Both of which also benefit the community. Sure, the B&B is their business, but they charge the minimum and the focus has always been promoting the community. Like, offering out-of-towners a place to stay when they come for the markets!"

Brenda's color wasn't abating. "I know! And I can tell you this: Frederick Clausen better hope he never runs into me around town, or I'll be giving him a piece of my mind! And I won't hold back!"

I agreed heartily. "Does this man even have a clue how hard that couple works for this town? They give and give! Their home is always open, they organize help for whoever needs it, they volunteer for everything—all they do is work for the people of Airlie Falls."

"You're preachin' to the choir, honey," Brenda interrupted. "Don't forget I've grown up with Clay and Fiona. And everything you're saying is correct. We've never had it so good since Clay took over, and Fiona directed the markets to the success they are today. We've got a good strong community and mostly due to Clay and Fiona—they got us moving in the right direction."

Her words died away as the screen door banged to a close

and Sheriff Frank Kinnead stomped in through the mud-room, his face lined and his eyes shadowed. He kissed his wife and nodded to me as he slung his hat on the hook just inside the door. Indicating the offending advertisement I was still holding, he said, "I take it you've read that? Bad business. Just plain bad business."

Brenda drummed her fingers on the wooden surface of the scrubbed kitchen table. "It's plain disgusting is what it is."

"Can't you do something?" I asked, desperation tingeing my words.

He shrugged. "What do you want me to do, Rosie? There's no crime in advertising—unless it's false advertising. I can't arrest a man for asking a whole lot of questions—no matter how much I want to," he ended on a mutter.

"Have you seen Clay?" I asked.

"No, but I swear I've seen or spoken to every other resident of Airlie Falls. There was a lineup at the station. People are outraged and baying for blood—and there's nothing I can do because there's been no crime committed. Now, if upsetting people was a crime, I'd have him dead to rights—but it isn't." He sighed. "I just swung by for a snack and to check on how Brenda here was coping with the news. And I may as well tell y'all, there's a town meeting tonight. Not sure what good it will do, but it's been called by *concerned citizens*. Seven o'clock in the church hall."

I nodded. "Thanks. I'll be there."

"And nothing will stop me, either," Brenda said, rising from her chair to give her husband a hug. He responded with a kiss to the top of her head before turning to raid the fridge.

Watching his back, I also wanted to quiz him on the discovery of the body, but I figured he looked stressed enough and my questions might not go down well. Just as well because his food foray was brief, and waving a chicken leg, he made his goodbyes.

Concern wreathed Brenda's face; it couldn't be easy watching your husband carry the troubles of a town on his shoulders. When he returned for one last kiss, she pushed that worry away, instead offering a beaming smile that I knew must be costing her deeply. "Hey, honey," she said softly, "at least one thing went right today. There's nothing wrong with our TV; just needed reprogramming. Got it done this morning."

His face lit up. "Yeah? This morning? Now, who do we know who's smart enough to do that?" he joked.

"You'd be surprised," she answered. "I surely was. And all it cost was a bottle or two of preserves."

Frank Kinnead left the building with a smile and a jauntier step than when he'd arrived.

"He loves his television," Brenda explained, eyes on the closed kitchen door as though she could still see him making his way to his truck. "Not that he gets a lot of free time, but when he does, it's TV and gardening that help him balance all that police stuff. We don't know a lot about these new-fangled electronics, and we thought the TV had up and died. Thankfully that wasn't so."

She fell silent and her eyes pooled with unshed tears that she rapidly swiped away.

Taking that as a cue to move along, I pasted on a smile, patted her on the back and said, "Okay, Miz Brenda, this isn't getting our work done. So, what's on today?"

She sighed, only the merest thickness in her voice when she said, "Probably the last of the blackberries. Frank said the bushes are almost picked over, but he still got about four gallons over the last couple of days."

My heart did a happy dance. Despite everything happening, excitement still managed to find a way in. It had been a dream of mine since teenage years to be able to grow food and then create from that harvest. Working with Brenda had been a joy and a brilliant education. "Jam?"

She nodded. "Just plain blackberry this time. We've got enough preserves and enough blackberry-and-apple jam and also spiced blackberry-and-apple jam, so I'm thinking also of maybe a brandy blackberry nip. I've got the bottles all ready. They'll make great holiday gifts. And they should be ready in perfect time for our fall and Christmas markets. You're so good at making the packaging pop, Rosie, and I can't wait to see what you'd do to tizz them up for the holiday gift-buyers!"

I grinned. What a fun challenge.

"It's my grandmother's recipe," she continued with a cheeky smile, and as I watched her, I saw the tension melting away. It wouldn't work for everyone, but for people like Brenda and me, creating in the kitchen was a surefire way to kill pent-up anxiety. Her cheeks glowed pink and her eyes sparkled like those of a mischievous child. "I have to admit I like a little nip of that nip in the colder months. Warms me right to my toes!"

We both laughed. Okay, now I couldn't wait to taste it myself, especially if it made me glow as Brenda just had.

"And…it depends on how many berries we have, but I have another idea." The sparkle was still in her eyes. I'd been encouraging her to experiment a bit, and each week now, she was adding to her selection, and it was really working. "I'd like to try a sauce recipe I found. It's a blackberry-and-port sauce, and it's for serving with meat. I believe it's delicious with pork, but I think it would be amazing with any hot meat. Even if we just make a couple of experimental bottles today…"

I clapped my hands. "Sounds delicious. And how good would it be with the Christmas ham? Oh—and Thanksgiving turkey!"

Brenda's eyes widened. "Of course! And that means it would be great with just plain old chicken!"

Laughing, I set to work, washing berries and snipping stems while Brenda prepared the pans and gathered ingredients. Like mine, her kitchen was big. Unlike mine, Brenda's was cluttered with jam and preserve-making paraphernalia—and in need of a makeover. Yet, despite the lines of jars and lids, the piles of labels, the pots, pans, and slotted spoons, the place was spotless. Though I didn't envy the job she had each day to keep it that way. Constantly moving all this stuff must be a nightmare.

Workwise, it wasn't a big day, and the last task was the sauce and we both attacked that, dicing the green onions and mincing the fresh thyme leaves. By the time we were finished, the kitchen smelled heavenly and my mouth was watering. We'd had a quick sandwich earlier, and watching Brenda lower herself heavily onto a kitchen chair, I felt justified that we'd earned a sweet treat. I unpacked my basket, leaving the peach pie intact for Brenda and Frank to share, and sliced the raspberry-jam-and-meringue-topped chocolate cake.

Moments later, Brenda's groan was one of pure delight. "You know, darlin', even if I didn't need help, I think I'd pretend to need you just so I got to experience your sweet treats. This is pure heaven."

I smiled my thanks. "Delvene has asked me to provide some of my desserts for the Bluebonnet Café. Do you think this one would go down well?"

Reaching for another slice, she nodded vigorously. "Oh boy! I can see that girl's profits soarin'!"

I was still smiling as I headed out to my car. We always traded product, and as I packed the jars and bottles into a box in the trunk, my mind was already buzzing with what I could create. Individual blackberry pies, muffins with cream cheese, and cobbler cupcakes, and then some desserts based on that jam-and-meringue idea. That was just the beginning. I'd edit and add later.

MIDGE HITCHED A ride to the town meeting with Jonah and me. She'd learned nothing new about the discovered body. Still no identification and still no firm theories on where he'd come from or what he was doing out there, almost in the middle of nowhere. But right then, it was this election business we were focused on, and all three of us were on edge. For Midge, this was business; she'd have to report everything that happened. For Jonah and me, it was personal.

It seemed everybody in town who could be here was present, and not surprisingly Jonah and I became separated as different people paused to catch up or greet us.

After one encounter I remembered my phone was on and called that I'd catch up inside after shutting it down for the meeting. The others moved forward on a wave. It was weird to be caught in such a crowd one moment and completely alone the next.

However, if I hadn't been alone I probably would have missed the strange activity on the far side of the churchyard.

A woman in a plain-styled print dress seemed to be being hustled into a large car against her will. I stepped closer, ready to intervene, to help—close enough to see the despair on the woman's face. It was a face free of makeup, and her hair was pulled back severely—and she was staring straight at me.

Confused I hurried toward the scene. Was this woman seeking my help? Did she want me to do something?

I was more than halfway to them when another woman, one who was well dressed and made up, caught the direction of the other's gaze and turned to me. She held up a hand to stop me coming closer. "Please—this is a family matter. We don't need assistance and would appreciate privacy."

Still confused I faltered. The well-dressed woman seemed so rational… So rational I felt I should honor her request. And yet? I tried to peer into the car, but the door was now closed and the smoky windows prevented me from seeing clearly.

What to do? The woman would call out if she really needed help, wouldn't she? The front car doors were still open. I'd hear her pleas. Or screams.

Despite straining to hear even the slightest noise—which didn't come—and considering I was often in trouble for poking my nose where it wasn't wanted, I figured I should clamp down my imagination and just let it go.

Although I'd still be watching out for any other strange behavior that might support my concerns.

Behind me the chatter indicated more people arriving for the meeting, and a prick of guilt pushed at me to get inside. My first duty tonight was to support Clay and Fiona, and that was where I should be. But I wouldn't forget this…

Inside I waved to Brenda and my friends, the Fab Four, from the retirement village. The latter waved me over, their faces animated and sparkling despite their combined age of close to three hundred and sixty years.

"Did you hear about the body?" Lori Sue—their self-appointed leader and Jonah's great-aunt—whispered, though I'm sure any passing astronauts probably heard her in space. "We thought of you immediately!"

The girls had helped me fill in the blanks during the last murders, and it had definitely added a spring to their step to have something to focus on besides what was for lunch each day.

"We heard it was drugs," E.T., aka Ethel Therese, chirped.

Betsy, who reminded me of Betty White, put in her bit. "I think it's moonshine! My daddy ran moonshine, and let me tell you there were a lot of strange disappearances out in the wilderness in those days!" she added with a wink.

Martha groaned. "Moonshine? Oh for Pete's sake, Betsy! This is the twenty-first century! Alcohol's been legal for at least ten years!"

They were always like this, and as always I stifled a smile. They were the best entertainment. After assuring them I'd pass on anything I discovered, I hugged each and made my way down to Jonah, who waved to his aunt Lori Sue before guiding me to our seats.

Sheriff Frank Kinnead and his deputy, Bobby Don McAuley, both in crisp tan uniforms, were watching people arrive, and their grim expressions indicated they were on duty as well as being interested members of the community.

Jonah's parents, Clay and Fiona, sat up near the front, and we made our way toward them, determinedly showing our support. They greeted us warmly as usual, even though I could see the strain on both their faces. The advertising leaflet had been an insult, and of course it was rubbish, but it had caused some cracks to form.

"What if others in town feel like that?" Fiona whispered. "Have they resented the way we've handled things?"

"Of course not!" I reassured her. "This is an outsider's view."

Fiona's usual composure wasn't so evident tonight, and I squeezed her hand as I watched the hall fill up. I expected all the faces I'd gotten to know, and one by one they filed in. Many stopped to pat Clay on the back or hug Fiona. But as the crowd swelled, I was noticing more and more strangers. At least half those assembled were people I'd never seen, and I could tell by the shock on Fiona and Clay's faces that they were thinking the same thing. Where had these people come from?

A group of about ten women walked in together, and I

noticed them not just for their numbers but for their simple style. Interestingly I recognized the outfits as the same as that of the woman being—perhaps—forced into the vehicle earlier.

I studied them more closely. The dresses were clean but serviceable rather than stylish, all cotton and loose fitting. In truth they looked cool in a room overheated by the number of bodies squeezing into it. The fans above were practically useless against this much body heat, but these women with their lack of makeup and simple hairstyles looked a lot cooler than I felt. The swirly patterned pencil skirt, black camisole top, and platform sandals I'd chosen had felt smart and suited to the weather when I'd dressed an hour or so ago. Looking at the group, though, I suddenly felt hot and imagined my clothes clinging to me.

Yet the more I stared, the more the image they were supposedly creating seemed wrong. Despite their clothing and simple style, there was a worldliness about them—and it wasn't just due to their bored expressions. I squeezed Jonah's arm. "Do you know those ladies?"

He looked across, raising an eyebrow before shaking his head. "No. No idea who they are."

I continued to stare at them. They fascinated me.

Especially the one who hadn't made it to the meeting. Why wasn't she allowed to attend? Was she, like, the Cinderella of the group? The others didn't seem stressed at all, just bored. They lolled in the seats; they didn't make any effort to chat—not even among themselves.

The only energy I saw came when a photographer stepped up to snap some shots. Interestingly some preened for the camera and some cringed away from it. From the latter faction came enough eye rolls to make an eighth grade class look like amateurs. And that was saying something. The more I studied them, the more confused I became.

My problem was that I was a mystery story addict and I saw mystery everywhere. Jonah often good-naturedly pointed out that I saw it mostly where it didn't exist. The barista in Dallas had had lint in his eye. He hadn't been trying to signal me that there was a gunman under the counter with him. That had been slightly embarrassing.

So was the partial note I'd discovered that I was convinced was part of a kidnap ransom. Of course it was Merline's seven-year-old granddaughter's note offering a reward for information on her missing cat, Chatty. The clients at Merline's beauty parlor had been entertained by that story for several weeks. Only their good natures and sense of fun had saved me from feeling like a complete fool.

Still, this time I was sure there was something…

In deference to Clay, though, I forced my mind to what was being said. Many locals were complaining about the leaflet, but just as many of the others were countering with their feelings of being manipulated by Fiona and Clay, asserting a feeling of distrust in their decision-making. They were all but accused of benefiting from the position of mayor. A position no one had wanted when Clay had taken over all those years ago.

I'd struggled to see Fred Clausen, until he stood. He wasn't as tall as I'd expected, and as much as I didn't want to admit it, his real-life smile held a boyish charm not evident in his photo—and that would draw people to him.

He introduced himself, and in a voice as smooth as honey, he apologized for causing so much distress. "I'm a citizen of this beautiful town—just like y'all—and I just want to see people get a fair chance. Everybody, not just a select few. I want *everybody* to benefit."

There followed a rumble of discussion until Midge's clear voice rang out. Pen poised she asked, "Can you give an example of how you think some have benefited over others?"

I frowned at this man being allowed more voice, even though I got that she was just doing her job.

"Well," Clausen began, "I believe that the Johnsons out on Redrock Road got a new roof on their barn last winter. Is that right?"

There were shrugs and nods. I'd been caring for Miss Alice at that time, but I hadn't actually been part of the community, so I didn't know.

Others did. "That's because it blew off during that big storm just after the holidays. Jack and Ellie had had a bad run for a few years, and we wanted to make sure it was solid for them and ready to store their crops. No law against it," Hank Henderson explained firmly.

Clausen nodded sympathetically. "That's mighty fine. But what about the Potters and Henry Obedan? They both suffered similar tragedies, and no one came to help them. Seems to me unless you go to the right church or support the right politician you don't get a look-in."

"What?" Fiona was on her feet, eyes blazing. "Who are these people? I don't even know them! They'd have gotten help if we'd known them."

Hank and Clay ushered her back to her place.

Meanwhile, Clausen was smiling—like the cat who'd caught the canary. "Now, that's a mighty shame, Miz Fiona. As the first lady and someone who seems to be in charge of who gets help around here, it's a sad thing when you don't even know your neighbors."

"But…"

Clay gently shushed her, and she took heed despite the fact that it was killing her not to argue. I figured he felt they were playing into Clausen's hands to argue with him.

But then he surprised me by standing and addressing Clausen. "Sir, this is simply a meeting for people to air their views. I don't think getting personal is going to help matters. As a council, we have always taken our responsibility very seriously, and if there are people in need that we've neglected, then we apologize and will set about rectifying that immediately. Just remember, though, this help we give is volunteered help. People around here don't have unlimited wealth."

Clausen again nodded. "Yes, well, speaking of that, I'd like to raise the subject of the funds used for these projects. I believe it comes from a fee Miz Fiona imposes on the stallholders. Ten percent of all profits, is it?" He didn't wait for confirmation. "These are successful markets—that must add up to a pretty penny. Now, what I want to know is where that money goes and how much is left."

Fiona was just about foaming at the mouth. To me she whispered, "It's not imposed. It's voluntary so that those who've had a poor sales day don't suffer any more than need be. It pays insurances and fees. And the rest is put aside to help people—like the Johnsons! That's where we get the money to help them!"

Clay was explaining almost that same thing, but Clausen was talking over him. "Mister Mayor, that's all fine and good. However, I believe a request was made to Council some three months ago, asking for those figures to be discussed and also a complete record of where every cent has been spent. To my knowledge those figures were never made public and we are none the wiser as to where that money has gone. This is what I mean, sir, about fully representing the community of Airlie Falls."

Clay's voice dropped to a tone I'd never heard from him before. Low and menacing. "Are you, sir, accusing my wife of embezzlement? Because if you are, I will personally tear you—"

Clausen's roar cut off Clay's words. "Ladies and gentlemen! Did you hear? Is this what you want? A mayor whose only method of negotiation is to resort to violence? He just threatened to kill me! To tear me apart! For what? So his wife can cover up her own sins? Where is the money, ladies and gentlemen? Where is the money?"

Clay was quick, but Jonah was quicker. He and Hank, with help from Deputy Bobby Don, managed to hold him, while Frank ordered Clausen and his crew out of the building.

The noise around us was deafening. Arguments abounded; voices rose both in anger and wonder. It was crazy, and my eyes darted from the crowds to those I considered *my people*—Fiona and Clay and Jonah.

Four people I didn't recognize had Hank Henderson cornered, and one was pointing a finger at him. Beside him, Clay was trying to explain something to another exasperated young woman I didn't recognize. But through all that mayhem, two images stood clear in my mind, creating two searing memories.

The first was Fiona Fencott's face. Fallen. Crushed. My heart was breaking along with hers. This was so unfair. And so wrong. Silent tears began to roll down her face, and she seemed helpless to catch them. I had never seen anybody so devastated.

Unless it was the woman I'd seen earlier.

She was the second.

Had I imagined that plea for help? Had she been begging me?

And what could I do about it even if she had?

Chapter Three

MIDNIGHT CAME AND went, and despite the amount of coffee consumed, I could barely keep my eyes open. I was even more amazed that Jonah was still conscious given his ordeal the night before.

Midge had gotten a ride back to the farm. She was anxious to do more research on Clausen for next week's story. And, of course, there was the mysterious body story to cover. I think for once she wished the *Gazette* was more than a weekly. Over the course of the week, she could be spending a whole lot of time researching things that might be settled and cleared away by the time she went to press.

When the meeting had finally broken up, a small band of us had wandered down to the B&B, and we were all gathered in Fiona's amazing kitchen around the table in the glassed-in nook. Hank, Clay and Fiona, and the Kinneads—as well as Jonah and myself. The same arguments were still being rehashed, though Fiona had requested restraint and respect for their one guest, a single woman who was booked in for a week.

My thoughts had been torn between what was happening

here at the table and the woman from the meeting. Since I could do nothing about the latter and Fiona and Clay were my chief concerns, I knew I was going to have to put her out of my mind. At least in the short term.

"Yes, we received that request for the figures, but no one ever came forward at a meeting to ask for a copy," Clay explained yet again. "For the past three months only the regular committee members were present, and they all waved away the paperwork each time I brought it up. These are hardworking people—they trusted Fiona and wanted to get the meetings over and get back to their families and chores."

Hank nodded. "I have to agree with that. I dunno who requested the paperwork, but no one came forward to claim it or check it over. Strange…"

Fiona yawned for the fifth time, and it was contagious. In turn, we each yawned. "Tomorrow I'll have the updated figures printed up, and I'll get you and Clay copies, Hank," she managed between gulps of air.

The lawyer nodded and then stood to retrieve the big white Stetson, now yellowed by the sun, that all the men in town and beyond seemed to wear.

It was a signal that we were all excused, and I was so tempted to accept Fiona's offer of a bed there instead of traipsing out to the farmhouse. Jonah had to check on his babies, though, and as his farm was out past mine and he had to drive right by, I chose to go back home.

As we drove, I was once more reminded of my very first

assessment of Airlie Falls. In many ways the tiny town resembled an English village with its town green in the center surrounded by stores and businesses, mostly all built in the late nineteenth to early twentieth centuries. The English would call it quaint, and while the Texan heat had taken its toll and some of the foliage and grass had taken on a gray, brown, and yellow aura, and it was unmistakably Texas, it had a similar appeal.

Away from the lights of the town, dim though they were, it was very dark, lit only by the vast sky and a million glittering stars. Headlights were a necessity, but I wished we could just navigate by the light of the sky. My exhausted brain was ruminating on this foolhardy scenario when suddenly Jonah hit the brakes, his wheels screeching to a stop and expletives slipping off his tongue.

In that same instant I was wide awake. "What's wrong? What is it? Animal? Something escaped from a farmyard?" That was a common experience in these parts. Goats, cows, bulls…

He shook his head, his face glowing an eerie blue color in the reflection of the dashboard lights. "I don't know." And then he was out of the car.

I followed suit, my eyes everywhere, searching for something—anything. "What are we looking for?" I asked again.

Jonah stood staring all around him. The air had lost its biting heat, and a slight chill flirted with my arms and any other bare skin it could touch. I watched him turn a full, slow, lazy circle, his eyes peering into the gloom around us. "I don't know. Something just ran out in front of me. It was white—and flowing." He rubbed his eyes. "I must be going crazy; I thought it was a woman."

He stepped closer to the wild grasses and brambles lining the road and peered even more intently. "I just can't see where she could have gone, though." He tramped at the grasses, flattening some as he stomped. I followed, swiping at the grass caught in the headlights, my fingers circling around something soft and dry that I absently picked up. But there was nothing else there. No one there.

I reached over to touch his arm. Personally I thought his mind was so tired that he'd simply imagined seeing something. My words were gentler. "Honey, I think you're too exhausted to search right now. So much has happened in the past twenty-four hours for you. Could it have simply been some kind of animal? A big bird?"

He shrugged. "I suppose anything is possible. And I admit I'm about as wiped out as I can get." He slung an arm over my shoulder and walked me around to the passenger side of the truck.

Once settled, we continued, but I insisted that he spend the remaining hours until daylight at my farm. It was the only way I could guarantee he'd actually be safe.

WHEN I WOKE in the morning, he'd already left, and I understood. The calves needed checking and he was facing another big day. I admired his fortitude; I was feeling the lack of sleep as I dragged myself into the shower. But with the water's reviving magic came a montage of images from the evening before.

Now that I was removed from the shock of the veiled accusations, Fred Clausen's performance seemed to be exactly that: a performance. A deliberately orchestrated, overdramatized act. He'd deliberately goaded Clay, knowing Clay would never stand for untruths uttered about Fiona. Drying myself on my outsize fluffy towels brought no contentment this morning; I was barely aware of what I was doing. Was this politics at work? And really, was this kind of dirty play really necessary in a sweet little town like Airlie Falls? I couldn't see those tactics working here. But then again last night, I'd seen confusion on faces where I'd never have expected to see anything except solid support.

So what was Clausen's agenda? Why was it really so important for him to become mayor?

Back in the bedroom, I dressed in jeans and a scooped neck, sleeveless shell top. The lemon color tricked me into thinking it looked cool—a foil against the heat. It took only minutes to make the bed and tidy the room, but I paused as I brushed a small piece of something off the nightstand and into my open palm. I was just wondering where it had come from when it suddenly hit me. Last night. When Jonah had feared he'd almost struck a woman…

My bedroom was light and airy; still I walked to the window to ensure I could see clearly. It was a piece of cloth. Only about two inches at the longest point of its jagged shape, and it was strangely familiar. It was a floral print—crisp blue on a white background. For a moment I thought it was from some cushions I had downstairs, but again, suddenly enlightenment came. And with it a little pang of concern. The dresses on the women last night… The fabric all their outfits were made from, including the woman outside the hall who'd looked anguished.

If this wasn't the same it was awfully similar, and if you added the fact that Jonah had thought he'd seen a woman…

That suddenly begged a lot of questions. Who was the woman? I had a strong feeling she was connected to Clausen. So, how? I grabbed the material scrap and trotted downstairs, wondering if Midge was still home, but a note explained she'd left early for a day trip to the city. I assumed it concerned Fred Clausen, although in truth, it could have been anything. Still, I'd be waiting for her to get back so we could pool our information.

Coffee and a blackberry muffin done, I considered the day ahead. The plan had been to attack parts of the garden that were so far only partially prepared for further planting. And even at just after eight, it was already later than I'd planned to begin. But as the sun rose higher, the events of the evening before had me changing plans.

My thoughts had been with Fiona and Clay all morning so it was no surprise that was where they centered again. And on Airlie Falls itself. In my short time here I'd learned a lot about the ways of the people, and I could sum it up in one word: caring. The Fencotts would be inundated with people showing their concern and offering help. So, I headed to the kitchen and my supplies cupboard.

Two ovens make a huge difference; still it was a couple of hours, plus some, before the six dozen cookies in three varieties and chocolate-caramel drizzle cake were cooled and ready to be transported.

I WASN'T SURPRISED to see the county sheriff's logo emblazoned on the side of the truck parked out front, nor Brenda's smaller truck; after all, the couples were old friends, but I was shocked by the reason.

Inside, I expected people would have already gathered, however, only Brenda Kinnead greeted me. "You're so sweet to think to bring refreshments, Rosie, but we're asking people to allow Fiona and Clay some time to sort some issues. Frank called, and I came over to help usher folks away for a while."

Baskets and box in hand, I could only stare.

"Oh, she won't mean you, darlin'. I meant other visitors," she explained. "And just until Frank's finished doing whatever he does."

Finding my voice didn't mean it came out well. "W-…
why? Fiona never turns anybody away. What's going on?"

Before she answered, Jonah tramped in through the
door, looking rushed and worried. "What's going on? I got a
call from Mom."

Footsteps from farther back in the house had us all turning to the little procession coming toward us. Clay was gray
under his usual tan and Fiona was so pale she was almost
ghostly. Heavy, dark circles shadowed her eyes, and her usual
fashionably messy up-do was just plain disheveled. Long
strands hung limply around her face; others tangled and
stood out at odd angles, like she'd been dragging at it, which
I assumed she had.

My gasp filled the room and I rushed to her. "Fiona?"

She folded me into a hug, which was the wrong way
around. I should have been hugging her, but our height
difference always made that more awkward. Jonah had
followed me and looked enquiringly at his father who was
flanked now by Sheriff Frank Kinnead and lawyer Hank
Henderson. Deputy Bobby Don McAuley brought up the
rear.

Clay swallowed. "It's the funds from the markets.
They're gone."

Jonah frowned. "What do you mean *gone*? All used up on
projects? That kind of gone?"

"No, just plain gone. Not there. There isn't even an account."

None of this made sense.

Clay gently guided Fiona into the gracious living room and lowered her into a chair. When the front door opened, I moved into the hall to greet the visitor and encountered an elegant, very well-dressed stranger. She was in her forties, I'd guess, and very well put together. Expensive clothes and enhanced red hair. Her alabaster skin glowed from the heat, although she looked neither flustered nor heat affected. In fact, her makeup was flawless.

"Can I help you?" I asked.

She looked up, startled. "Oh, no, dear. I'm fine." She held out her hand, and when I took it, her grip was as strong as that of any man I'd ever met. "Simone Grant. I'm a guest here." Noting the crowd in the adjoining room she raised an eyebrow. "Oh, am I interrupting something private?"

I shook my head, trying to be gracious to Fiona's paying guest. "Oh, please forgive me. I'm Rosie Hart. And," I said, tilting my head to the lounge, "this is just a family issue we're ironing out. Fiona would hate it if you were inconvenienced, so please go on through."

She nodded and smiled, but as she made her way up to the next floor, I had the distinct impression she was listening to what was going on below her. Her steps were slow and measured, and her head was tilted slightly in our direction.

I wondered who she was and what her connection to Airlie Falls could be—and what would keep her here for a week?

When it was appropriate, I'd endeavor to find out.

There were way too many strangers in Airlie Falls at the moment.

Walking back into the lounge and spotting Fiona perched on the edge of one of her sofa chairs rocked me all over again. It frightened me to see how shaken she was. All the energy seemed to have been sucked out of her; her movements robotic and her stare almost trance-like.

Everyone had followed, taking seats on the various sofas and chairs all arranged to offer a sense of welcome. Of comfort and security. But this morning, even this ambient beauty, the gentle greens and blues, the fresh white, and pops of yellow failed to have an effect. Fiona's pain trumped it all.

Fiona was always the take-charge one. She would have been bustling about here normally, being the voice of reason and ordering people into action. And instinctively, I knew her current reaction wasn't due to this being about her; she'd faced adversity before and still taken charge. No, this was because she must've felt she'd let others down. That was the only thing that would fell her. That other people would be harmed or hurt by this.

Jonah waited until I chose a chair and then propped himself on its arm, one hand resting warmly on the back of my neck. He looked over at his dad. "I'm lost. You're sayin' the money's not there and the account is closed. Right?"

Clay sighed, his eyes weary as he looked back at his son. Frank and Bobby Don had elected to stand, but now the sheriff was shuffling from one foot to the other. His wife glared, and he settled. Still, Clay couldn't seem to find the words so Hank jumped in.

"No, Jonah. Not closed. Let me start at the beginning. Fiona called me to come over and get these figures and paperwork for the market stalls. The charity fund. After last night she wanted no shadows or doubts concerning the money. But"—he cleared his throat—"when I got here and we went into the office, the ledger wasn't there."

"Wait, I thought Mom had an online account for that money. You'd get a copy there," Jonah inserted.

Hank shrugged. "Fiona keeps double records. We talked it over many years ago, and it was a precaution. Once a year she has an accountant—and myself—check it over to see that it's all on the up-and-up."

"So…?" Jonah prompted.

"Well, when we went online, there's no record of the account. It's been wiped completely."

My hand automatically went to my mouth. "You've been hacked? Oh my goodness! But I don't understand where the ledger is. You're so organized, Fiona!"

Her eyes, so empty this morning, just looked over at me and again, she allowed Hank to answer. "It's gone. That and all the receipts. Everything."

"Stolen?" I said stupidly. "That makes no sense. To be hacked and then have books stolen—what are the odds of a coincidence like that?" Then it hit me. So much for my mystery radar. I was about ten seconds behind everybody else. "Oh. Oh my... No coincidence, right?"

Hank was nodding. "And just to be clear, this wasn't just a garden variety hacking. This was a very professional job. All our inquiries so far indicate the account never existed."

I couldn't even get my head around how that could be possible.

Jonah and I began speaking at the same time, but we were coming from different angles. I waved him forward. "How much money are we talking about?"

Clay shrugged. "About eight thousand rounded off is what we had left. Of course, there were some insurance premiums coming up due."

"I can cover that, Mom," Jonah said quietly. "I don't want you to worry."

Clay smiled. "Thanks, son. It's not the money. We can cover that, too. It's your mama's reputation..." Tears filled his eyes as he wrapped an arm around her. "It's just plain not fair. She gives so much—and to have that integrity questioned? It's just...just..."

Jonah nodded, his own eyes glistening. "I know, Dad. I know..."

Frank cleared his throat, and I guess, knowing what was coming, Bobby Don glued his eyes to his shoes, unable to face his friends. "And I hate to be the bearer of worse news, but this goes further than reputations. This is a crime and it carries a hefty punishment. Your mother could be facing jail time over this."

Chapter Four

J ONAH LURCHED FORWARD, his eyes darting from Frank to his parents. Clay, however, remained seated, his eyes down, his hold on Fiona even tighter. They already knew this.

Meanwhile, I battled between struggling to breathe as I comprehended this latest news and corralling the questions that were building in my head. I clasped my hands together and closed my eyes, focusing on finding calm.

Hoping for clarity, I ventured one question. "Didn't I hear you say last night that Council had copies of the figures? Can't they be retrieved?"

Hank sighed. "Rosie, they were just copies of the ledger, not any official bank statements. Any court would say they could have been fabricated. They mean nothing." At my frown he explained, "You've got to remember nobody has ever questioned this before. I think Fiona just assumed someone wanted to know how much was in the account— and it's not a secret so that's what she provided. If they'd wanted more she would have provided that as well."

I nodded. "It bothers me, though. Eight thousand is substantial enough, but it's hardly enough for such an elaborate operation, is it?"

Frank stared in that way he has that made you feel like you were pinned to a board like a moth. Or maybe that was just how he sometimes made *me* feel. "What are you sayin', Rosie?"

I shrugged. "Just maybe that this whole thing is meant to make Fiona look bad, so we have to look at who benefits from that. And the only person who seems to benefit is Frederick Clausen. He seems determined to set the town against Clay and Fiona."

Clay's eyes fired. "If he's behind this—so help me I'll…"

"Take it easy, Clay," Hank ordered.

"I'm with Hank, Clay. As your friend I'm asking you to remain calm and let us find out what's behind this. As your sheriff, I'm ordering it. Stay away from Fred Clausen."

The silence that followed the order was awkward and tense, and it was almost a relief when Bobby Don's pager crackled a message that only he seemed to understand. For some reason we all seemed fascinated, making Bobby Don more self-conscious than usual. He was a nice guy, but it was no secret he was a far better chili cook than he was a deputy sheriff. Flushed, he spoke briefly to Frank, and they made immediate farewells.

At the entrance to the room, Frank hesitated—his sheriff's voice evident. "Now, if you remember anything else—anything at all—call me. No matter what time or day. Y'all hear?"

Despite the fact that Brenda, the sheriff's wife, was still present, the atmosphere was slightly lighter after the law enforcement representatives had left. For me personally, it freed me up to satisfy some of the things that were hammering at my brain.

"Fiona, do you remember the last time you had the ledger?"

She nodded, seeming to force herself to speak. "The day after the last market. I always tally up and record everything that day, and I always go to the bank on the Monday following the markets."

"So, you're saying your checkbooks are gone as well?"

Clay sighed. "Everything."

That was the trouble with the wonderful things about small-town life. It had always charmed me that people didn't lock their doors and left their keys in their cars when they were shopping or visiting—or at church. Airlie Falls was like that. The *trouble* being that occasionally it was going to come back and bite you. Like now. No one would have had to break in. All they'd have had to do was turn the knob and stroll in.

"So, the markets are due again this weekend—in four days, to be exact—which means sometime in the past nine days, someone came in and cleaned you out of all your records. How much time would that have taken do you think?"

Clay offered a disgusted snort. "Minutes. Seconds!" When I frowned he said, "Rosie, you know how organized Fiona is! Well, all the market information has its own filing cabinet—so labeled—and everything *in it* is labeled so clearly that it would have been child's play. Frank thinks that's one reason we didn't realize anyone had been in here. There was no mess—didn't have to be because no one had to search through wads of paper or files to find what they wanted." He shook his head. "I didn't ever think I'd see the day when such an honorable trait would be the cause of such a downfall."

"Forgive me for asking so many questions, but—"

"Don't apologize, darlin', just ask," Jonah assured me. His gravelly voice was low and even deeper today due to the gravity of the situation. "We've got to find answers somewhere."

I swallowed, wishing my mouth wasn't so dry. Picking up the cue, Brenda excused herself to prepare some refreshments. "When were we first aware of Fred Clausen being in town?"

Clay scratched his chin. "I'm not rightly sure. If it was him behind the requests to Council, then that takes him back three months—but I was only aware of him in the past few days when he started his campaign for mayor. And I'd bet money on the fact that the twelve hundred new voters registered this week were due to him."

Jonah and I both jumped. He got in first. "Twelve hundred! That's double the entire population of Airlie Falls!"

What was going on? This was ridiculous. "When did you get this news?"

"This morning," Clay answered.

"Isn't that called stacking the votes or something? It can't be legal," I argued.

Clay sighed. "It could be perfectly legal if all these people are bona fide residents. The thing is that we don't have the time or the manpower to check that many registrations."

My head was buzzing with questions. "And what about this property he owns. Does anyone know anything about it?"

Dismally, everyone shook their heads. And my frustration began a slow burn. It was ludicrous to think a stranger could come into a tight-knit community like Airlie Falls and cause such chaos, literally, overnight. And yet I was watching it happen.

"And so," I said, moving back to the more serious issue, "we have no idea when the robbery could have taken place so we can't even work backward. Do we know when the house was empty?"

"Fiona's given Frank a list of her comings and goings—as precisely as she can anyway," Hank answered.

The wonder in his voice wasn't lost on me. Keeping track of Fiona would be like tracking a fly or a mosquito. She darted through life—and her only saving grace in this situation would be her diary, which was diligently followed—at least for official or planned events.

Like Clay, Fiona was a committed member of multiple committees and associations. I had never been able to decipher how she juggled them all and really cared and worked for each of them. My mind began to list some: Markets. Founder's Day. Keep Airlie Falls Beautiful. Women's Committee. Fourth of July. Garden Club. Farm Outreach. (Tiny) Airlie Falls Elementary. (Tinier) Airlie Falls Nursery School. Library. Book Club. Riverbend Retirement. And those were just the ones I could remember.

On top of that she was the self-appointed benevolent caregiver who visited the elderly and ill to ensure they were okay, kept a lookout for families in distress and raised funds to be able to help them. Her door was always open as was her heart. And people appreciated it. She was discreet, and they could offload or seek her counsel. I knew because I'd seen it happen all the time when I'd lived here with her and Clay.

She also organized the men's dinners that Clay had instigated to bond farm and ranch people with townsfolk to ward off isolation and build relationships. More recently she'd talked to me about her plans to propose an annual literary weekend, an art weekend, and an antiques week. And she was assisting four more townsfolk set up B&Bs to cope with overflow.

The woman was a marvel. And yet someone dared accuse her of theft and being self-serving? That person had no idea who Fiona Fencott was.

When Brenda reappeared with a loaded tray, Jonah and I both jumped to help. He took the tray, and as soon as it was settled, we three began distributing coffee and food. Clay and Fiona had always been the biggest fans of my baking. It was due to Fiona that my desserts stand even existed. When I'd, briefly, lived here it was a joy to create for them, and they'd always shown their appreciation with hearty appetites. Today, I watched both push cake around their plates. Not a crumb made it to their lips. The cookies sat untouched. Brenda and Hank were the only fans today.

I cleared my throat to break the silence that had begun to feel odd. "Fiona, Clay? I'm not sure what I can do, but I won't be letting this sit. Midge is off somewhere today, and I've got a feeling she's looking into Clausen's background. I know she'll help me do everything she can to get to the bottom of this."

At the mention of Midge's name, Brenda gasped. "The paper! This will all be in next week's newspaper!"

I held my breath, expecting to see even more shock bombard Fiona, but amazingly she was calm about it. She waved away the concern, finding her voice at last. "Clay and I have worked hard to promote this town and build a community to be proud of. That community needs a newspaper and an ethical editor. We admire Midge, and we're glad to have her. It's her job to report the news. This is a situation where we have to accept the bad if we want to maintain the good."

Clay nodded and gave his wife a tight squeeze of approval. "Rosie, honey? We'd appreciate it if you pass that on to Midge. Tell her there's to be no clash of conscience. We trust her to do her job and we expect her to do it." The words were delivered more stiffly than normal for Clay, but I knew he was sincere. And I could see what this whole ordeal was costing them both.

Tears filled my eyes. "She'll really appreciate that. It's going to be hard for her—so thank you."

As Jonah began to speak I turned to see him directing his words at his parents. And I wasn't surprised to see that my big, tough cowboy's eyes were also glistening. His deep whiskey voice was rougher this morning. "I'll give Ben a call. Bring him up to date. We don't want some fool blabbering gossip at him before he's got the facts. Or someone handing him a local paper."

Fiona smiled her thanks, and Clay rose to hug his younger son. Their eldest, Ben, was completing his medical residency at an Austin hospital, and all three Fencotts worried about his workload and lack of time. For all his gratitude, though, I could sense the tension still evident in Clay. His mouth was set and his movements stiff.

Brenda, caught up in the emotion, sniffed loudly. "And don't forget we also have the markets this coming weekend. I know you may not be up to coping with it all, Fiona, and I'd be happy to stand in for you."

"I don't know all the behind-the-scenes issues, but I'd be

happy to be Miz Brenda's assistant, if that helps?" I offered.

Fiona's brokenness was still evident, making her smile of gratitude all the more brave and appreciated. "I won't be hiding away, but I'll happily take the help. Thank you."

Those words were almost like a signal to Clay who suggested crisply that maybe Fiona should rest, hinting to the rest of us to allow her to do that. As much as I'd have liked to stay, I had market preparations—as well as a burning desire for answers.

One of the things I'd forgotten to do was check out Clausen's address. I imagined Clay and Fiona knew it by now, as would Sheriff Kinnead, but I didn't think he'd be happy to share that information. We were friends; in fact, he could be quite fatherly toward me; however, he'd made it clear months ago that he didn't like me meddling in police business. Even if I had basically solved three murder mysteries. Two current and one that was over sixty years old.

Gratitude would be a nice thing.

JONAH FOLLOWED ME back to the farmhouse, and we made ham sandwiches topped with sweet homegrown tomatoes and some of the tangy cauliflower mustard pickles I'd put up a month or so ago. Sitting on the deep veranda with icy lemonade and a hint of breeze coming up from the nearby river should have brought a level of contentment, but the woes of Clay and Fiona were hitting us both hard.

"Do you think they'll be okay?" I asked quietly.

Jonah put his half-eaten sandwich down and sighed. "I've never seen them so beaten." He leaned back in his chair. "You know, from the outside it looks like they've had it good. And they'd be the first to say they've had a great life. But like everyone, they've faced some harsh things, crushing things that would have broken others. And every time I've watched in awe as they pulled themselves together and kept walking boldly into the future. This time, though? I don't know…"

"Do you think it's because it involves others?"

He nodded. "Possibly. Other times have been personal tragedies, but this time others have been hurt. Mom will be beating herself up that those people worked so hard for the money they entrusted her with. She'll feel she's failed them. And that won't sit well."

"I want to help them; I just don't know where to start. As soon as Midge gets back, I need her to tell me everything she knows. I know Clausen's behind this." I paused. "I'm really worried about your dad, though, honey. He's pretty wound up over this. So angry that someone's hurt Fiona…"

"I know," Jonah answered, reaching over to take my hands in his. "But, darlin', he's sensible. He's mad as a hornet, but he won't do anything to make things worse. He's too smart for that."

After we'd said our goodbyes and I wandered into the

kitchen to make inroads in my to-do list, all I could do was hope Jonah was right.

I also hoped some quiet hours baking would help clarify my scattered thoughts. The tray-bakes—brownies and bars—had done well at my stand; they were easy to consume while walking and often people then came back to buy boxes of several to take home for later because they were also easy to transport and carry.

For the most part, they were also things I could make ahead and freeze. Or at least the bases could be frozen. The brownie with its soft chocolate, coconut, peppermint topping on a cookie base was a good example. While four bases baked, I flicked through my baking bibles to make my lists.

By five in the evening, I'd put all the baking aside to focus on preparing a meal I could take over to Fiona and Clay. Jonah was going to meet me there later, and we'd stay and share it—mostly to encourage them to eat.

THE NEXT MORNING I was up way before daybreak. Last night when we'd returned, there was evidence that Midge had come back from her trip, but she'd gone out again before I could catch her. We didn't keep tabs on each other, and as this was Airlie Falls and not the city, we never overly worried if one was home late. But she'd had a big day and for once I *was* worried, although if she'd hooked up with an old friend or it was some kind of romantic liaison, then she wouldn't appreciate my interference. The dilemma had kept me tossing and turning. The last time I remembered looking at the clock last night had been 2:02, and she still hadn't been home.

In the early hours, I was awake—and it was then I remembered the strawberries I'd picked two days ago that were sitting in the storeroom refrigerator. Before all this nonsense, I'd intended to make another batch of strawberry sauce for bottling. I'd begun adding a few longer-life merchandise items that still fit the general dessert category. They looked so pretty on the stall, and unless I sold out, I didn't have to reproduce them every market. They were proving to be popular and I was glad to have a good stock of chocolate, peach, and peach-and-brandy sauce as well as the strawberry. Well, I thought a little later, as I hulled the lush little jewels, I might have *if* Jonah didn't consume all the peach-and-brandy sauce! Poured over hot pancakes, that sauce had become a fast favorite for him.

Thankfully, this strawberry version was an easy project, and as I added sugar and vanilla, I was overcome by a sadness that was hard to shake. The aroma wafting through the house was incredible. That sweet, clean summery scent that fresh fruit offered was such a gift; a reminder of all the wonders of the season and always made me feel alive and energetic. And so fortunate. But today there was a block to that wonder. It was so tragically sad that someone like Clausen could have such evil in his heart, could cast such dark shadows over things that are good and wonderful. Could cause such pain.

Frustration built rapidly and I knew I needed something to do, something to help work it off before I let it consume me. As soon as the sauce was bottled and in the water bath, I made a plan.

It was too early to check on Midge and too early to go and do any investigating, but I'd put off clearing out a particular garden bed and this morning seemed like a good time to rectify that.

I wanted it ready for end-of-summer and autumn planting especially since I had some broccoli and beans and some squash and cucumbers to get in the ground. Clive, our tenacious postman, was a great gardener and had given me a heap of seedlings, and not only did I not want to lose them but I also wanted to reap the harvest before the cold really set in.

More to the point, I wanted to get to it before Jonah so he'd be able to take it a bit easier this weekend. He'd been spending most weekends working on my house and yard, and he'd already done so much. The gauzed enclosures to prevent critters feasting on my produce—while still allowing maximum sun—were a stroke of genius and saved me one problem.

With Tiny at my heels, I wandered down the back, tools,

hat, and gloves at the ready. The tomato bushes were really getting messy. I'd had such a good harvest, and I didn't want to risk losing any now. The tangy aroma washed over me, and like a two-year-old I rubbed my face in the foliage to absorb as much as I could. I smiled as I picked off some dead undergrowth and then popped a lush ripe tomato into my mouth, letting all that summery goodness squirt around my tongue. The basil, its companion, moved in the slight dawn breeze and joined in to add its perfume, lulling me, urging me to forget all the bad stuff for just a moment.

Sighing, I straightened, knowing I could only keep it at bay for such teeny periods before it all flooded back. Aiming to focus on the practical, I noted I'd need to harvest today as well and was thrilled when a shiver of the usual excitement scooted through me. I couldn't have imagined a life I could love as much as this. Simple and fulfilling.

All the little things that gave me delight lined up in my mind to be admired. Like the completely spontaneous little squeal of delight every time I walked into my preserves larder. The rich red of the sauce and preserved tomatoes. The spicy summer vegetable sauce—great on meat or over pasta. The chili jam and relishes added to the jewel-like display, and until two days ago, I'd been so excited that I was going to add some onion jam and caramelized-onion preserves as well. All this and a man I loved. Life had seemed perfect.

Then Clausen had come to town.

My shovel hit the earth. The soil was rich and dark, and

I dug through it with more ease than I'd expected. Or perhaps I was just exerting more force. When pain sliced through my right shoulder I realized it was the latter and knew instinctively I had to step away from the emotion of what was happening and look at the whole situation objectively.

Having resolved to do that, I somehow I managed to focus on the work at hand and was surprised to see the sun high in the sky when I was ready for a break. The morning was as hot as predicted, and I'd worked up a sweat. Wondering whether to keep at it for a bit longer or be satisfied with what I'd achieved was another dilemma solved by the sound of a truck rolling into my driveway.

The gardens were out back, and given all the land I'd inherited, they weren't right up close to the house, so it was a bit of a walk back.

Frank Kinnead was peering through the front windows when I turned the corner of the house. "Sorry, Rosie; I was beginning to think there was no one home."

I smiled as Tiny loped to the man she considered a friend and heavily thumped a giant paw against Frank's thigh. "Gardening—out back." I indicated the wicker chairs. "You want some lemonade? Iced tea? I'm going to take a break myself now."

He shook his head while continuing to pet Tiny. "Well, that kinda depends on if Midge Moylan's at home."

I explained not seeing her the night before. "To be honest, I'm not even sure if she's here or not. Why do you need her? Anything I can help with?"

"I was really hoping to talk with her." He looked pointedly at the door. "Would you mind checking to see if Midge is in?"

"Oh. Sure." As I made my way up onto the porch I crossed my fingers and launched into a question of my own. "Seems you've got your hands full. I don't suppose you've heard any more about that mysterious body?"

His eyes narrowed. "Now, Rosie, I surely appreciate your help with the murders last spring, but this is police business. You know that, right?"

I nodded. "I'm just curious, like the rest of Airlie Falls."

He looked like I'd just tried to make him a great deal on the Statue of Liberty. "Right. Hmmn, of course you are." Then a tired little grin cracked to the surface. "Well, this is nothing the rest of the town won't know as soon as that sister of mine finishes work," he said referring to Janet, his receptionist. It was also said with a resigned sigh. "That said, I'd at least like one person to get the real story and not the embroidered one that'll no doubt be the preferred version. The facts are that the man had a prosthetic leg and, as you probably know, those things are numbered, so it shouldn't be too long before we have an identity. That was a bit of luck. Relying on dental records can take a load of time. Dallas and Austin don't have any leads of who he might be, so we're thinking he could have come from out of state. But that's purely speculation at the moment. And that's as much as we have."

His tone said, *Now, I hope that keeps you busy and quiet for a while.* I felt like a kid being given a cookie in exchange for good behavior, but the sheriff was a father and grandfather. He should've known that didn't always work.

I grinned my thanks and was rewarded with a brief, amused shake of his head that disappeared even faster than it had appeared. And I didn't miss the pointed gaze he directed at my door.

Getting the message, I hustled along. Despite our little chat, Frank seemed serious. Worried, even. The house was cool and quiet, and my footsteps clattered across the hardwood floors of the wide hallway. As I skipped up to the next level, questions stacked up with each stair rise. *Why Frank want to speak to Midge? Was he wondering if she' uncovered anything about Clausen? Any information? Maybe the mysterious body?* By the time I knocked on her bedroom door I'd convinced myself this was the case.

Once again, she wasn't there. *Where was she?* Dragging out my phone, I punched in her number, listening with my heart in my mouth when it went to voicemail.

Really worried now, I tore downstairs to beg Frank to put out a missing person's bulletin.

Frank scratched his head. "Considering there's only me and Bobby Don and a coupla other junior deputies, I'll let them know and we'll keep an eye out, but I doubt we need to file a report just yet."

"Frank, she hasn't been seen since the night before yesterday! The night of the town meeting. And she'd not answering her phone."

He nodded, but I didn't miss the speculation in his eyes. He was brushing me off; however, there was something else going on in his head. "That's right—but she also gave you a good explanation as to where she was going—and there are a hundred worthy reasons she might still be where she said she'd be." Winding down, he ran a hand across his face. "As I said, we'll keep an eye open for her."

"Sheriff? Is everything okay?" I prompted.

Again he shook his head. "I've been waitin' for you to ask me somethin' else, but it's clear you don't yet know." He sighed. "Seems to be my morning of revelations. It'll be all over town before we know it. And seein' it's impossible to keep secrets in this town and you're gonna hear anyway I might as well tell you: Fred Clausen was found dead this morning."

"No! Really?" Hearing of a sudden death is always a shock, but—blame it on the sun—a strange giddiness came over me. Surprise wrapped in relief. "How? Is it too much to ask that he choked on his own nastiness?"

Frank raised an eyebrow, and I was immediately sorry for my disrespect. "No," he said. "He was murdered. Banged on the head with something mighty heavy. Real nasty."

"Oh…" This time I had nothing more.

"And, Rosie? This is something for the sheriff's department. You were lucky last time, but I shouldn't have to remind you that murderers are dangerous." And with that, he tipped his hat and started back down into the sunlight. "Thanks again for the offer of refreshment, Rosie. I'll take you up on it next time. For now, when Midge returns, if you could tell her I need to speak to her, I'd be mighty appreciative. You have a good day, now."

As he trudged down the deep, wide stairs I always felt were so welcoming, I sensed his step was heavier and those broad shoulders more stooped. For a man only in his late sixties he sometimes seemed like he'd seen too much of society and didn't always like what he saw.

I couldn't blame him. My own head was going crazy. Clausen had been murdered? I didn't like the man, but to be murdered? My thoughts immediately went to Fiona and Clay. How were they feeling? Were they relieved? It was completely understandable if they were.

I watched the sheriff head back out my long driveway, deciding my next move. Clean up, get to the B&B, and track down Midge. It didn't take much thought, really.

And even less to decide to add a basket of food.

Chapter Five

O N MY WAY to the B&B, I called Jonah, who was on a
job about twenty minutes away, and then put in three
calls to Midge. On the third call, she answered, and it was
evident she was either drugged and being held captive—or
she was half asleep.

It was the latter.

"Where are you?" I almost screamed. "I've been worried
sick! I haven't seen you for days."

"Hi, Mom," she answered sarcastically.

Despite my worry I grinned. Obviously she was okay.
"Sorry. You know me and my imagination. So, I'm guessing
you're at the office?"

I sensed her nod through the fluctuations of her noisy
yawn. "All night. Better internet here—and besides, all my
notes are here."

"Your car isn't there. Frank checked."

Her sigh was deep, and I figured she was shaking her
head. Probably even contemplating banging it on her desk.
"You had Frank try to find me?"

"Actually he was looking for you first." She didn't immediately respond to that, and I moved on. "So where's your car and what's kept you up all night? Notes on Frederick Clausen?"

"Car's in getting that oil leak fixed." She yawned again. "And uh-huh RE: Clausen. It's pretty interesting. I expected whispers of corruption, and I can't find much at all. There's the mystery of his wife, of course, and his sister…"

"And the mystery of his death," I added.

"*Wh…?*"

I wished I was there with her. Silently I counted the three. One: Momentary confusion. Two: Dawning comprehension. Three: Got it!

"What?" All signs of her weariness had disappeared. "Dead? But… How? Why? When?"

"Yes, dead. *How?* Head injury. *Why?*" I sighed. "Really? Do we have that much time? *When?* I'm assuming last night."

"Head injury?" she repeated. "So, he fell?"

I shrugged. "Not unless he fell onto a blunt instrument that was coincidentally being propelled at him at great speed."

I heard her gasp. "Are you saying he was murdered?"

"Yes indeed I am, ma'am. At least that's what Frank Kinnead said," I added more soberly. "And, Midge? He— Frank, the sheriff—came out to the farm to find you. Said he needed to talk to you. I'm guessing he wants to pick your brain on what you've discovered."

The answering silence on the other end was so drawn out I had to check she was still there.

"Yes, sorry. Got lost in my head for a moment." She drew in a breath. "Yes, let's hope that's what he wants to talk about."

Her tone was so serious I was immediately on alert. "Midge? Is there another reason he might want to see you?"

Again, her reply was long coming. "Unfortunately, Rosie, there is…"

And then the line dropped out. Timing!

I ARRIVED AT the B&B, and as frustrated as I was that Midge and I had ended the call on that enigmatic note, my attention was captured by the sheriff's truck once more parked in Fiona and Clay's drive. Slipping into a spare space, I parked and dove out.

Inside, the atmosphere was exactly like I'd experienced a few months back when I'd visited the families of the recently deceased with Fiona. At least a dozen people sat or stood around the spacious living room, but instead of sharing stories about a lost loved one, all were enveloped in a grim silence. There'd been an effort made to offer refreshments, even though it was evident Fiona's heart wasn't in it. She hovered near the door leading into her study, her focus completely on that closed door, her hands absently murdering a handkerchief over and over.

Spotting my friends from the retirement home, lovingly known as the Fab Four, was a surprise. I hoped Lori Sue hadn't driven again. It took the four of them to manage the vehicle and negotiate the road and the traffic—and it was terrifying to watch. The octogenarians, who were all tapping on the nonagenarian door, were huddled and hadn't seen me yet. Making my way to them I saw that Martha, E.T., and Betsy were supporting Lori Sue, who was really upset. Hurrying the last couple of steps, I dropped to my knees at Lori Sue's feet and took her gnarled hands.

"Oh, darlin'," E.T. said brokenly. "We're sure glad to see you. This is just terrible."

"What? What's terrible?"

"It's my darlin' nephew, Clay," Lori Sue began, breaking off to fight back another round of tears.

"What about him?"

"He's been accused of murder!" E.T. explained.

Then, true to their shared style of conversing, they each added another layer to build the picture. "Of that awful man from the meeting," Martha added.

"He's gone and gotten himself dead, and they're blaming Clay!" Betsy finished off.

Clay? Murdering someone? It didn't make sense, and yet a part of my brain was arguing that it made way too much sense. Clay didn't have a murderous bone in his body, but he had threatened Frederick Clausen. Or at least, Clausen had accused Clay of threatening him. Truth be told, Clay hadn't actually completed his sentence even if the intent had been there.

"Where is he?" I asked, though I could guess fairly easily. Fiona still hadn't moved away from that door.

Martha pointed. "In the study with Sheriff Kinnead."

Pushing to my feet, I offered each of them a peck on the cheek and went to Fiona. Reaching up I put my arm around her. "Is Hank with him?"

She nodded. "If it goes beyond questions, though, he's going to get a criminal guy to come in and take over. Just like they planned for you." Her sigh was heartfelt. "Oh, Rosie honey. Clay didn't hurt anybody! It's just not in him!"

I patted her back. "I know. So, did I hear you say they're just asking questions? He hasn't been charged?"

"Yes. Just questions." A little cry of anguish escaped her lips, and she pressed the damp handkerchief against the tip of her nose. "Oh, it's just so unfair!" Her words were uneven and broken, interspersed by little catches where she struggled to drag in air. "All...all he wanted to do was talk to the man! Talk, one-on-one, away from everybody. He wanted Clausen to know we wouldn't be fighting him or be drawn into a dirty fight, that we had no intention of spreading stories about him. We hoped it would calm him, so we could just get on with a fair election."

"So, Clay went to see him? Last night?"

Again she nodded. Oh dear. This wasn't good. "Did they

speak?"

"For short while, yes. Clay even said he was quite civilized about it all." Her eyes narrowed in thought. "Clausen said something about things going back to normal, told Clay not to worry. He—Clay, that is—was quite cheered by that."

Vicki from the general store came to offer Fiona a hug and I moved away, but my head was still in the conversation with Fiona. What had Clausen meant by that? What kind of man causes all that havoc and then waves it away by claiming it was all going to be okay? My thoughts were scattered. Should I call Jonah? I'd promised to keep him updated, and the accusation against his father was pretty serious—the kind of thing that brought people undone. I ought to know. I'd been there myself last spring.

My fingers were on my phone keypad when he walked in. Coming straight to me, he leaned in for a kiss and then turned worried eyes toward his mother, who still hovered near the study door. He read the question in my eyes. "Village drums. Once the gossip mill starts, it's a power to be reckoned with. Lori Sue called me as soon as Frank arrived to talk to Dad." He nodded to where the "girls" had clustered in a group of chairs near the AC unit, casting wise eyes over the group and chatting furiously. "They'd come to check on Mom and Dad."

"Bless them. I've only just arrived myself. I've spoken to the four *girls* and to your mom. At this stage it's just questions, but, Jonah"—I turned to fully face him—"your dad went out to see Clausen last night!"

Jonah rubbed a hand down his face, his palm rasping against the beginnings of regrowth, even though it was barely midmorning. "Holy…"

His words died as he looked around. Others were watching us and listening. Glad of the basket I'd packed and left in the foyer, I suggested we serve refreshments. I'd hoped it would give us some privacy to talk in the kitchen, but I should have known better. As though awaiting a cue, two women jumped up to help.

That seemed to lift the gloom, and quiet chatter resumed. The subject of the mysterious body came up and Betsy was holding court with her moonshine theory, much to the entertainment of all. That, of course, led to the other dead body and lots of speculation about who might have murdered Clausen—still, the unspoken threat Clay had directed at the man hovered. And each time the mood darkened.

Jonah and I were starting to become concerned. They were all well-intentioned, but Fiona didn't need this. So, it seemed right that after a reasonable time we gently ushered people away with a promise of keeping them updated.

Just as I was closing the door I felt a forward push, and I released my hold. It immediately opened, and I was just as immediately enveloped in a cloud of expensive perfume.

"Oh dear. Excuse me. I didn't expect anyone on the other side."

Simone Grant's smile appeared to be genuine until you noted it didn't exactly reach her eyes. Eyes that were now casting a speculative look around the living room. "Have I interrupted something again? I'm so sorry."

It was Jonah who stepped forward, and I admit to a tinge of alarm at how her eyes lit up as she looked him over. Well, gosh, gee whiz. I understood that. Jonah was a man who unintentionally incited that kind of reaction; I didn't have to like it, though.

Her hand came up, but her eyes remained latched on to his. "Well, hello. I'm Simone Grant. How do you do?"

He took her hand. "Jonah Fencott. You're a guest here?"

She nodded. Still smiling.

"My parents are your hosts, and no, of course you're not interrupting. We've just been entertaining company—though *entertaining* doesn't quite seem the right word…"

I was hardly able to believe my ears. Jonah was hardly the loquacious kind. He never made idle conversation. There was always a purpose, and yet here he was blathering. Not good. I wanted to kick him and remind him she was at least fifteen years his senior and that was being kind!

"No?" she encouraged. She also flicked back those long red locks. "What word would be better?"

Whoa? *Was she flirting?*

Jonah's smile deepened. "I'm not sure really. Maybe, *commiserating?*"

"Now what would you have to commiserate about?" she

purred.

Spreading his arms, he feigned misery. "Death actually…"

Her eyes narrowed. "Death? You've had a family tragedy?"

He rocked back on his boot heels, wondering, I could tell, how to answer that question respectfully. "Not quite."

I'd had enough. "Just a local. I doubt you'd know him. Frederick Clausen. He was challenging the mayoral position in the election. He's dead, and people had just gathered to"—I glanced back at Jonah—"to commiserate."

I expected her to throw herself at Jonah to offer her sympathies. Physically, of course. What I didn't expect was for her normally perfect alabaster skin to suddenly suffuse with color. Red color. It clashed horribly with her hair. "Dead? But…"

I frowned. "Did you know him?"

Simone regrouped quickly. "What did you say his name was? Clausell? You were correct, Miss Hart, I've never heard of him."

I forced a smile. "Clausen. Frederick."

She shrugged. "Never heard of him. Now, if you'll excuse me?"

I watched her hurry up the stairs. At the mention of Clausen's name, she'd forgotten her flirtation with Jonah to the extent that he may as well have been invisible. I turned to him. "She knew him. She knew Clausen…"

Jonah nodded. "Yep. So, what's a compatriot of Clausen's doing in my parents' home?"

"I don't know… But hey, don't say anything to them right away," I suggested. "I'd like to do some digging first. There's something about that woman I don't fully trust."

He grinned. "Apart from the fact she was flirtin' with me?"

"You knew? You rat!"

"Of course I knew, and I also knew it was irritatin' you, so I went along for a bit of fun. Sweetheart," he whispered in my ear, tickling the tender flesh there, "you sure are cute with steam coming out of your ears."

Of course I responded maturely and punched his arm, which of course he thought was hilarious. "One thing, though," I said when we came back to the present. "I don't think she knew Clausen was dead."

He shook his head. "Don't count on it, honey. Women like her have as much feeling as a two-bit coin. What I saw was a mighty fine act. Trust me on that."

I did. No doubts at all.

I followed him back into the living room, where he began clearing away dishes and napkins. I took care of the food, and as we loaded up, a plan formed in my head. I was ashamed to admit I was so preoccupied with how I'd carry it out that I hadn't really made any connections to Fiona being absent from either room until the study door clicked open and five people emerged. Obviously she'd been called in.

They were a sorry sight. Frank Kinnead looked like you'd expect a cop to look after grilling one of his best friends on a suspected murder charge. Fiona and Clay were drawn and tired. Hank looked irritated, and Deputy Bobby Don, the town's chili king, looked like he'd rather have been bare-handedly chopping chilies for the past two hours. The hottest ones.

Every one of them looked too wired or jittery for coffee, so I made soothing iced tea while Jonah stacked the dishwasher. They all waved away food, which was testament to how upsetting the ordeal had been for all of them. There was no talk of the murder—or the other death—and small talk was stilted. It was almost a relief when Hank announced he was taking Fiona and Clay to some out-of-town place for lunch. It would get them out of the town's line of fire for a while; food was a poor secondary consideration.

It was a great idea. Especially from my perspective.

After they'd all left the house and Jonah and I completed the cleanup, he reluctantly announced he had to return to work. Like a good partner, I made all the right noises, but secretly I was delighted.

"I'll walk you out," he said as he put out the last trash bag. "What are your plans this afternoon?"

I shrugged. "You go on ahead. I need to hang around here for a few minutes."

His eyes narrowed. Jonah was equal rights all the way, but he hated me doing anything dangerous—or stupid—

which was sweet, just ever so slightly annoying at times. "And why would you do that?"

More shrugging while I frantically improvised. "There's—a—a recipe I want to find."

His roar of laughter shook the rafters. I swear it did. "A recipe? In *my* mama's house? The queen of the kitchen wants a recipe from my mother, the queen of burned water?"

I lifted my chin, and yes, there was defiance in the action. "It could be one Brenda gave her!"

More incredulous laughter followed. "Brenda would never give my mother a recipe, and you know it. What are you really going to do?"

Rearranging some decorative canisters was better than having to face him. "I just need to check a few things."

His eyes rose heavenward. "About our Miss Grant?"

"Maybe."

He took my hand and pulled me close. "Darlin', tell me you're not going to do anything dangerous. I don't care if you snoop through Mom's B&B files—they're my parents, and I want to know what's going on and that they're safe, just like you do. But I want you safe as well."

His kiss almost convinced me to let it go. Almost. But no one was that good.

I waved him off and crept into the study. After gleaning all I could from the records there, I set about waiting. Fiona always kept a store of the latest magazines for her guests to browse through—and then they went to Clay's dental surgery to do double duty. I added a third duty when I used them to help pass the time.

It wasn't too bad. An hour ten. I stayed well out of sight as Simone Grant came down the stairs and went out the front door. Creeping into the living room, I watched from behind the drapes as her car pulled away. Then, fingering the master key, I ran as fast as my legs would carry me.

The problem with sneaking into someone's room was that you didn't really know their intention on leaving. Was Simone Grant going out for lunch? Out to meet someone? For business? All of these were good reasons for her to leave; they indicated she'd be gone for a considerable time. Time enough for me to check out her room. But what if she was just going to the general store for gum? Or candy? These were bad reasons—from my perspective anyway.

Speed, therefore, was my friend.

Her room was the same one I'd been given when I stayed here last spring, which was a blessing as I knew the layout well. Still, my nervous fingers slipped on the doorknob as I passed inside. Then stalled. Of course, it was a suite, not just a room. I knew that, but in my haste I'd momentarily blocked that fact. Tension ramped up inside me as I contemplated all the extra places I'd have to search—suddenly turning this little venture into the opposite of a blessing. I needed to be fast. Very fast. Heart pounding, I imagined her purchasing gum and turning back to the B&B. On her way—right now. Kicking me into action.

Quietly closing the door, I checked her suitcase first and, seeing she'd unpacked everything, I tiptoed to the closet and then the bureau in the main room—the bedroom. She was very neat, which made things difficult because I had to be very careful, and that slowed me up. Such a neat person would notice if things were disturbed. I was a neat freak—according to every person I'd ever lived or worked with—so I knew that for a fact.

Despite there being no one in the house I endeavored to be as quiet as possible, straining to hear anything that might warn Simone was returning. Several times I paused, sure the pounding in my ears was something more.

The closet held nothing I could find of interest. The bedside tables, ditto. The bureau was my biggest hope, and on the third drawer I hit pay dirt. A little bundle bound with rubber bands. It was hidden at the back of the drawer under some T-shirts and soft foldables.

On top was a photo ID card with Simone's face staring back at me. That red hair was unmistakable. Except that the name didn't match. This person was apparently Norine Westerling. Norine had a whole set of identification cards, so I immediately figured Simone Grant was really Norine Westerling.

Until I got to the next card.

And there that face—shrouded not by that fire-engine red hair but long, dark, loose curls, not unlike my own—smiled back at me again.

Only this time she was called Erica Penfold.

"What?" The whispered word seemed to echo around the room. Or perhaps just around my head. "What is this about?"

My heart was thundering so hard I thought it might burst. A quick flick of the pile below showed no fewer than three other identities. Some accompanied by more supporting forms of identification than others. *What sort of person has stuff like this?* My hands shook. What to do… I could photocopy some? Frank should know about this, but then he'd want to know how I came by the information. He'd be livid if he knew I'd been *poking my nose in* again. To say nothing of the fact that I'd broken into the woman's room and was illegally snooping through her belongings.

Seconds were ticking by. I couldn't waste any more time deliberating. I had to make a decision. It was in those moments that panic ignited, and I knew I'd lingered too long. There it was—a footfall in the hall. Then another. Fiona and Clay had rooms on the other side of the house. There were no other guests expected until the weekend.

That meant only one thing.

Simone Grant had returned.

Move! The word seemed to scream inside my head. My eyes were everywhere, searching for a safe place and finding none. The tiny balcony seemed too obvious, but it was my only chance. All I could count on was the fact she, hopefully, didn't know I was here and maybe wouldn't be too suspicious.

There was no time to wonder how I'd get out of there without getting caught if she'd returned for the day.

The sun was cutting in on that side, blazing down and searing my skin as I crouched in the corner of the small space. Uncomfortable as it was, it worked in my favor because at least it meant the drapes were pulled closed. Not that I was safe.

Focusing intently, I tried to follow her movements by mentally tracing her footfalls. She was a woman who moved quickly and purposefully, which made her steps heavy. I'd kind of placed her, then sensed her pause. It was a longish pause, and basically she'd stopped mid-room. It could have meant anything, but I had a bad feeling.

The next few moments were possibly some of the longest of my life. I lost track of her movements; it was like she was deliberately moving quietly. My heartbeat was so crazy I felt the quaking through my body.

I swear I'd aged by the time I heard the soft click of the door to the hall. Pushing to my feet I went to peek through the minuscule crack where the drapes didn't quite meet. Mid-step I paused. What if that had been a trick? Shuffling back, I waited, thinking—and hoping.

Eventually it was the heat that forced the decision. Even olive skin burned if it was overexposed—and I was feeling mighty overexposed. Taking a huge breath, I crept to the opening. I could see nothing except furniture, so, closing my eyes to send up a little prayer, I forged forward.

The room was so cool I almost cried out in relief. Cool and silent. And seemingly empty. I ventured a few steps forward, eyes on the outer door but with every step expecting to be halted by a voice—or worse. When I'd almost made it and hope surged, I paused long enough to look back, and what I saw puzzled me—then scared me. The drawer I'd found the identities in was partially open; open enough for me to see the pile of evidence I'd discovered was gone.

That was enough to push me out the door and into the hall, where I almost ran the remaining distance to Fiona's front door and out into the street. If anyone had been chasing me they'd never have caught me. It was only when I was well on my way home that I allowed myself to think about all that had happened. First and foremost on my mind, surprisingly, wasn't that I'd found all those identifications, all or most of them false, but why that drawer had been left open. Simone Grant, or whatever her name, was super neat. Why did she leave the drawer open? As a message? To let her intruder know she knew someone had been there?

"BUT WHY WOULD she think I'd return?" I'd arrived home and had hurried inside, relieved to find Midge home, and not just because I needed company. I also needed a rational viewpoint.

She shrugged. "My guess? Obviously she suspected or knew someone had gone through her stuff. She probably left some kind of trap that would warn her if she'd been infiltrated."

"Like what?"

"Maybe," she answered, "a hair or piece of invisible tape or something strategically positioned?" She took a moment to ponder that. "And probably, again, once she realized that she'd been sprung, she suspected that person would come back to retrieve what they'd found?"

"So she left a message." I shrugged. "Of course, this is all speculation, and," I added, suddenly feeling foolish, "the thing is, I have no proof it was actually Simone who came into the room." As soon as that thought was out there, I discarded it. "No, that doesn't make sense. It had to be her. The person didn't creep up to the room; he or she had a key—and entered with purpose and confidence. It was her."

Midge blew out a sigh. "Well, you're just dead lucky she didn't suspect you were still there and decide to wait you out!"

"Exactly. And also lucky she must have had to hurry away and not hang around. Which again brings me back to what someone like her is doing here in Airlie Falls."

"To say nothing of discovering her real identity—and especially right when we've had two suspicious deaths." Midge reached for a notebook. "Can you remember any of the other names?"

Unfortunately shock had chased away most of what I'd read, and while I could provide scant information, I couldn't be sure how much of it was accurate. Still, Midge was hopeful something would come up in her research.

While I made some tea, I finally got to the issue I should have addressed as soon as I saw her. "So, what gives with you and Sheriff Kinnead? Why would he want to see you?"

Her eyes remained on her mug, and I watched her fingers tighten around the smooth white porcelain. "He—ahhh—probably discovered I went to visit Fred Clausen last night before I went back to the office."

"You did *what*? *Why?*"

Her eyes lifted briefly. "Well, I do run a newspaper, you might remember."

Okay, that made sense, but her response didn't. As a journalist she had legitimate reasons to talk to the man. So why was I getting the feeling there was more? Because she seemed unnecessarily jittery about it.

I pushed a bit more, but she kept shutting me down with the same answers about getting a story. "So, what did he have to say? Clausen," I clarified, "what did he say?"

She shrugged. "*No comment.* That is, he didn't say anything because he didn't answer the door. I didn't get to speak to him. It was pretty frustrating actually."

Well, I could relate to that.

Fortunately for me that frustration didn't have a whole

lot of time to burn because the sound of a beeping horn reminded me I wanted to catch Clive, the mailman. I'd been trying to catch him for days and kept missing him.

It was a surprise, therefore, when the waving arm that greeted me through the open truck window was accompanied by the jangle of bangles and bracelets, and the long fingernails on the hands were decorated with a glistening candy-apple red that could have stopped traffic.

"Clive?" I asked hesitantly.

Chapter Six

"HOWDY!" THE VOICE boomed back. "Now, do I look like a 'Clive,' honey?" The words were followed by joyous laughter that was quite contagious.

I smiled back. "Well, if you are Clive, you've spent a heck of a lot of money. That's quite a change!"

Her laughter rang out again and her ample cheeks happily wobbled along. Her short, spiky blonde hair was highlighted with purple tips. The hand angled toward me. "Aileene Langtry. How do ya? I'm fillin' in for Clive. He and his wife won one of those charity sweepstakes. Thing was, they had to take it right away, so they've gone off on a cruise to the Bahamas if you can believe it! Went last week. Lucky cats!" She waved her free hand in front of her face. "I'd sure like to be treated to some of those cooling ocean breezes right now."

I couldn't place the accent. It wasn't purely Texan. Not purely southern. Maybe there a hint of mountain country there—I couldn't be sure. "Please to meet you, Aileene. I'm Rosie Hart. I can't provide ocean breezes, but I can offer cold lemonade or iced tea if you've got the time?"

She didn't even look at her watch. "Always got time for a chat and refreshment," she said as she climbed down from the truck.

I was considered small—*petite* was the term. And I hated it. Five-four (barely) in flat feet was quite respectable in my book, and my height and small frame had never hindered me in any way. But Aileene was even shorter than me. I swear she barely made five feet and was quite round and cute to go with it. She was older than I'd first thought, maybe late forties. It was hard to tell, and anyway, I was always bad at guessing exact ages.

It was too hot on the porch so we went inside where the air conditioning was doing a mighty job fighting back the heat. After she cooed her appreciation, Aileene took a stool at the kitchen island next to Midge, and the two chatted while I made up a plate and some cold drinks. I overheard her say she'd moved about a lot, which explained the accent and probably the tattoos on her inner wrist. One was a star—the Lone Star, I figured. It was a popular tattoo here in Texas—for obvious reasons. On the other was an animal. A dog? A wolf? I'd love to ask her more about that. I knew that in some cultures the wolf symbol meant power—and then there was the wolf guide, the protector. I wasn't into tattoos myself, but if you had to have one, it made sense for it to be symbolic.

She was a nice lady, and I was starting to feel guilty. I could see her relaxing and trust building, which was so wrong when I was about to ask questions that she probably wasn't supposed to answer.

I started easy. "So, have you been with the post office long?"

She waved a bejeweled hand that jingled like Christmas bells as she spoke. "Most of my working life. Even won a few service awards," she admitted proudly. "Got me some pretty pins."

She scrolled through her phone to find a photograph of herself in full postal uniform and passed it over. Her jacket, pulled tight across her ample bosom, boasted a dozen or more shiny pins down the right lapel and beyond. In her left hand she held a certificate of appreciation and honor.

"Wow," Midge murmured. "Impressive."

I agreed. "You must be proud. Not many people get that kind of recognition. Keep this up and you'll be running the postal service!"

She lowered her eyes. It was cute and coy. "I guess I just like doin' what I do. Helpin' people—or that's how I like to think of it. And being a fill-in means I get to move around. See places. Meet people."

"Must be hard delivering in an area you don't know well," Midge suggested as a way of continuing the conversation.

She shrugged. "Not so difficult. Everybody knows everybody in small towns, so that helps. If something's not addressed correctly and I get stuck, I just ask and people guide me."

I nodded. "I suppose it helps, too, that we don't have many strangers in town."

She leaned back on the stool. "I bet you'd be surprised there. Funny how many times strangers are right there on their doorsteps and people don't notice. My job is to fill in for postal workers who go on vacation, and I've seen it a whole pile of times." She paused, excited to explain something. "I took this job because up till recently I was a wholly single woman, so I didn't exactly have anybody I had to go home to but," she continued, waving a ring with a small diamond flanked by two blue sapphires under our noses, "that's about to change. I'm getting married!"

We made all the right noises and asked all the right questions.

"He's handsome," she said dreamily. "And successful, too!" She was one excited woman—and so she should've been.

After what I hoped was a reasonable time I said, "I'm just fascinated by what you were saying about strangers under our noses. Surely there aren't too many in Airlie Falls?" My personal feeling was that there were way too many strangers here in town for my liking at the moment, but I wanted her perspective.

She winked. "Well, there's a woman who's staying with her cousin over on Arcacia Street. And a couple at the Goodmans' B&B. They're just retired folk travelin' through.

One at the B&B in the main town square." She stopped counting. "That's four right there! Bet you didn't know that!"

Midge shook her head in feigned wonder, but I kept my own face turned away. Focusing on preparing the snacks.

Perhaps worried she hadn't impressed us enough, she added, "Though I'm not sure that cousin is having such a happy visit. I overheard a conversation there that sounded like they were charging the woman to stay there! It didn't sound like either party was very happy with the arrangement. I wanted to tell that cousin to just go on back home where she was really wanted and leave those sorry relatives to their own misery." She paused. "Of course, it's none of my business so I said nothing."

Which is exactly what I did. I said nothing. However, I filed that information away for future perusal. Would you really treat a relative that way? I certainly didn't know everybody in town but I knew most, and hospitality seemed to be their bylaw. It was the way of the south. Unless she wasn't a relative at all…

Hmmn. Two strange women in town who possibly weren't who they said they were? I brushed the thought aside. Airlie Falls was hardly a hive of espionage.

Conversation had suddenly halted, and I was doubly grateful when Midge brought up the murder of Fred Clausen. In truth it was probably the topic of conversation in every home and place of business today, so it wasn't all that awkward.

"I suppose you get to deliver the mail out there?" I asked conversationally as I joined the chat and handed out drinks to go with the loaded plates of sweet treats.

"Sure I do," she answered through mouthfuls of brownie.

"Does—or *did*—he live alone out there?" I continued, noting the sharp look Midge sent me.

"Oh, no! There's a whole pile of 'em. Now, I've only been on the job this past week, but you can see 'em all out there working on those produce patches. Behind the wire fencing. Women mostly." She nudged Midge. "Maybe he had himself a harem!" Inside the house I expected her laughter to rock the drywall, but strangely it was more subdued. Maybe she was respectful inside. Or maybe the laugh was a cover for loneliness or shyness because now with us beside her it even sounded a bit strained.

Or maybe she was feeling she'd said too much. While I was surprised at her candidness, she'd only offered her observations. She hadn't broken any rules or laws. Still, I was intrigued, and my mind immediately slipped back to the woman I'd seen at the meeting. "Could it be some kind of commune?"

She nodded, and I noted Midge's interest was pricked as well and she leaned forward as Aileene answered. "I guess. I s'pose it looks a bit that way."

"Did you ever meet Clausen?" Midge asked.

Aileene foraged for crumbs, and as always when someone

obviously enjoyed my food, I couldn't ignore a little jolt of pride. "Can't say I had the pleasure." Plate clean, she looked at her watch, a frown starting to form.

Obviously she was thinking she should be getting back to work, but I was hoping to dig some more. "Hey," I said, turning to Midge. "Aileene might be able to help us!"

"Really?" Midge's tone was cautious.

"Sure!" I turned to Aileene, who was now tracking crumbs along the bench. "Say, you haven't delivered mail to the Fencotts' B&B in town, have you? The one opposite the Green in the town square? You just mentioned it before." I assumed a goofy, dumb brunette expression. "It's just that there's this guest there and I've been introduced to her three times and I just can't remember her name! Have you delivered any mail to anyone other than the Fencotts? I'm just so embarrassed, I can't ask her again! Did you happen to notice a name? Midge and I have been just scraping our brains trying to remember!"

Midge nodded weakly. "Just scraping our brains…"

Aileene looked up then, her face clouded. "No, I can't say I have. Sorry." And she began to push down from the stool, her glass still half filled.

Shame flooded me. I'd gone too far. Pushed her to break some kind of postal service code. I could feel it. "Oh gosh, I'm sorry if I put you in a difficult position. I didn't mean to, I just—"

She waved away my apology with a smile, but the sparkle

had gone from her eyes.

I pressed the icy glass into her hand. "Please, take this. Sip it as you work. You can return the glass any time. I don't need it. No rush!"

Her eyes held mine for a long moment, and then she accepted.

There was no booming laughter as she drove away. No jangle of bangles and bracelets.

And I felt about as bad as it was possible to feel. Midge and I had probably lost the opportunity to make a new friend. Rats! Why did people have to murder each other and force us to ask awkward questions!

Well, force *me* anyway.

Somehow I'd have to try to prove to her that we weren't as callous as we'd appeared. I'd prepare a box of brownies—or maybe cookies—and try to catch her next time. Maybe it wasn't too late to make amends.

Back inside the house, Midge was scribbling furiously, her worries over a pending visit from Sheriff Kinnead put to one side for the moment.

"How much did you see when you were out at Clausen's property?" I asked.

"Nothing much. It was dark. I went to the main house. Nice place, if you like ultramodern." Obviously Midge didn't. It was there in her tone and in the shake of her head. And in her next words. "Stands out like a goat with two butts. I remember thinking it seemed like no expense was spared."

I picked at a lone leftover piece of brownie. "So, you didn't see anything like a communal setup?"

She shook her head. "As I said, it's pretty dark out there. It was obvious there were other buildings, but I couldn't make them out properly. I saw the wire fencing because it was lit at intervals down the side of the property. Bit like a prison, really." She shuddered before continuing. "Creepy. The long drive up to the house didn't alter that feeling."

"Gates?"

"Yeah, well, that was the odd thing. There were gates. Electronic, by the look of them. But they were wide open. I didn't have to buzz to be allowed access." She stared off into space for a moment. "The reason I thought it was so strange is that a van with a logo from a security firm pulled in as I was leaving. I remember thinking that the guy—Clausen— had wire fencing topped by what looked like razor wire all around the side perimeters and a security firm on hand—yet the gates to the front were wide open for anybody to access. Didn't make sense."

A thought niggled at me as she described the setting. "Midge, is it possible Clausen didn't answer the door because he was already dead?"

Her gaze sharpened. "You're saying the gates were open because Clausen opened them for someone he knew? And they killed him and left—leaving the gates as they were?" She dropped her head, studying the granite bench top momentarily, then looked up again. "It makes sense."

We both knew the next step. "I don't suppose you re-member the name—"

"Of the security firm?" she finished, reaching for her phone. "On it."

As intriguing as all this was proving to be, and despite all the questions building in my head, I was also acutely aware that market time was closing in on me. And I still had a mountain of things to prepare. And Delvene was expecting an order to be delivered to the café in time for her weekend market crowds.

A moment of panic catapulted me off my stool and into the walk-in store cupboard.

That was the only downside of having a fresh-food stand. Apart from the few desserts I could freeze or preserve, little could be prepared ahead, so the last couple of days prior to market weekends were always frantic.

As I worked, it wasn't the first time I considered getting some help. There was that girl who'd tried to get work with Miss Alice last year. She'd be off to college in the fall... Peggy? Meggy? Megan? My hands moved like lightning—stirring, rolling, cutting... The more I thought about it, the more sense it made. Right after the market, I'd find her and see if she'd like some summer casual work. If she was interested, it would tide me over until I could find someone from town who wanted a permanent part-time job.

And I told myself my decision had nothing to do with the fact that I was fairly sure Peggy/Meggy/Megan lived on Arcacia Street.

WHILE A BREAK from the heat would have been a relief, the dry weather held for the markets, which was a good thing. The evening markets proved popular in summer, so this weekend was an extended version. Friday night, Saturday, and Sunday morning.

With everything going on, not the least of which was the shadow over his involvement in Clausen's murder, Clay had voluntarily stepped aside from his mayoral position. Understandably the council had postponed the election, with Hank Henderson assuming temporary leadership for the short term until everything settled. It was a sensible decision, and it allowed Clay and Fiona to leave the worries of the town in his hands and focus on their own predicaments.

General opinion was mixed, though, and as the afternoon wore on and more locals arrived I watched them gather in clusters and didn't have to actually hear their conversations to know what they were all talking about. Hands and arms waved and heads nodded or moved from side to side in denial or disgust. In my heart, I believed most folk still supported Clay, but two deaths in their community—one suspicious, one murder—plus the shadow over the market funds still hanging over Fiona had left many confused, and I understood that as well. Even so, I wanted to shake everybody and urge them to remember what Clay and Fiona had done for the town and so many in it.

Fairy lights began flickering to life as the sun set, as always lending a festive air. There was no dance this weekend, but some good ol' boys had set up in a corner and their music added to the sense that we were all at a big party. However, as usual it was in the aromas that got me. Spicy barbeque, ribs, chili, hot dogs, fried chicken… If you could carry it and eat, it was there. And those mouth-watering aromas carried that message to the far corners of the township. If you thought you weren't hungry, you were about to be proved otherwise.

At my stand, business was brisk. It was never easy choosing what would be the most popular due to crowd preferences changing with each market. Tonight I knew I'd be wishing I'd baked more salted caramel cupcakes and more meringue-topped chocolate cake. I was selling the cake in bars already pre-cut and protected by a hard, clear plastic packaging, but I wondered if I should have altered the idea to make meringue-topped cupcakes instead. I'd play with that and see how they went. There was always the fear they'd be too dry.

While those two were selling the fastest, everything else

was getting a good nudge, and I could see a very early morning in my immediate future if I was going to have enough stock for another day and a half.

Jonah came by with a long cool drink and a cup of Bobby Don's chili and also an offer to stand in while I took a break to enjoy them. I usually didn't need a reason to hug him, but the one he received was extra tight. As fun as the markets were, they could also be tiring. To say nothing about what those teasing aromas were doing to my digestive system.

Taking my dinner, I moved to the shadows at the back of the stand. As anticipated, the food was good and I was happily mopping up the spicy stew with thick crusty bread when I thought I saw someone I recognized. The woman from the meeting? The one I had been sure was being harassed. I made to move to her when I suddenly realized I was mistaken. They were alike, but it wasn't the same person. Thinking of Midge and me and our uncanny likeness without being related, it wasn't surprising to find someone who resembled another so closely.

Disappointment, however, flowed through me; and just as I made to return to the stand to take over, something else caught my eye, and instinct told me to stay where I was.

A group of women who'd also been at that meeting were working their way through the crowds, stopping to pick up the odd thing and then put it back. Their simple floral-printed dresses identified them right away as those who had supported Clausen at that meeting and reminded me again of the scrap of material still sitting on my bedside table.

As they reached my dessert stand, I watched one of them stop and run her fingers over the sign I'd had created—*From the Hart*. From my position in the shadows at the back of the stand, there was something disturbingly voyeuristic in my fascination with them, but I couldn't turn away.

The other women had slowed and were staring at the confections before them. Smiling, Jonah started talking to them, obviously describing the various selections. Their return smiles moved from tentative to intent, although I wasn't sure if they were all for the food or for the server. Either way, it was evident they were tempted.

A surge of protective pride tempted me to call out that whatever they chose would be good, but instead I continued to watch silently. And was rewarded by further insights, which, while interesting, confused me even more. Did they have no money or amazing willpower?

I was too far away to make out their faces clearly in the evening light, but as suddenly as I wondered at their motivation one stepped forward, seemingly disgusted with the rest and pulled out a wallet. And she bought up a storm while others looked on. In delight? Disgust? Or awe? I couldn't tell.

Amazed, I stayed back in the shadows and simply watched. Watched Jonah's big work-worn hands fumble a few times but never once damage the delicate confections.

Watched him pack a mountain of desserts for the one girl. Possibly she was going to share—I wasn't sure. It was weird.

So what was going on there? Surely these women were from Clausen's—where else could be from? Especially if I added that clothing into the equation. Those identical dresses screamed *commune* to me, though maybe not a very equitable one. Did they all have money or just one? The women appeared to be content and to have a level of freedom to come and go from the compound.

Although, maybe all except one had that freedom. My "friend" from the meeting wasn't there. So, where was *she*?

It was only when they'd moved out of sight and I stepped out of the shadows to wrap my arms around Jonah that I silently realized as fascinating as it all had been and as appreciative as I was, my stocks were now more depleted and I'd be closing the stand early.

"Was that as weird as it looked from back there?" I asked, leaning my head to catch the cooling breeze that had drifted in.

He lifted my hair off my nape to allow it, too, to enjoy the breeze, and I almost moaned with pleasure but I didn't want to miss his words. "Weirder, probably. I wasn't sure they were going to buy anything until that girl stepped forward. And I'm pretty sure she said something about being sick of the others and something about a test? Another said something about some guy being furious."

I turned to look up at him. "A guy? Do you think they

meant Clausen?"

He shrugged. "Could be. Then again, he's dead, so what would it matter? Why would they care?"

"And why would you need to hide it in the first place? If it's your own money, then what does it matter to anyone else if you spend it?"

There was no time to speculate. A surge of customers moved in, followed by more and then more. Jonah stayed to help, and by the time they'd all moved on I was down to my last half dozen random items, and I quickly packaged them together, hoping to sell them as a boxed selection. Amazingly, that happened as I was sealing the transparent box, and it freed me to check on Fiona.

She'd been wandering through the market, past all the stalls, nodding and smiling. But for the first time in my experience, that smile was tight and it didn't reach her eyes. Perhaps in deference to the problems she and Clay were experiencing, the stallholders solved their own problems and no one was harassing her with queries or complaints as they usually did. I wondered if it would have been better if they'd stayed true to form because with nothing to do she looked not only miserable—but also lost.

Having cleared away and shut down, Jonah and I set off to find her. We hit pay dirt by finding both her and Clay plus Hank and Sheriff Kinnead at Brenda Kinnead's preserves and jams stand.

From a distance it looked like any simple gathering of old friends; however, as we neared, it was evident there was a whole lot more going on. Frank looked like he was aging before our eyes, and Brenda had been crying. Her friend Merline, from the beauty parlor, was serving customers while the others chatted.

I hurried forward, slipping in behind the makeshift counter to help serve the waiting customers. Merline flashed me a grateful smile and a wink, and we worked silently together until that little rush had passed. Looking around for Jonah, I saw him with his parents, who were still grouped with the others. He held out a hand, indicating for me to join them. Merline saw and paused filling the depleting display stacks. "Go on over, honey, I'm fine here."

Tentatively I joined the group, fearful I was intruding, but that was immediately brushed aside by the welcome I received.

"I don't understand where that stranger could have gotten hold of my preserves!" Brenda was saying.

It must have been something she'd been repeating because I could sense Frank's patience waning. "Anyone around here could have met that guy and offered him food, Brenda! Or maybe he or his family or friends had been here prior and purchased some then. Maybe he brought his own stash!"

Fiona frowned. "The dead man traveled with a stash of fruit relish he had a severe allergy to? That doesn't make sense and you know it, Frank Kinnead."

Shrugging, I looked up at Jonah, who filled in the blanks for me. "Your mystery guy. Cause of death has been identi-

fied as a fatal anaphylactic episode. Specifically, as a result of
consuming a component in fruit relish. Even more specifically, possibly consuming *Miz Brenda's* fruit relish."

"They know that already?"

"It's an early call, but it's looking that way."

"Why Brenda's preserves?"

His forehead crinkled into a frown, "I don't know all the
details, but it wasn't a commercial product and given how
much of this stuff Brenda supplies around here Frank offered
a jar for comparison and it matched. Doesn't mean it's
definitely Brenda's, however, it's certainly homemade and
contained an unusual ingredient she uses."

My hand went to cover my mouth, but not fast enough
to catch the gasp. Miz Brenda's preserves? Possibly some I'd
helped to make? If I was feeling suddenly unwell at the
possibility of having created a weapon of death, how bad
must Brenda have felt? Jonah's arm tightened around me as
my eyes darted to my friend and baking partner. On the
surface she seemed to be taking it well. Until you noted the
shaking hands, pale color, and sweat beading her upper lip
and brow—all of which I suspected had nothing to do with
the heat of the day—which was already fading as night made
its claim.

Turning back to Sheriff Kinnead, I asked, "Is that all that
was in his stomach? Just preserves?"

"Looked like it was part of a snack," he answered. "He'd
had a sandwich, which was probably how the relish was
consumed—inside the sandwich. And coffee with cream. At

least that's what the report said."

"So," I continued, thinking out loud, "I guess the Blue-bonnet Café is the most likely place…"

Jumping onto my train of thought, Fiona supplied the answer. "Frank just explained that the man didn't go the café. At least, no one remembers waiting on him."

"So, that leaves two options. The first being that he brought his own food, which is unlikely, and the second that he had a private meeting with someone—probably in their home… Someone who served him fatal refreshments."

Frank cleared his throat. "Ahem, I *am* here you know, Miss Rosie, and as sheriff, I *have* actually thought about these things myself, you might like to know!"

My face suddenly burned, but the chuckles from Clay and Jonah helped to cool me down. "I'm sorry, Frank. I really was only thinking out loud."

His answering sigh almost drowned out Clay's words. "Don't go getting all het up there, Frank. Rosie's just trying to help, and you gotta admit it must be better than someone who's primary thoughts all day long are how to improve his chili recipe!"

At the mention of Deputy Bobby Don, a second sigh, this one less vehement and more of agreement, preceded Frank's reply. "Well, you're right. It is a nice improvement. Just remember, though, you're not police, Rosie, and as I keep telling you, this is dangerous work. You were very lucky last time, but Jonah and I might not be around if you got yourself into hot water again. You hear?"

Of course I heard. And I had no intention of putting myself in danger. That didn't mean I couldn't do a bit of innocent snooping, however. And if ever there was an oxymoron—that was it right there.

Sidestepping his point, I asked, "So, still no ID?"

Frank shook his head. "Though they tell me it's not far off. They're narrowing it down as we speak."

"And I guess no one is admitting to entertaining the mystery guy on his last day?" Jonah asked.

"No, and what's more, no one in town saw him, either. I reckon I've asked near everyone, and the way gossip flies around here, if it was an innocent meeting or sighting, someone would have heard about my questions and come forward."

"Which leaves us with the supposition that he was entertained out of town. At a farmhouse?" I paused, adding quietly, "Or a compound?"

"Now, Rosie…" Exasperation tinged Frank's words. Actually, way more than *tinged*. "Don't go adding two and two and getting five. Our mystery guy's death has nothing to do with Clausen's murder. It's purely coincidence they both happened around the same time. The only reason we are even havin' this conversation is because Brenda's preserves are likely involved. Apart from the fact he was moved, this is a straightforward tragic—but accidental—death."

I stared into the older man's eyes, and despite what I saw there, I held my tongue. Frank Kinnead didn't believe in coincidence any more than I did.

Chapter Seven

THE WEEKEND PASSED in a blur. On Saturday most of the summer crowds drifted in after the sting of heat settled into the cool of evening. A million stars twinkled in the night sky, adding to the magic as the music played and smiling customers filled their bags and baskets with home-grown produce and goodies. They weren't the only stars; *From the Hart* had its own stars that gentle evening—specifically double-choc-nut brownies and marshmallow bars.

That part of the business did my head in a little bit. I tried to go with the flow and find excitement in what each day brought, and to some extent that was how I operated. But I couldn't ignore the fact that if I had an idea of what the preferences might be, I could save myself a lot of time and stress. Times like these, the crazy thoughts came out to play. Like, maybe I should hold out for an assistant who also had clairvoyant powers? Someone who could predict what the crowds were going to prefer on a given day? Right... As if...

Maybe one day a pattern would emerge.

Although, in fact, one pattern had already emerged. It didn't help my baking choice dilemma, but it was comfortably predictable. Being a half day, Sundays had traditionally become a day of bulk buying rather than individual treats. Families and singles alike chose boxes of desserts to take home for after their evening meal or even to have through the following week.

Once I'd sensed this pattern a few markets back, I'd begun packaging the baked goods to suit and had such fun sharing tips on what could be frozen for later as well as serving and accompaniment tips to take the desserts to the next level for special occasions.

And I was learning from them as well. Returning customers excitedly shared their own serving suggestions. One lady served the cheesecake bars with chilled poached peach halves from her garden and then filled the seed indent with homemade chocolate-coated ice cream balls (that she called *pearls*). She topped the whole thing with my peach-brandy sauce. My mouth watered, and I couldn't wait to try that!

Another customer, a man in his sixties—I knew because he told me his age—proudly told me how he loved to cook but wasn't so hot at the baking side of things. He described a special dinner he'd made for his wife of forty years for their recent anniversary. Not confident enough to bake his own dessert, he'd purchased the marshmallow bars from my stand and reshaped them into hearts with a cookie cutter, grated some chocolate curls over them and added fresh strawberries and my strawberry daiquiri sauce on the side. He said his wife was still raving to their friends. He even had photos to show me. The delicate pink of the marshmallow worked so well with the richer pink sauce and rosy strawberries that I was genuinely impressed. Impressed enough to consider making heart-shaped marshmallow bars for the Valentine's market. He was so thrilled when I asked if he'd mind me using his idea, he even offered a copy of his photo to use as a serving suggestion.

This was the community and life I had so yearned for— this connection with people and a feeling of being accepted. And to top off all that magic, my first orders started to trickle in from the returning customers. New customers, listening in, encouraged by the rave reviews started ordering as well. Oh heavens. As I carefully made notes, I realized that getting an assistant was suddenly less a whim and more of a necessity.

WHEN I WOKE on Monday morning, my muscles were stiff from standing all weekend, and my lips still tingled from where my cowboy had made his pride in me very clear, and in a very tangible manner, before he headed back to his farm. My fingers moved slowly over my lips, which were smiling at the memories of the day and night before. For a fleeting moment, I recognized this as contentment as I lazed in that post-adrenaline lethargy that accompanied the acknowledgment of knowing you'd done something right. A few somethings, as it turned out.

Sadly, it was a brief moment. If I wasn't so worried about Fiona, Clay, and Midge, I doubt I'd have been able to wipe the smile off my face for a week. As it was, that cloud outweighed any contentment I was experiencing, and my mind was again fully focused on how to prove Clay and Midge were both innocent of murder and to prove a link between the missing money and accounts and Clausen.

My limited experience and success in this area told me there was only one way to prove someone innocent—and that was to uncover the guilty party. That is—to prove someone else guilty.

Easy.

Not.

Last time, my lists had proved to be useful, even for just clarifying my thoughts, so after getting myself ready to face the day, I grabbed a coffee and padded into the study, missing the sound of giant paws padding along at my heels. Gathering up a couple of markers, I set up my whiteboard and flung open the French doors to let the cool of post dawn drift into the room—bringing with it the evocative scent of the potted, creamy gardenias that lined the wide steps up to the house.

If Tiny had been there she would, as usual, have wandered out to sniff around. Her tail would've been wagging, and she'd play for a minute before settling into a comfy position just outside the door. She always thought she fooled me, but I knew she was making sure she kept me in sight.

Still, today she'd be experiencing doggie ecstasy. Jonah had taken her last night so he could drop her at the local pet beauty parlor for a spa day. It was an extravagant treat, but she loved it and thankfully I could afford it. And such a small reward for all that beautiful dog did for me.

What a life. And once more I gave thanks for the wonderful turn my life had made all due to one woman's generosity. *Thank you, Miss Alice…*

It made me all the more determined to protect that life and those I'd come to love who shared it with me.

Forty minutes later, I knew the list had helped. Six names—or at least six people—were listed. Two I would stake my life on being innocent of Frederick Clausen's murder, but they had to be up there for the sake of clarity and to create an accurate time line. Listed with those two, Clay and Midge, were Simone Grant, the houseguest at the B&B, because there was something very suspicious about her and my gut told me she was involved somehow. The so-called relative who was visiting in Arcacia Street—simply because she was a stranger. And because, if our mail carrier was correct, she was no more a visiting relative than I was. The fifth entry was the woman I suspected needed my help—the one who (I was pretty sure) had made eye contact with me outside the meeting. Because, again, if my instincts were correct and she needed help to escape from Clausen, then maybe she'd been forced to take action. Fatal action. At the bottom of the list, I used a space to include all the women (and men) who were involved in the commune—or whatever it was.

Surely a murder such as this would have been committed by someone close to home? Like one of his followers? Was Clausen a stereotypical, power-driven cult leader who preyed on the innocent and weak? Could this have been retribution? Or simply someone who'd had enough and snapped?

The names themselves—such as they were—didn't help much at all. And it clarified how little information I'd gathered. Basically it highlighted the glaring blanks, but it gave me a solid starting point. I knew, for example, absolutely nothing about Clausen's business affairs nor about his commune. I didn't even know exactly where it was, although hopefully today, all that would change.

I also had to ascertain the identity of the woman from Arcacia Street as well as see if Peggy/Meggy/Megan was interested in a job. And, of course, there was the guest at the B&B.

Breakfast was a peach smoothie riddled with ice chips that I happily crunched through after they were dragged up through the oversized drinking straw. The sweetness of the peach combined with the tangy orange juice, tart yogurt, semi-sweet strawberries, aromatic mint leaves, and crunchy ice was perfect. Healthy, refreshing, cool, and filling—it hit all markers.

Even better, it was mobile, and fifteen minutes later I was on the road complete with an extra smoothie for Midge, who was going to be my first stop.

"You were up and gone early this morning. I was up just after dawn, and you'd left the house," I said as I pushed through the heavy door that led into the offices of the *Airlie Falls Gazette*.

The space was neat as it always was, but despite the bowl of fresh flowers that graced the countertop, the distinctive smell of newsprint mingled with coffee permeated the air and overwhelmed the sweet scents of the flowers. It was like it had seeped into every pore of the building—into the walls, the flooring, and furniture. Along the walls, various headlines mounted in aged, dark wood frames depicted a history of Airlie Falls and it would be fascinating reading if ever one had the time.

Midge reached for the drink, not even pretending to be surprised I'd brought it along—and took a long appreciative draw. Smacking her lips, she cooed her delight before launching into an answer. "Tomorrow is publishing day. Loads to do. I need to be ready."

I caught sight of the front-page headline and pursed my lips. No doubt about it, Midge was as ethical as they came. EDITOR AND MAYOR BOTH QUESTIONED OVER CLAUSEN MURDER.

She followed my gaze and shrugged. "If it was someone

else, I'd have to print it—I'm no exception." She sighed. "At least I've got the inside scoop on this one… Nothing like interviewing yourself for the front-page news."

I leaned in to give her a hug. "We'll find the answers, Midge. We'll get through this."

She hugged me back. "Thanks, Rosie. It means a lot to know someone has my back."

"Don't sell yourself short. A lot of people in this town appreciate you and love you. Your aunt Merline, for one! They know murder isn't your style."

She laughed. "Not with a blunt instrument, anyway. Don't they say 'the pen is mightier than the sword'?"

"Don't they also say 'research is the answer to all that ails us'?"

Her answering expression was incredulous. "No, I don't believe *they* say that at all. You made that up."

I had no remorse. "I know. But I had to get you on track. I need answers. Starting with what you learned about Frederick Clausen."

Before answering she glanced at the work set out before her. Glanced longingly, reminding me that she had a load of work to do.

I cut off her response. "You work. Do you have a file on him or something? Notes I can look over?"

Relief evident, she passed over a manila folder and a flash drive. I balanced the folder on my right palm, testing the weight. It was much lighter and thinner than I'd have liked or imagined. Surely someone with an ego as big as Clausen, and as manipulative as he appeared to be, would have generated more headlines or print space than this? Maybe the bulk was contained on the USB? I started with the paper file, reading over the scant news articles. They were all pretty general.

I chanced a darted look across at Midge, who caught it and shrugged. "I know… I know exactly what you're thinking. I said from the beginning that there was precious little to dig up. It's very confusing and doesn't seem to sit with the man we met. That Clausen came across as a powerful big shot whose love of the sound of his own voice was surpassed only by the marvel of his own cleverness. Both of which were wildly overrated, in my opinion."

"Whereas," I added, pointing to the file before me, "*this* Clausen seems to be a mild-mannered man who appreciates privacy and eschews the public eye."

She tilted her head to one side. "Do you suppose Clausen isn't really Clausen? Like, he's a double or something?"

I felt my eyes literally pop. "Hey, isn't overreacting and overdramatizing my modus operandi? You're supposed to be the voice of reason and logic." Her expression was still thoughtful, and I rushed on. "You can't believe that, Midge? That would be something straight from a mystery novel."

"I'm certainly not saying I believe it," she answered. "However, I am saying it's something to consider. Identity theft isn't new or unheard of. It happens."

"But not like this!" I argued. "Despite liking his privacy, Clausen was a public figure. And his stab at the mayoral position would have made him even more public. It's one thing to assume an identity of some mom or pop from say"—my mind struggled for a random place name— "Hicksville, Arkansas, who hasn't got a clue they've been violated, but it's quite another thing to assume a stolen identity and then stand for mayor. Even if that mayoral position is somewhere as hicksville as Airlie Falls, Texas!"

She said nothing, just watched me.

"The position of mayor," I continued, "is surely a position that has to be recorded. Documented. If Clausen wasn't really Clausen, then that would be one heck of a risk. He'd spend his whole time looking over his shoulder. Expecting any minute that the truth would be revealed." I shook my head. "No, I can't accept that one. Too extreme, even for me," I added on a grin. "Any more ideas?"

She sighed. "You made some valid points, but at the moment that's the only idea I have. Weak as it is."

I gathered up the papers. "Can I take these with me?" When she nodded, I asked, "And I assume the address of the commune or whatever is here in this package somewhere?" Again she nodded. "Okay, I need to get out of here so you can work. I'll give you a call later, and if it's going to be a late night, I'll drop by with dinner. Okay?"

Her thanks echoed behind me as I made my way back to the car. I needed to go over these papers again and find out what was on the flash drive as well, but now that I was in town, I wanted to pay a call to some people in Arcacia Street.

FIRST STOP, THOUGH, was the tiny local library, where Mary Struthers had held the position of librarian for almost fifty years and claimed to know everyone in, and everything about, Airlie Falls.

"Rosie Hart, the good Lord created colors to be shown to their best advantage and she'd be smiling to see how you brought that glorious sunshine inside with you today. Your only competition is the roses in my garden. Darlin', you are a sight for sore eyes."

I couldn't help glancing down at the yellow, fluted, off-the-shoulder top I'd chosen for its softness and ease. And I smiled my thanks because, like Mary, I'd always believed this color paid tribute to the brilliant sunshine we enjoyed down here in Texas. And yes, yellow roses and Texas and all that; despite me being an Oklahoma native originally, that tune immediately struck up in my head. Any other day that song and Mary's words would have been enough to keep my smile in place all day long.

"Aww, that's so nice, Miss Mary, but now I feel bad that I've come to blatantly extract information and not just for a friendly chat!"

The older woman looked down at me over her half-moon glasses. "Are you intending to be unfriendly during this so-called extraction?"

I flushed, then giggled. "No! I just meant—"

"Honey," she said, cutting off what would have been a feeble response, "you can ask me anything at all as long as we're being friendly to each other. Any conversation can be pleasant if we make the effort to make it so. It's the way of the South. Am I correct?"

I grinned again. "Yes, ma'am. You're correct."

Her own smile grew wider. "Now, what is it you need to know? Or should I say, *who* is it you need to know it about?"

"It's an easy one—I hope. A young girl who lives in Arcacia Street came out to Miss Alice's looking for part-time work last winter. If she's still available I'd like to offer her some work as my assistant, but I can't remember her name. She'd be just college age—freshman year. I think her name was something like Peggy or Meg or Megan? Maybe more exotic than that. Do you know her and maybe her home address?"

She thought for only a moment before answering, "Makaylah Williams. Her daddy is the head of the math department over at Eastwood High School. And her mama is an opera singer, Jada Williams, though she doesn't do much singing anymore."

"You really are a marvel. You truly do know everything about Airlie Falls!"

Mary beamed. "Oh, honey, that was an easy one. Makaylah—actually she calls herself Mackie—is a lovely girl. She was probably looking for work with Miss Alice because she's trying to get as much nursing practice as she can. Wants to study nursing," she continued in that clipped way of hers, "maybe even medicine later on."

"Oh—then maybe she won't be interested in kitchen work. I thought she was looking for any kind of work."

Mary shrugged. "You can only ask. And if she doesn't need the work, she might know someone who does. She's that kind of girl—always willing to help." Mary leaned forward. "Just the other day that woman who's staying with the Lipskies came in to use the internet on one of our computers and she was thoroughly lost. Young Mackie noticed her distress and sat with her for hours helping her navigate her way around the internet. When the woman left she couldn't stop singing Mackie's praises. Though she was disappointed that she couldn't find as much information as she was hoping for. I offered to check our archives, but we didn't have much about that Clausen man, either. And then he went and got himself killed! I couldn't believe my ears."

She looked to me for comment, and I had to force myself out of my shock. Mary Struthers had just inadvertently given me the answer to the second part of my puzzle without me even asking. "Um, yes, terrible news."

She lowered her voice and leaned even closer. "Well, more terrible for some than for others. That Clausen was making a lot of bold promises. Telling folk their land value was going to triple if he got elected mayor. And that there'd be people swooping down on this town willing to pay any price just to live here. He was promising big salaried jobs and college scholarships for the kids of this town. And I gotta say because it's true and fair: The folk here are nice people but they're human, and some saw those dollar signs and were suckered right in. Hermie Bryce's wife was telling me how Hermie had promised her one of those four-month round-the-world cruises, and that's best part of forty thousand dollars! When I asked where they were going to get that kind of money, she said Hermie told her it'd come from Clausen. It wasn't the only story I heard like that, either."

Belatedly I realized my mouth was hanging open. "I…um… Oh wow. Miss Mary, do you think that one of these people found out that maybe Clausen wasn't being completely honest about his promises and maybe murdered him? Perhaps accidentally?"

"It wouldn't have been an accident if I'd been around!"

The voice startled us. Neither of us had been aware of the other woman who'd come into the empty library and had obviously heard our conversation. She was a small woman whose cheeks were flushed from the heat, and brown wispy hair clung to her damp forehead. However, the dampness on her cheeks and red-rimmed eyes had nothing to do with the heat outside.

"Jayne! Honey, what's wrong?" Mary was out from behind her desk in a flash and pulled the other woman into a hug, while I stood awkwardly to the side.

Jayne sniffed and I at least felt useful when she accepted a tissue from the box I nabbed from Mary's desk. "I heard what you were saying about this C...Cl...Clausen fellow, and it seems he was playing p-people," she began brokenly. "That story about house prices tripling? Well that wasn't what my Johnny and others in *our* street were told. I've been away with my sick mama, and I've come home to discover that this man, this Clausen, tricked them into signing over our properties for way less than market value. He's taken our homes!"

Mary rubbed the woman's back. "Oh, you poor dear. Come and sit down and tell us how on earth he did that."

While Mary settled Jayne, I scooted over to the water cooler and grabbed a cup of water for each of us.

Jayne was again grateful, and I felt less awkward as I settled onto the seat on the other side of her. "He was slick and sly, that's how! He apparently showed them some kind of proof that a paper was about to be released that proved there was something dangerous in the soil beneath our homes. It meant the government could reclaim our land and homes and not have to compensate us. Or so he said. Johnny said he had some fancy lawyer with him who verified all that."

She paused for breath, and selfishly I willed her forward. It was Mary who muttered, "I don't think I like where this story is goin'..."

"And I think you'd be right, Miss Mary," Jayne muttered

back. "Just as you've probably guessed the residents were told their land and homes were worthless, but he wanted to help the people of *his* town, and he'd found someone who was willing to buy them out for a low price. They were told it was better than getting nothing. And they all believed him."

"Are you sure he wasn't telling the truth?" I asked—and did so without choking on my words. Barely.

Her laugh was bitter. "Oh, very sure. I work for a lawyer in Dallas. Thankfully I can work from home most days. Anyway, if I'd been home I would have asked my boss, David, to sit in on these meetings, but of course I wasn't here. As soon as I heard about it, I went straight to David, who investigated. He went directly to the right officials, and they've confirmed they know nothing about any harmful soil issues in this town or anywhere in the vicinity of Airlie Falls. We were all cheated out of our homes."

Out of habit, I covered my mouth. "Oh my goodness. This is terrible!" Leaning forward I put my other hand on hers, trying so hard to convey the sincerity of my sorrow for her situation. "Miz Jayne? You don't know me. I'm Rosie Hart, and I have a vested interest in discovering all I can about Frederick Clausen. And your shocking news plays right into my opinion of the man."

She nodded sadly. "I know who you are. My family has come to love your desserts. Not that we can probably afford them now…" She stopped and shook her head. "Forgive me. Self-pity never helped anyone, and I'm not lookin' for sympathy."

Mary clucked her concern. I nodded, maintaining eye contact and making a mental note to send over regular baskets of food. It was the least I could do. "Well, I think you have reason to expect sympathy. This is a tragic story. Do you mind me asking when this all happened?"

She scrunched her face in thought. "Maybe five days ago? It was all rushed through as they were told the buyer had to leave the country and it had to be done quickly or they'd miss out. They signed overnight!"

I was thinking very bad words to describe Clausen, but I tried to contain them. "Did you speak to him?"

"He died the day after I got home. But I had already passed on the news to the others by the time I got back. Johnny couldn't get hold of me until the contracts were already signed because I was in ICU where no phones are allowed. But I went straight to my boss, David, when I heard the news."

"So, your neighbors already knew they'd been cheated before you got home?"

"You don't think…?" Her expression changed. "Please, they're not murderers. They're just hardworkin' simple people trying to pay their mortgages and put their kids through school."

I was saved from having to address that when Mary snapped her fingers. "Jayne, isn't your young sister…" She paused and thought. "Ally! Isn't Ally interested in becoming a chef?"

Jayne rolled her eyes. "Don't. It's all we hear about. And now with this and our Luke off to college in two years, I don't know how we'll afford culinary school for Ally, too." Looking at me, she frowned as she tried to explain. "Ally was a 'late in life' baby. Our mama died when Ally was only thirteen, our pa had already passed, and so she's lived with us ever since. She's a great kid—well, she's twenty-two now—and she finished her teaching degree, but her heart is set on culinary school because she wants to combine both careers. She helped us so much with babysitting and all that when she was younger, and I promised I'd try to help her, but now…"

Mary made eye contact with me, urging me to make a move, and admittedly it did seem like a perfect plan. "Um, Jayne, what does Ally do now?"

She sighed. "Anything she can! She's had some substitute teaching work, although now it's summer break, that's dried up."

I nodded. "I'd like to meet her if I could. I've got a part-time job available, and if she suits, maybe she'd be interested?"

The transformation in her face was something I will never forget. It was amazing. "A part-time job with you? Baking?" The woman almost kissed me right there. I had to remind her we were just going to talk—that nothing was concrete—but she didn't care. She kept saying she just knew

Ally would be perfect. And maybe she would be, I thought. And, too, I guessed it was the least I could do after all I'd learned in that one visit.

After settling on a time to meet up with Ally and also securing the Lipskies' house number in Arcacia Street, I left to find a quiet corner in the Bluebonnet Café. I had a lot of thinking to do and a lot of notes to make, which equated to a lot of tea drinking.

I was almost there when I saw a woman heading toward the café from the other direction. It wasn't just the familiarity that caught my attention. It was the hurrying. No one hurried in Airlie Falls. Hurrying was for city folk—at least that's what they all said.

I stopped, watching. Her head was down. Simone Grant. Almost at the entrance she slowed and looked up and locked eyes on me. For once she looked rattled. It was only for a second, and only when she first set eyes on me. Immediately her eyes turned to the café door, and with barely a step out of time, she picked up her pace and continued past the entrance.

As we passed by each other, only then did Simone Grant smile. With a nod, she bid me good day and hurried on.

Instinct told me she'd been going to enter the café. So, what changed her mind? It seemed my presence had been the catalyst for the decision, but why? Was it as simple as not wanting to be in my vicinity? Or something else? Something like not wanting me to see who she was meeting? So much to think about.

As usual, the café was crowded, but a quick glance didn't offer an answer to a possible secret coffee date meeting with Simone. No strangers. No one sitting alone. Did that blow my theory?

Hardly.

I didn't give up on ideas that quickly.

I headed toward the back to an empty table to mull things over. I'd been seated for about ten minutes when irritated looks from the people at the table next to me snapped me back to the present. I didn't need to question the irritation and mouthed a humble apology. It was my habit of absently tapping my pencil against any surface while I was thinking. The more intense the thoughts, the more furious and forceful the tapping. Obviously this had been a particularly intense session. I placed the pencil firmly on the table and clasped my hands while I waited for my iced tea.

So, Clausen had been involved in some shady deals— telling one side of town they were about to get rich while fleecing the other side. To what purpose? Did Clay know any of this? Did the sheriff know?

Because right there were a whole slew of potential murderers with far stronger motives than Clay or Midge.

But again, why would Clausen do that? I understood

cheating the poor souls who'd potentially lost their properties in so much as I got that he was gathering up whole parcels of land for almost nothing.

So, what was the deal on the other side? All I could think of was so that he could shore up support for himself. After all, I suppose if someone made you a load of money and reduced your financial burdens, he was going to be your lifelong friend, right? You'd support him no matter what, right?

"Unless his name is Satan," I muttered quietly.

"Excuse me? Did you say something, Miss Rosie?"

I looked up into the smiling face of Emmy Kaye, Delvene's teenage assistant, as she placed my iced tea on the table. I smiled back. "I was just wondering what else I should order," I prevaricated.

Actually, looking up into that pretty young face had reminded me I still had business in Arcacia Street. And that, yes, I could definitely use some fortifying as I continued on this discovery tour. The special of the day sounded like just the thing: poached Atlantic salmon with lemon dill sauce. And maybe I'd even treat myself to some ice cream for dessert.

How was I to know my appetite would die before I'd even had my first mouthful of food?

Chapter Eight

I AUTOMATICALLY GLANCED up as the bell on the outer door chimed the entrance of a new customer. The woman glanced casually around the spacious café space, smiling and nodding at various acquaintances. My own smile was already in place, awaiting my turn. Liz Pauling, an artist, and her husband, a sculptor, ran a small hobby farm out of town.

I'd purchased some of her artwork, and we'd become friends. So far that had been restricted to the odd coffee date, but I'd promised to join her yarn-and-knitting group as soon as the weather cooled. And to bring Midge as well.

Her gaze was nearly upon me and I almost stood to wave her over. Thankfully I didn't because when that gaze reached me, the smile died, and flustered, she instantly looked away.

Hurt, I didn't know what to do. Pretend I hadn't noticed, or try to get to the bottom of her reaction? Had I done something to offend her? My mind tracked to our last meeting. No, I was sure nothing had happened...

Mesmerized, I continued to watch her. Liz—who was always so graceful and sure of herself—dropped her purse and then in retrieving it, almost collided with a tray-bearing waitress. Amid the apologies, confusion, and cleanup, I realized something was very wrong.

Drawing a breath I rose and went to her. "Liz, are you okay?" I took her arm. "Come and sit with me. Have some tea."

Her eyes were wide as she looked at me. Backing away, she said, "No, I ca—" Then just as suddenly as she'd backed away, she stilled and straightened. Closing her eyes momentarily, she sighed, opened them, and nodded. And just like that, she was following me to my table.

Emmy Kaye arrived silently with another iced tea, and I let Liz compose herself while I sipped at my own. Even then, I didn't speak, giving her time to decide what she wanted to do.

Finally she was able to look at me, and in her eyes I saw sadness and regret. "I'm so sorry I reacted that way. I've been hoping I wouldn't see you."

I frowned. "Why?"

"Because I knew if I did, then I'd have to tell you."

I sat back in my chair, mentally wading through my confusion. "Well, first, I'm not going to force you to tell me anything, and secondly, what on earth could be so bad that you'd be afraid to mention it?"

Then a light bulb started blinking at me. And with it came a chill. "Is it Jonah? Something about him? Or the Fencotts?" I added as other thoughts darted in.

She shook her head. "Oh dear, this is so hard. No, it's

not Jonah or the Fencotts, but it is about someone you care about."

Beside us, the occupants of the table moved on and others replaced them. I didn't look up. Tracing a pattern on the table with my finger, I found it was distractingly pleasant to realize that for the first time in my life there were several people who fell into that category. People I'd come to care very deeply about and who cared for me in return. But if not the ones I'd mentioned, the next down would be Midge. Or Hank. Or Brenda…

When I mentioned Midge's name, Liz nodded. "Oh, Rosie, it's been awful. I know Midge is a great girl and she'd never hurt anybody, but the thing is, I overheard her threaten Frederick Clausen."

I sat up straight. "You what?" From that moment, it was like everybody else in the room ceased to exist.

"It was late and her office lights were still on. Rory was having an exhibition in Dallas, and I wanted to put a notice in the *Gazette* about it, so I thought I'd drop in. Her inner office door was open and I could hear voices. I turned to go, then I realized she was upset and so I hovered, wondering if I should help her."

"And you heard what was said?"

She nodded. "I recognized Clausen's voice. Just recently he'd called out to the farm to introduce himself. Rosie, that night I heard him—he was threatening to take the paper away from her. Said he knew stuff about her and could close her up. And that's when"—she paused to gather herself—"that's when she told him she'd kill him if he tried."

I shook my head. "That would have been just a bluff! An angry response! Not a real intention of murder. Midge would never mean it."

Liz nodded. "I know, I know. But, Rosie, she sounded so deadly cold when she said it! And that Clausen? He just laughed! He was moving about and I figured he was about to leave, so I scooted out of there. And the next thing we hear, he's dead!" She was shaking her head. "I haven't known what to do. I didn't go to Sheriff Kinnead because, like you, I don't think she could murder anybody. And yet, I heard her say those exact words right before he was murdered."

I reached across to take her hand, my head screaming as it refused to accept the information it was being served up.

Now she'd started, Liz couldn't seem to stop talking. "I've been sick with worry. I've wavered between guilt at not reporting what I know—and loyalty to a friend. Certainly she's a new friend, but she's still a friend, and besides, I know you'd never be close with someone you didn't fully trust." She sighed. "You're the only one I could tell, Rosie; I've just been hoping and praying the sheriff would find the real murderer and I could forget about it. Hoping I didn't have to tell you. I left it in God's hands. I told him if I saw you, then it was a sign I had to tell you."

God was in on this, too? Did He not know I had quite a lot on my plate right now without adding a solid murder motive for my best friend? Of course she didn't do it. In spite of what Liz had just said, my stance on that hadn't changed. But it scared me because if it got out, Midge would be in a whole lot of trouble.

My food went back to the kitchen, cold and barely touched. We chatted for a while longer, but it was stilted and forced. Weather and pets. More tea was brought over, warm tea, and Liz drank most of it. Everything seemed to stick in my throat and stay there. By the time we said goodbye, I had the queen of all headaches and I was reconsidering my trip to Arcacia Street. I needed my wits about me to try to find information without seeming like I was doing it, and I wasn't sure that was something I could pull off right then.

Alone at the table, I blinked and looked around. I felt like I'd been in a cave, like Liz and I had just emerged into the light after being locked in the dark. There was nothing metaphorical about my thoughts. I sincerely felt like we'd blocked out our surroundings and completely forgotten where we were. At least I had. My head felt fuzzy and thick, and I almost tripped over a chair belonging to the table closest to me, which was thankfully empty. Feeling clumsy, I tried to push the chair in under the table but something blocked it, and that's when I lost my balance. And fell. Heavily.

Of course, there was a fuss.

Delvene, her waitresses, even her cook and barista all came running. It was chaos. Someone calling to get an ambulance. To call Jonah. Other voices ordering me to be still. Not move.

It took far too long to convince them the only thing hurt was my pride. Which, in fact, wasn't quite true. I'd twisted my ankle ever so slightly when I'd kicked the chair, and it was throbbing along with my head, which had hit the floor.

But these were minor issues that would be cleared up by the next day, I was sure of it. However, the embarrassment (and secret pride) in being scooped up by my own muscle-bound cowboy was something that would take a lot longer to live down.

In a wild fluke, Jonah had finished a job early and had called in to his folks before heading out to my farm. So, he'd been a mere half block away when he'd gotten a call from Delvene. And yes, he insisted on carrying me the entire half block back to his parents' B&B.

Laughing to cover my embarrassment over the whole affair, I bid farewell to the assembled crowd of well-wishers, offering my thanks and my version of a royal wave. We were almost at the door when my laughter died. There, in profile leaving the café, was the woman from the commune. The one who'd tried to signal me! Except it wasn't...

Well, it was, although now her hair was much more stylish and her clothes were also stylish and modern. She was wearing makeup and... A sense of déjà vu settled over me. I'd been here before. At least, I'd been in this situation before: thinking I'd seen her when it wasn't her at all.

It had looked so much like her, though. She paused to glance at the outsized watch dangling from her slender wrist, darted a look in both directions, and then headed out.

Blame the bump on my head, but I suddenly had the craziest thought that she'd been stood up. And I was pretty sure I knew the identity of the culprit.

Simone Grant.

And if my theorizing was correct it was because she didn't want me to see her with the mysterious woman. Mysterious woman? The Arcacia Street lady? The "cousin" of the Lipskies. That thought pushed me to the point where it took all my strength not to groan out loud. Why was it I kept finding more questions but never any answers?

I tried to hurry Jonah, who was enjoying his role as rescuer way too much, but by the time we were on the sidewalk there was no sign of her. Which may have been a good thing because once I hit the bright sunshine my head began to ache in earnest, and I had to wonder whether I'd hit my it harder than I'd thought.

The weekday traffic in Airlie Falls could never be described as heavy, but as Jonah strode down the sidewalk, grin on his face, it seemed every vehicle in town passed us on that short walk. Good-natured calls and whistles met us, and there was a constant accompaniment of car horns, which I guessed in a way was kind of cute. Or maybe it was the cute look of pride on Jonah's face. I wanted to be a bit mad with him for doing the whole he-man thing, but really?

So much had happened in the past couple of hours, so much information to process, and my head hurt anew just thinking about it. For the moment, maybe the sensible thing was to just lie back and enjoy what was happening and worry about it all a bit later.

The last vehicle to blast its appreciation was Clive's mail truck, and the now familiar bangle-and-bracelet-clad forearm, complete with fingers tipped in candy-apple red, waved as it passed. The sharp jab of an unpleasant memory speared me and was quickly washed away by guilt. I had some making up to do to that woman. Sighing, I just added it to my mental list, wondering how to juggle my love life, my friends, my business, and discovering the identity of a murderer with my responsibilities and life in the community.

As soon as we entered the B&B, I expected to be swamped as I always was, with appreciation for Fiona's skill in creating such homely elegance. The color scheme of soft blues and greens supported by gentle lemons and all highlighted by the pops of brighter yellow was both welcoming and sophisticated. It was all complemented by the gleaming dark wood furniture and the artfully arranged bowls of cut flowers that added a sense of freshness and life as well as their calming perfume.

Yet as aware of this as I expected to be, it was Simone Grant who took center stage in my thoughts. Midge hadn't mentioned if she'd discovered any information yet, and being here made me itch to push that along.

Even that, though, was thrust aside at the sight of Fiona sitting in the living room. In the months I'd known her, the only time I'd ever noted that woman to be seated was to eat or in her office surrounded by the endless streams of paperwork that came her way. I'd never seen her just *lounge* before, and the sight of her, slumped shoulders, energy seeming to have been drained from her, was downright scary.

She jerked forward when she saw me in Jonah's arms. "What's go—"

"This isn't how it looks." I quickly wriggled free to show her I was okay. "Your caveman son is just showing off. I'm fine. Truly. Please don't worry."

Jonah grinned. "Hey, if the world had more cavemen—"

"There'd be more women with headaches?" I finished for him.

His grin gave way to a chuckle. "Sweetheart, seems you can do that all by yourself." His fingers gently probed my skull. "How's the bump coming along? Delvene seemed to think it was going to be a beauty." He winced along with me when I couldn't control the *ow* that filled the room. "That bad, huh? Better get you some ice and painkillers. Pity we didn't have a category for biggest bump at our annual fair. You'd be a certainty to take the blue ribbon."

"Jonah, stop being a tease and let's get her attended to." I would have argued at my need for treatment, but seeing a spark of the old Fiona, bossy and in control, filled me with warmth and hope. So I went along with it. "Honey, what happened?" she continued as she helped Jonah get me seated.

"Just another example of my gracelessness, aka my clumsiness. This is why I could never have taken up ballet. I trip over my own feet."

My joke fell flat as Jonah frowned. "I thought you tripped on a chair leg that hadn't been pushed in properly. That's what Delvene said."

Things happen so quickly that it's often hard to remember the exact sequence, and as it had been such an insignificant event, I'd barely examined it. Now, though, I forced my mind back. "You're right. But it wasn't that the chair leg was sticking out so much as that something was preventing it from being moved forward. The only weird thing is that I couldn't remember anyone sitting there. But then..." I stopped. The conversation I'd had about Midge was something I wasn't ready to share even with those closest to me. Not yet.

"But then?" Fiona prompted.

I forced a smile. "Then Liz Pauling popped over to join me, and you know what it's like when two gals get gossiping!" Both watched me, and I hoped they put my evasiveness down to a headache. Part of which was completely true, I noted as the thumping in my head began to rival the ferocity of a base drum in a rock band. Instinctively my hand came up to my forehead. "Truly, I'm fine. It's not the first time I've tumbled headfirst, and it won't be the last."

Fiona ignored me and looked up at her son. "Water. Aspirin. Ice bag. I'll get a pillow and blanket."

These people were too precious to me. I couldn't deceive them. "Fiona, please. I'm really okay. Yes, I have a headache, but a couple of aspirin and a glass of water will do the trick."

"But, darlin'…"

I smiled and reached out to take her hands. "I've never felt so loved as I do here in this town—in this home." I slid a glance in Jonah's direction to ensure he got that message as well. "And you've cared so well for me when I've needed it, but today, I can't let you fuss because I'm truly okay."

"You know I love fussing over you, darlin'," she replied. "Clay and I knew the moment Jonah brought you into this house that you were meant to be here with us all. But," she sighed, "if you insist you're okay, I'll back down." She paused and her expression changed, and it was pure Fiona of old. "Just this once. Hear me?"

I laughed, then blinked back a shaft of pain. "Deal. But now let's get those pills!"

As it was, I made a mockery of my own bold speech by dropping into a light sleep after I'd had the pills. One minute I was sitting on a soft sofa and the next my feet were up and I was in snoozeville. When I woke, I was shocked to see how much time had passed, and Fiona was pressing a late afternoon snack on me. I declined coffee, and she made hers while I nibbled on a chicken salad sandwich and Jonah went to answer the phone. "Is there any news?" I ventured when we were alone.

She sighed and dropped heavily into a white wicker chair in the kitchen nook. "Nothing worth reporting. The authorities have brought in experts to trace my banking paths. So far they've not found anything helpful. And as Frank pointed out, even if they find the money was withdrawn, there's nothing to prove it wasn't me who did it." She fiddled with her cup. "And of course, they'll then say Clay murdered Clausen so he wouldn't push to have the accounts revealed."

"But it's a relatively insignificant amount! We're not talking millions of dollars here!"

"The thing is, Rosie, that amount *is* significant to a lot of folk around here, and they won't take it lightly that someone took it. Whether it was me or someone else, the money they'd worked for—and, except for their generosity, could have used for themselves—is gone, and it's a heavy blow to them. Their trust has been violated and I don't blame them for being upset."

I leaned across to steady her hands. "But, Fiona, no one will believe you did this!"

Tears filled her eyes. "I have friends and supporters, darlin', but human nature is fickle. Once a story or idea gets out there"—she waved toward the front of the house and town in general—"it grows legs and soon it grows a tail. It starts to sound real, and so folk make pieces fit. Before you know it, doubt has sprouted and it's fed by more stories and suddenly it's taken over. Even with people I've known all my life. You can bet your bottom dollar that every mistake or bad judgment call I've ever made since nursery school has been taken out and aired off and discussed and analyzed. It's the way it works."

"Oh, Fiona, I can't believe that…"

"That's the way of it in small towns. For the most part it's wonderful, but this is the downside. People talk to each other—really talk, and that can be good—and it can be bad." She shrugged, brushing it off and looking up expectantly as Jonah reappeared.

His face was strained, and I guessed we both knew it couldn't be good news. "That was Hank." He dropped to a squat beside his mother. "Mom, I hate to be the one to relay this news, but the market committee has voted that you stand down as manager." He held up a hand to ward off whatever was coming. "Hank did say to reassure you it wasn't an easy-won decision. The vote was close, and it only tipped the scales by two. That means you still have a whole lot of people who believe in you, Mama."

She nodded. If it had been me, I would have fallen apart, but not Fiona. She straightened her back and forced a smile. "It's okay, honey. I expected this would come, and I understand it. I'll let them know I don't blame them and that there are no hard feelings on this side. It's just business. We've all worked hard for this, and no one wants to see it jeopardized."

Jonah wrapped his mother in a hug. "You're one in a million, Fiona Fencott. You know that? One classy dame."

She shrugged, but tears burned my eyes and I was happy to let them fall. Before I could add my own respect for her, Jonah turned to me. That wasn't all he had to pass on. "Rosie honey, he also said that Frank got a tip of some kind, and they're headed on out to your farm. They've got search warrants."

"What? I never even spoke to Clausen. What kind of tip?"

He was shaking his head. "Not you, sweetheart. It's Midge."

"Midge?" My brain was racing to join all the dots. "But... I don't understand. What do they expect to find?"

He shrugged those broad shoulders and moved to join me on the wicker sofa. "I don't know, honey. But as tragic and shocking as this is—there's a bright side." He looked back to Fiona. "Hank says this will take the heat off Dad."

Like me, I saw the conflict in Fiona's eyes. "That's great—in a way," she said quietly. "Getting the heat off your father is an answer to many prayers, but even your father isn't going to be happy that the spotlight has now landed so forcefully on young Midge." She banged her hand on the table. "Oh, this is just terrible. It's a mess! A complete shambles! Good people are being hauled into this evil, and they shouldn't be!"

I agreed wholeheartedly, but then that dark secret I'd just learned today was lying heavily on my heart, the same heart that clenched painfully as I thought of Liz. Would this be enough to prompt her to step forward and share her knowledge with the sheriff? As my pulse picked up speed I could only pray she held off. For just a while longer, at least.

"We need to get out to my place," I said looking up at Jonah and moving to grab my purse.

"My truck. I'll drive."

We all went. Fiona as well. It was a quiet trip, with the other two as lost in their own thoughts as I, and so it was a surprise to them when I suddenly blurted, "Fiona, what do you know about this Simone Grant? Your B&B guest. Do you know what she does? For a job? Or why she's here?"

Chapter Nine

CONFUSED, FIONA SAID, "Well, I believe she said something about farm insurance. Said she'd be out meeting a lot of folk about their policies. Ensuring they're adequately covered." She sighed. "I didn't like to tell her that many around here can't afford insurance policies."

Her eyes suddenly darted to the roof of the truck, an expression I'd seen many times before. Fiona had had an idea. "Oh dear," she continued. "Why didn't we think of this before? We should try to get some kind of group deal. Something affordable. I'm sure it can be done—even if Council chips in. Right! I must make a note for Clay to raise this at the next meeting. We'd need to get some company representatives down here. Perhaps even Simo…"

Jonah and I remained silent. It took only a moment for reality to kick in and bring her back to the present. "Oh dear, that's not going to happen, is it?"

Turning slightly, I squeezed her hand. "Not this month, Fiona, but next month, when everything's back to normal." I tightened the squeeze. "See? This is why you and Clay are such a good team and so good for this community. You're always thinking about what's best for the residents. Always trying to help them. I just hope people remember that."

She said nothing more. Just nodded. Her thoughts were clearly elsewhere, and I figured I knew where. Changing track, I went back to the original question.

"So, Simone's in insurance. Do you know which company she works for?"

Shaking her head as though to clear it, Fiona said, "Not really. I think I saw a reference to Reno on a card she flashed at me, but to be honest I can't be sure. Oh, wait… I think it's Columbus! Yes! That's the company." She paused, her face wreathed in confusion. "Why do you need to know, dear?"

I looked across at Jonah, who nodded and took the lead, his eyes back on the road ahead. "Rosie and I have a suspicion that Simone Grant knows Clausen. He could even be the reason she's here."

Fiona's surprise stirred my conscience, and I debated coming clean about the multiple identities but in the end, I held my counsel. Perhaps this wasn't the time. Besides, that would require a lengthy explanation and we were almost at the turnoff to my driveway. That was my excuse, anyway.

BOTH BOBBY DON and the sheriff had their trucks parked in my drive. Midge's little car wasn't around, and as she was standing on the deep front porch in earnest conversation with the sheriff, I could only imagine she'd traveled out with one of them. My knowledge of police procedure was scant, but I didn't think the suspect had to be home when a search was carried out. It would be just like Frank to afford the person some dignity, though.

Bobby Don wasn't around, and I shuddered at what mayhem he might've been causing in my home.

Fiona stepped straight up to the two on the porch. "Are you okay, Midge?" Turning to the sheriff, she said, "Frank? What's going on? We heard you had search warrants. Can we do something to clear this up?"

Frank scratched his forehead. "You might have been inadvertently led astray there. We don't have a warrant, but we do have to search and Midge here has offered her compliance."

Jonah and I moved in close as well. I instinctively hugged Midge, who was holding herself as stiff as a rock. "But why are you searching? What are you looking for?"

Frank sighed and it was pure frustration. "You know, in any other jurisdiction the sheriff wouldn't be expected to hand over private police information. Why is it the people of my town think differently?"

"Because you're a good, honest cop," Jonah answered. "You play fair."

Frank wasn't the only one burning with frustration. My levels had jumped from zero to self-ignition stage in the beat of a minute, but the sheriff had his dander up. "In answer to your question, Miss Rosie, we'll know what we're looking for when we find it."

Fiona groaned. "And you're trusting Bobby Don to find this mysterious thing? I hope you don't have any chili recipes hiding in there, Rosie, or he's likely to get distracted and leave us hanging here for hours. Days!"

Frank had had enough. He held up a hand for silence. "Why is it I spend most of my time feeling more like a schoolmaster than a sheriff?" he muttered as he shook his head at us. In a clearer voice he said, "The fact is, we're acting on intel that has come our way, which means we're just doin' our job."

He sounded confident, but we all noticed how he peered inside the house following Fiona's chili comment, obviously trying to check on Bobby Don. If I hadn't been a bit riled, I would have laughed when he eventually called, "Bobby Don? You finished in that kitchen yet?"

Jonah had less self-control and sniggered. Loudly. I didn't blame him. It *was* funny. And he and Bobby Don were good pals, so they'd laugh over this at some later stage, but I just didn't feel like laughing.

And I still needed answers. "You said you got 'intel'?" I was suddenly feeling sick. Had Liz done this? "Jonah said you got a tip? Who? Was it—" I stopped. Abruptly. Too abruptly.

The sheriff's eyes narrowed, and I had his complete attention. "Please continue, Rosie. You were sayin'?"

What had I done? My heartbeat picked up speed and ferocity. Oh good grief, could Midge sense it? I didn't want her alerted, either. Crossing the fingers of my free hand, I cleared my throat and shrugged. "Sorry, something caught in my throat." I faked another cough, and the lift of the sheriff's right eyebrow told me it was overkill. Still I plowed on. "I was simply going to ask if it was anyone we know."

While everyone else looked on curiously, Frank continued his silent perusal of me. I forced myself not to squirm; he shouldn't worry—he was very good at this cop stuff.

Finally he broke the eye-lock, and maybe I passed muster because he sighed and pushed his hat farther up onto his head. "If you must know, it was an anonymous tip. Happy?"

No. As a matter of fact, I wasn't. "Anonymous! I thought cops didn't pay heed to anonymous tips! This could be someone who's bored and gets their thrills seeing cops chase their tails."

Ridiculously, now I had people soothing *me*! Even Midge, and I was supposed to be comforting *her*. She was patting my arm and whispering hushing noises, and Jonah had taken up the other side and was squeezing me in tight against him. He knew better than to shush me, though.

In front, Fiona was fist-pumping me all the way. Bless her.

Frank turned lazily from right to left. "And where is this thrill seeker, Rosie?"

The air was starting to seep out of my anger balloon. Your boyfriend stroking your back could do that. No matter how angry you got. "All right! No thrill seeker. But it still could be a troublemaker. Someone doing it just for the heck of it."

He nodded. "Could be. But this person had some specific information. Some of which Midge has been able to verify."

I looked at her, and she nodded before hanging her head. I closed my eyes momentarily. This wasn't good. Really not good.

And it got worse. Bobby Don came pounding down the stairs and out onto the porch waving something protected by an evidence bag. "I got it, Sheriff. It was right there hiding under some—ahem—underwear. I—ahh—brought the items around it along in case, well you know, in case… Oh, and I found this, too. It was stuck down behind a dresser."

I stared at him wondering what to be more amazed at. A deputy sheriff who blushed and stuttered over the word *underwear*, or that he'd actually found something. Frank leaned in and I stepped forward to take a look as well. "Let me look at this other thing first," he ordered.

Being the one with the gloves, Bobby Don held it for Frank to examine. It was a box of some kind. A very well-crafted box, and quite wide. If it had been stuffed behind a dresser in my house—which it obviously had been—it would have stuck out a mile. At Frank's nod he lifted the lid and revealed black satin lining that covered various slots purposely created to hug specific items—but they were all empty.

I was completely flummoxed. "What's that for? A fishing kit? Some fancy paraphernalia that has to be assembled?"

Frank turned to Midge. "Perhaps Midge can tell us?"

She shrugged. "Don't look at me. I'm as in the dark as anyone. I'd say maybe some kind of glamorous hair appliance set? Straighteners? Curling wands? Sorry, that's my best guess." She paused and glared at Frank. "And no, I've never seen it before. That *was* your next question, right?"

I swallowed a grin. It took a lot to rattle Midge.

Sighing, Frank asked for the next item. As Bobby Don produced it, I grabbed for it. Snatching it away from me, Frank struggled with the bag. Turning it one way and then the other to ascertain its contents, his frown growing deeper by the second. "For gosh sakes, Bobby Don, other than underwear, what in tarnation did you find? I can't see anything but this pink, silky, spotted thing and—"

"What?" This time I wasn't going to be pushed aside. I forced my way closer, determined to see that bag. "Where did you get this *mysterious thing*, Bobby Don? Because I certainly didn't give you permission to go through *my* bureau!"

The sheriff sighed. Again. "Explain yourself, Rosie."

"Happily. Sheriff, this is my underwear, and I repeat, I did not give permission for anyone to go tampering with my things." I pointed at the bag. "Secondly, anything you found in that drawer would be mine and therefore not relevant to your case."

Jonah stepped up behind me. "Sheriff? Frank?"

Shaking his head, Frank moved to the table and chairs just a few feet away and sunk heavily into one of the padded wicker chairs. "Only way to solve this is to see what in the heck Bobby Don found." After dragging out a pair of evidence gloves he slipped them on, the plastic snapping against his wrists as he pulled them tight.

We all gathered around him, Fiona—I noted—clasping Midge's hand in support. I didn't blush as two tiny, frothy pairs of sheer underpants, one polka dot, one striped, fell from the bag, but Bobby Don did. Jonah simply cleared his throat, and I wasn't exactly sure what that meant—although I could guess.

Any other reaction was short-lived as all focus was suddenly on the sheet of tightly folded paper that followed. Three things hit me. One, that it wasn't mine, no matter where it had been found. Two, I had never seen it before. Three, it had dried blood on it. Quite a bit.

Fiona gasped. Midge frowned. The others stared. I was taking in all reactions.

Frank had pulled his mouth into his kissy-face pose. "Midge? Miss Moylan. Have you ever seen this before?"

Midge—who I thought couldn't be rattled—paled and hesitated, which I was sure wasn't a good sign, but I understood moments later. I saw her sway first and then her lips seemed to change color ever so slightly.

"Quick, get her down. Inside would be better. It's cooler."

Without hesitation, Jonah scooped her up and hurried to the kitchen/family room where he laid her on a sofa there. I grabbed juice and a couple of cookies, and Fiona helped her eat them while Jonah and I began on something more substantial. Having spent so much time here, Jonah had seen these attacks before and knew what we were going to do.

Bobby Don looked lost while Frank just looked confused. "Is she sick or something?"

"Not really," I answered. "Low blood sugar. She forgets to eat sometimes, and it catches up with her. She just needs to rest a bit and get some food into her. We'll get her a sandwich."

"Is there any chance she's faking this? It seemed mighty timely," Bobby Don asked.

Jonah jumped in before me. "Does she look like she's faking it, B.D.? Can you make yourself go pale on command? And I'd say it *was* timely. Very timely. On top of no food, I'd say the shock of what's going on contributed greatly to this reaction."

I glanced up from slicing a tomato. "Thank you for that." To Frank and Bobby Don, I added. "These aren't really common, but Jonah, Fiona and I have all witnessed her have these attacks before. The doc says she just has to remember to eat regular meals—but you know what it's like when you get busy."

Jonah shot me a stern look. "Yeah. Like someone else I know…"

"Hey, I work with food. I nibble all the time."

Jonah was about to argue, when Midge held up a hand. She was still a bit pale, but color was slowly returning. "Sheriff? I'm not faking and I'm happy to try to answer your questions. However, the first is a tricky one." Even though she was partly lying on the sofa I saw this take its toll. She stared straight ahead, her back rigid and upright, her chin lifted high. "Yes, I've seen this article before, but no, I have never seen this piece of paper before."

I hadn't had a chance to see the paper properly, but I did see her photo and a heading that mentioned something about theft and assault. And I knew without reading it that whatever she was accused of wasn't true. It couldn't be, and I wouldn't believe it.

"Can you tell me how it came to be in your possession?"

She didn't change her position. "It was not and never has been in my possession."

I started to intervene, but Frank held up a restraining hand. "Bobby Don, could you please describe the position of the room in which you made this discovery?"

Bobby Don assumed a stubborn expression, which I presumed was his "tough cop" face. "The room to the left at the top of the stairs. It's the first one you come to on that side. It faces the front of the house and is—kinda—all whitish. Lots of lacy pillows—and things. Maybe it's got some pink… Smells good. Like Rosie."

Frank sighed. Yet again. "The first left at the top of the stairs, facing the front." He looked back at Midge. "Midge, Miss Moylan—can you please tell us which room you occupy?"

"Right-hand side of the house. Faces the back. The third door down the hall. The one that's not all completely *whitish*," she added with a glare at Bobby Don. "Okay, it's a bit whitish, but it's got some grayish and maybe a few bluish accents. And if it smells like me at the moment it would smell like something's burning!"

The sheriff ignored her jibe at his deputy. "You sure of that room, Bobby Don?"

He nodded. "Sure, sir. I didn't even get to the others yet."

"Rosie, have you seen this before?"

I glanced at the paper, noting that Midge wouldn't make eye contact with me as I did so. "Never seen it before."

"Do you have any idea how this got into your room?"

For the first time I felt out of control. "No, I don't. I mean," I added shrugging, "we don't lock doors—just like everybody else in town—and we're both often out, so I guess it could have been planted at any time."

"You're assuming an outsider planted this?" the sheriff asked.

"Well, of course I am! Neither of us"—I included Midge

with the sweep of my hand—"did this!"

"Hmmnnn. Don't I recall Tiny lives here now? Jonah's guard dog?"

Jonah jumped in, frustration clear in his tone. "Yes, but occasionally she has time with me. Last night, for example, and then all day today, she's been at the dog spa."

Frank lifted his brows at that but let it pass.

Sudden panic surged through me, "You were supposed to collect her!"

He leaned in to touch the tip of my nose with his finger. "It's okay, sweetheart. I called Dad. He's on the job."

Relief washed over me. Since opening the market stall, *From the Hart*, I couldn't carry Tiny in my car. As clean as she was, it wasn't hygienic, so Jonah had to take her in the truck if we all went somewhere together. Or if she had an appointment or something.

"If we could get back to the point," Frank interrupted, moving slightly to make room for the refreshments Fiona had been busy fixing.

It amused me for a moment to watch Bobby Don. He swooped on a brownie, then at Frank's raised brow began to slowly put it back. But then when Frank rolled his eyes, Bobby Don resumed taking it to his mouth, holding it there for moment waiting to interpret the next eye command. All the while never taking his gaze off his boss, who eventually turned away. That was obviously the sign he'd been waiting for, and not only one but two brownies disappeared faster than you could say *piggy*.

Her job done, Fiona finally sat down and turned to Frank. "So, what is this thing that you've supposedly found, anyway?"

I saw Midge's mouth tighten, but then it was she who answered. She spoke in a monotone, low but clear. "It's a news article about my involvement in a major theft several years ago." I went to stop her, but she raised a hand. "I need to get this out," she said quietly.

Taking a seat next to Fiona at the table, I let her continue. "My involvement couldn't be proved. I want transparency on everything here. That point needs to be very clear. What I'm saying is that I was never found innocent; there just wasn't evidence to prove me irrefutably guilty."

What was she doing—*incriminating herself?*

She went on. "I was at a city paper working with a guy who kept pestering me to introduce him to a friend who worked for a firm that invested pension funds among other things. I thought he just liked her. But he used us both. Me as an *in* to get to her, and her to get to the computer files. She was a bit wary at first, so we all hung out together for a while. It was that friendship that brought me under suspicion. Emails that could be interpreted to mean something other than they did. Same with texts."

"What happened?" I asked, even though I could guess.

"He eventually got her passwords and all the other information he needed and stole a whole bunch of money.

Pensioners' monies. It took a few weeks, and at first no one noticed because money gets moved around. Then my friend got charged. All the money was gone. And somehow I knew, just knew it was him. He'd started cooling the relationship. Ghosting her. It all made sense. He'd finished with her. Didn't need her anymore. Plus, I'd accidentally discovered he was leaving the country."

"Did you confront him?" Jonah asked, as intrigued as I was.

She nodded. "He laughed. Said I couldn't prove anything and besides, according to him, my friend looked good in orange so all would be okay. I was livid. I hit him with a stapler. A big heavy-duty one. He went down. I was immediately asked to leave my job, and the next thing I knew, the police were knocking on my door, accusing me of being an accomplice. And of assault."

I felt so ill for her. "Oh my heavens!"

"Did they catch him?"

"Eventually, but not before my friend suffered." She seemed to pull herself together. "So, that's what this article is about, and if the people prefer me to leave town, then I will."

"Oh, darlin'!" Fiona said, rising to hug Midge. "Oh, you poor baby. Nothing will happen, sweetie, because we already knew all this."

"You did?" I asked.

"You did?" echoed Jonah.

"What? No! Really?" That was Midge. "What does that

mean? How could you know?"

Frank cleared his throat. "Well, Midge, you might not like this, but I can't apologize. This is a good town. We're proud of it. And a newspaper is a very important part of that town—any town. When it went up for sale, we looked into the folk who showed interest. Yes, I know," he said raising his hand, "it's a breach of your privacy, and we're guilty."

Midge frowned. "You had me investigated?"

"That we did. Only Council folk knew any of this, by the way, and they're decent, fair folks. Back to the point here—newspapers are very influential, and we had to know that whoever took over was ethical and honest."

"But..." She pointed to the paper on the table.

"Everything we found pointed to you being a good person innocently caught up in a bad situation. It was Fiona and Clay who convinced us you were deserving of a new start."

Mouthing her gratitude, she then rubbed her hands over her face. "I can't believe I've worried you'd find out. It was one of the reasons I started to look for my grandmother out here in the first place. I wanted a new start—to find myself again after all the mess."

My heart broke for her, for what she'd suffered. I moved to comfort her, but a hand on my shoulder held me in place. I looked up into Bobby Don's face, and he was gently shaking his head.

And then the sheriff cleared his throat one more time, and this time it sounded different. He looked different as well. "See, Midge?" he said softly. "It wasn't worth committing murder over, was it?"

What?

No, no, no!

I wasn't sure whose protest was the loudest. It didn't make one jot of difference as Midge was taken away with Bobby Don and Sheriff Kinnead.

And it was so wrong. So wrong.

This had to stop! There'd been a huge mistake…

But they drove away.

I was never so glad of Jonah's support as he held me close to him. Never had I felt so useless, ineffective. However, I couldn't just stand by. Surely there was a way to stop this? There had to be. My brain whirled for a valid reason to make those police trucks turn around. But there was nothing.

I was barely even aware of Clay turning into the drive, not really until Tiny was whimpering at my feet, her huge head nudging me. Like she was saying, *What's up, Mom? Who do you want me to get?*

Equally, I was barely aware of Clay and Fiona's farewell. Clay's grave and quiet. Fiona's wet and devastated.

Inside the house Jonah grabbed a soda, poured it over a glass of ice, guided me to a sofa and then the glass to my mouth. "Drink."

As he lowered himself down beside me, the cold bubbles fizzed through my veins, bringing with it awareness, sensory feeling—and anger. "This is a huge mistake, Jonah. Midge couldn't have murdered that man!" That was quickly followed by another thought. "Oh, Jonah! We need to call Hank! He has to get that criminal lawyer!"

Jonah pulled me in tight and kissed my forehead. "I've already got Hank on it, darlin'. Midge is being looked after. Our focus now is you. We want you rest up a bit. We're worried about you, too."

I lay there against him, enclosed in his arms for a while, my thoughts twisting between guilt that I was here, safe, and anger that my friend was being so unfairly judged. But as thoughts are wont to do, they started to drift further, and abruptly I sat up. "Why my room?"

Jonah leaned back on the sofa. "Say again?"

"No, listen… Jonah, why was that note found in *my* room?" Excitement rushed through me. "Because the person who planted it didn't know us! Didn't know which room was which! That's it! They're both large, both decorated in a fairly feminine way, meaning that if someone was rushing to get something hidden, they had to make a random guess as to which room was mine and which was Midge's room."

"Okay…" Jonah said slowly. "Yours is the master, though…"

I knew I was correct on this. "Yes, but perhaps someone doesn't know which of us owns the house? Or maybe if they did, they might have assumed I'd let out the master. Obviously, I mean—someone who didn't know Midge is my guest and not a paying tenant."

"So, we're saying this is someone who doesn't know your setup? A stranger to town? This is what you think?"

"Jonah, it has to be! And it supports my earlier theories! Someone from the commune—or whatever it's called—or Simone or the lady from Arcacia Street are my picks. But which one? I need to get a pen. And a pad! I've been going around in circles, getting bits of information, but not anything in its entirety. I've got to make a list of questions..." I started to push to my feet. "Where's that pen...?"

Strong arms gently eased me back onto the sofa. "Honey, I love that you want to help Midge so badly, but we have to remember what happened last time you were determined to outdo the cops and get answers."

His eyes locked on mine, the concern there melting me, making me forget what I had to do. Most times I was lost at this point. At least for a while. This time was different. The magic was working—until a random thought boldly pushed to the front of my mind. And started flashing. I straightened, pulled back. "His wife!" I grabbed Jonah's shirtfront. "Midge said there was something about Clausen's wife, but we didn't get to finish that conversation."

I swear if the back of my sofa had been made of any hard material I would have heard his skull shatter against it. That's how hard his head hit the padded fabric. Hard and heavy. Almost as heavy as the exasperation in his tone. "Rosie. Honey." He shook his head. "Darlin', this is dangerous stuff! It's not one of your books."

"Ouch! *Et tu, Brute?* Wow, you really know how to sting a girl."

He was totally unrepentant. "Did it work?" When I didn't reply, he swiped a hand through his hair, even more exasperated if that was possible. "You can't let it go, can you?"

I took both his hands, running my thumbs gently against his work-roughened skin, the remnants of that hard work reminding me again of his strength and determination—and that contrasted so vastly with the gentleness in his eyes and touch. "Jonah, it's Midge. Our relationship might not be a long one, but that doesn't mean it's not precious. She's become as close as a sister." He went to speak, but I held up a hand. "I trust Frank Kinnead; he's a good cop. No matter how it looks, though, he's dead wrong this time, and I can't stand by and watch."

He sighed. "I can't argue with that, darlin'. Or with you." Another sigh heralded his next words. "So, what can I do to help?"

My heart swelled with relief. "Thank you."

I even managed to smile when he added, "But, Rosie? Promise me you won't go doing anything crazy." If he noticed I didn't respond—or promise—he didn't say, but I knew he was too quick to miss that omission.

Besides, we were suddenly busy. Jonah grabbed pen and paper while I went to get the Clausen files Midge had loaned me.

And Tiny nudged her food bowl. Noisily.

Chapter Ten

THAT WAS ALSO a reminder that we hadn't eaten, either, and it was starting to get late. I wasn't all that hungry under the circumstances, but I figured Jonah would possibly be starving. He confirmed that by mooching over to the icebox and rummaging through the contents.

He was munching on a triple chocolate brownie when I pushed off the stool I'd snagged and went to the freezer. "Here, let me thaw these steaks. We can toss them on the broiler. While they're thawing I'll do a couple of baked potatoes." I checked the date on the sour cream and then reached for the bowl of produce I'd picked yesterday. "And green beans?"

"Honey, that sounds pretty much like heaven right now."

I darted into the preserves larder where a second, commercial-sized freezer stood, returning with my prize held high. "And peach pie for dessert!"

His head lolled back, his face radiating what I presumed was an expression of bliss. "I'm yours."

I loved cooking with Jonah—despite Fiona's declaration

about his chili being a disgrace to Texas, he was actually pretty handy in the kitchen. And it was always such fun. Tonight, though, was more subdued.

When we'd finished the main course, he began the cleanup while I printed off the stuff from the flash drive and perused the paperwork from Midge. "Clausen's wife is missing."

Jonah paused stacking the dishwasher and watched me, waiting for more.

"It's a brief newspaper clipping that Midge has included." I frowned as I read down the small print. "There aren't many details, just that apparently she hasn't been seen for several weeks. She and Clausen are estranged." I flicked over a couple of pages. "Seems it's not that odd; she's a very private person who eschews the limelight and has been known to disappear for short periods before," I quoted.

Jonah wandered across and leaned over my shoulder. "Julia Savage-Clausen?" He whistled, obviously incredulous. "Clausen is married to Julia Savage?"

"*Was* married. Separated, remember? And now, well, he's dead, so…?" I flicked my pen against the granite countertop. "Why are you surprised? Is that significant?"

He shrugged. "Maybe. Maybe not. They weren't divorced, so maybe that's significant in some way. The Savages represent big money with a capital *B* and a capital *M*. Huge international transport company. But that's just one part of their empire. Oil, mining, media… They've got more fingers in pies than a nursery school in a mud pond." He paused, one eyebrow arched high. "I'd say if Miz Savage-Clausen wanted to get lost for a while, she could afford to do it in style. Old man Savage passed on a few years back. The mama was long gone, so…"

I joined the dots. "So, Julia owns the company?"

"Apparently so. I think there's a sibling, though I'm not sure if it's a brother or sister. Or maybe I'm wrong on that, come to think of it. I really only know of Julia because one of her companies was involved in a small building project I quoted on a while back and her name was on the paperwork."

I nodded. "Did you ever meet her?"

His hand stroked the back of my neck, sending delightful shivers down my spine. I'd pulled my curls up into a topknot, which would last only until I began moving about, then strands would escape and dangle down around my face. And what he was doing to me would certainly make me wriggle around if he didn't stop. Much as I hated pulling away slightly, I did so. Not for my hair's sake, but because I needed to concentrate. "No," he answered, oblivious to my internal battle, "I've never seen her. My involvement with them was all done via phone and email—and naturally with her project managers."

After firing up my laptop, I came to the conclusion that Jonah was in the majority there. Despite her wealth and position few people had ever actually seen her. Google images gave up precious little. "Gosh, even I must have more photos on the internet than she does! Well, especially after last spring when I was accused of murder!"

"Suspected. Not accused."

"Meh. *Potatoes, potahtoes.* Felt the same to me." I scrolled farther, my attention again fully back on my subject. "Amazing. Obviously quite a few photographers have tried to get shots of the elusive—and very rich—Julia Savage-Clausen, but they're either very bad photographers or very unlucky! Every photograph is either shadowed, she's got her hand covering her face—or all we see is the back of her head."

"Maybe she's really shy."

I responded with an eye roll. "You think? Jonah, this is almost obsessive. Let me get out of images and have a scramble around the Web."

It seemed to take forever, but finally I found one little mention that gave clarity and context to the whole elusiveness. "Oh wow, Jonah. There was a kidnap attempt on her when she was a baby! The kidnappers were caught, but their intention was to hold her for ransom." My hand went to my heart. "How can people do that? To parents? To innocent children!"

"It explains a lot." Jonah was back at my shoulder, this time after placing a serving of warm peach pie dripping with creamy vanilla bean ice cream in front of me. "Says farther down that her parents, especially her father, went to great lengths after that to shield her from the public. I suppose that's what she's used to. Staying out of the public eye."

I nodded. "It could also explain why she got caught up with Clausen, too. I mean, if she didn't have a whole lot of experience with people, maybe she didn't spot him for the creep he is. *Was.*"

I took a bite of pie, instantly being slammed by two reactions. One of pride in the juicy filling that just oozed summer coupled with that golden crumbly pastry that melted in the mouth, and one of shame for speaking ill of the dead. If anyone upstairs—*way upstairs*—was keeping tabs today, then I just scored two black marks against my name. Drat. And if my grandma was correct, that meant I had to do four good deeds to get that slate swiped clean again.

Clearing Midge's name would surely be my first. I hoped. My heart clutched each time I relived that moment when Frank arrested her. She was a good person, yet someone was intent on playing cruel games. Deadly games.

"Jonah, do you think it's possible that Julia Clausen is dead? That maybe Clausen murdered her?"

He whistled. "That's a huge leap. And besides, you read yourself that hiding out for a while is a common thing for her to do, so—"

"I think," I said, interrupting him, "that the article said she goes away for a few days. Didn't it?" I scanned down the page again. "Something like that, right? Well, this is saying she's been missing for weeks. Not a few days, Jonah. Weeks!"

"Honey, I'm glad to go along with you on most things,

but I'm reserving judgment on Miz Clausen's disappearance. At least for a while. Okay?"

I nodded. Of course he was right. For starters there was no big story, just a mention. And everyone interviewed—staff, mainly—seemed to think there was nothing strange about her behavior. So, why even publish it in the first place? Midge would probably say it was a filler. That there hadn't been enough news that day.

The thought of her brought another question to the fore, one I should have thought of a lot earlier. "Jonah, why Midge? Why did someone target Midge?"

He shrugged. "Because they knew about her past, I guess."

"Yes, but who would know that? Apart from the council, that is?"

His spoon scraped the last of his dessert and he glanced once, speculatively, at the remaining pie before answering. "You're discounting the council members because you're convinced this is a stranger at work, right?"

I nodded. "It doesn't make sense that it's a local, Jonah. The murderer has to be an outsider." The irony of my comment wasn't lost on me. One of the reasons I'd been suspected last spring—apart from the whole means, motive, and opportunity thing—was that I'd been a stranger in town. Everybody automatically assumed the murders couldn't have possibly been committed by a local. And here I was, doing the same thing. Although I hoped my own reasoning in this regard had more substance than just because I didn't believe a local could be responsible for murder. Because, I knew for a fact, they could.

"You know, I had an interesting"—I paused, reaching for a different word—"no, *scary* conversation with Liz Pauling today. You know—my artist friend from out at the old Tetley property?" I loved how "local" that made me sound, even though I was only repeating the description the real locals used. He nodded, and I continued, "Well, I was really hoping I didn't ever have to say this out loud because I know how bad it sounds, but Midge did threaten Clausen's life. Apparently."

I relayed the conversation, and like me, Jonah wasn't shocked or outraged—or even concerned that it made Midge guilty. "Loads of people make that threat when they're mad or cornered. Under normal circumstances most people forget they've said it or that they've even been threatened if they're on the receiving end. It's a pretty stupid, pointless thing to say, unless that person turns up dead."

"That's what I thought, too. But Liz was so upset and confused as to what to do. She's feeling really guilty she's kept quiet, but now I figure that once she hears about Midge, she'll tell Frank."

"Rosie, I *want* to say Frank will see through that, but cops tend to take threats seriously." Rubbing a hand across his jaw, he said, "So this conversation happened at the café?" When I nodded he continued, "And Liz caused a bit of a scene nearly bumping into the waitress right? So it's unlikely she was missed by anyone there. I mean, all the patrons would have seen her there. Honey, is it possible someone could have overheard this conversation?"

"I get where you're going, but I just don't know the answer. I was so shocked that Clausen had threatened Midge that I admit we—Liz and I—sort of went into our own world. It was deep stuff. I guess someone *could* have been listening—we were pretty oblivious. I remember coming back to the present like coming out of a fog or tunnel."

"But you don't remember anyone close by?"

I replayed the scene in my head. "There was no one right beside us on one side," I said, picturing the empty table, "but the other? The one closest to me? It was kind of partially behind me so I really can't be sure. And yet there's something. Something I just can't put my finger on…" My voice trailed as I tried to bring back that elusive something, but it was futile. "Of course that was when I hit my head."

Jonah winced. "How is that by the way? And the ankle? With everything going on, I've hardly been a great caregiver."

I leaned back against the handcrafted iron backrest of my stool—and folded my arms across my chest. Classic offense position. "You forgot my injuries? You forgot my head and my ankle?"

He bared his teeth in a silent *eek* fashion. "Maybe, kind of… Yes, I admit, I did. But I can make it up to you," he finished hurriedly. "What do you need?"

I held his gaze, unblinking for as long as I could. "You think you can just make it up now?" I said quietly.

His eyes narrowed, became uncertain.

I couldn't do it. I had to let him off the hook. "Oh, honey," I said, unable to hold in the laughter. "You've fed and watered me. You've held me and made me sit. You've cleaned. And you've listened to my ramblings. Nonstop ramblings. It's okay. I think you get to keep your caregiver badge."

He ran a hand across his forehead in a grossly exaggerated fashion. "Phew… Thought I was in for it then."

I laughed again. "I got to admit something, cowboy. I forgot about my injuries as well—which obviously indicates they were hardly worthy of being called injuries."

"Ahhh, is that so?" he said menacingly, moving toward me from his side of the bench. "So, pretty lady, are you sayin' you faked those injuries to get my attention? To trick me into coming to your rescue? To get me to carry you back to safety? You did that on purpose?"

His steps had intent. His eyes were twinkling, his hands outstretched.

"Jonah! No! Not the tickles! No!" I was laughing so hard I could hardly get off the stool. His hands were fast, and I dodged once. "Aaaack! Don't you dare! No fair. I hit my head remember? I'm an invalid."

His response was a deep, evil chuckle. "Too late, little

lady. You just admitted you're perfectly fine, and so now you have to pay for that stunt."

I eluded him but only for a second. His arms and legs were way longer than mine.

And in truth, I may not have been running too hard or fast...

THE NEXT MORNING I was up early but feeling edgy and alone. Jonah had gotten a call about midnight to say one of his longhorns was out on the main road, and he wouldn't let me go help him. After he'd left, I found myself too wired to sleep so I dragged the laptop upstairs and worked from bed until I couldn't keep my eyes open any longer.

Gritty-eyed, I sat out on the porch nursing my coffee and watched the sun rise with Tiny at my feet. The notes I'd scrawled last night sat on the table beside me, but still, even after all this, I felt all I had was a load of disconnected information that sent me in a dozen different directions. And I didn't have time to be going in a dozen different directions.

Every moment Midge sat in that jailhouse would be killing her, and I knew she'd be counting on me to help prove her innocence.

Restless, I gulped down the last of the coffee and went to the mudroom for my boots. I was a sight in my skimpy pajama shorts and spaghetti-strap camisole with my dirt-and-dust-caked boots, but I didn't care. As yet, I didn't even have any livestock, so there was no one—man nor beast—to witness the spectacle. No one except Tiny, who jumped around excitedly as soon as I pulled on my boots. I simply had to do something to burn off the edginess right then or burst.

I had a list of phone calls to make, but I had hours to wait until offices would be manned, meanwhile tomatoes, cucumbers, and beans didn't work to set times. They were on duty twenty-four seven, so it was to them, basket in hand, I headed.

Tiny ran on ahead of me, tail wagging wildly. She loved trekking down through the yard, feeling very tough as she scared off the butterflies and brave as she poked her nose into places she shouldn't.

As always, I was captured by the aromatic magic of the tomato bushes, basil, rosemary... And it momentarily stilled me. I lifted my face, feeling at one with nature as the dawning sun gently brought us all into the day. And as always I buried my face in that magic, feeling some of my tension melt away.

My basket filled and images of salsas and sauces whirled through my head. The cucumbers and chilies were going crazy, and I mentally listed those I could share them with. I hoped to meet up with Ally today to talk about the possibility of her working with me. With her family having it so tough I put them at the top of the list, and with that came the solution to filling the next few hours: I'd bake some goodies to share with them as well.

Baking not only calmed me, it also allowed me time to mull over my problems. Many a problem had been solved by an apple pie. Or peach pie. Or cherry. Or a crumble or… It always seemed the magnitude of my problem could be measured by the amount of baking that session yielded. Back in the days of apartment living in Dallas and working nine till five, my neighbors and colleagues prayed for me to have problems because they all benefited.

Still, this morning it was quite a shock to find it almost nine thirty when I finished cleaning my kitchen. The house smelled as good as the garden had earlier, although this time, it was the sweetness of sugary, fruity concoctions that filled the air. Banana bread cooled alongside pies and chocolate mint bars, peanut crunch cookies, and a rich chocolate mud cake halved and filled with fresh kirsch-soaked cherries blended into whipped cream. Along with the produce from my garden, there was probably way too much for one family, but I figured they might have neighbors to share with— neighbors in similar plights, from what I gathered from Jayne's conversation.

I was so caught up in my thoughts that I actually jumped when my phone rang, springing Tiny to attention. I patted her head and punched the speaker button, jumping again, but this time deliberately, when I heard Midge's voice.

"Oh my Lord," I squealed. "Are you okay? Is this your

one phone call? What do you need me to do? Whatever it is, I'm on it. Let me grab a pen." Dropping the phone, I scooted across the room, sliding back into place with such speed, I swear I left burn marks on my hardwood floor. Heart pounding, I took up the phone again. "Okay, shoot."

"Are you sure? Sure it's okay for me to speak now?"

Stunned into silence, I realized I hadn't let her get a single word in. "Oh, sorry… I've just been so worried."

I heard the smile in her voice. "I know you have, honey. But I'm ringing because I need you to come and collect me."

"You're free?" Needless to say, I squealed anew.

Her reply didn't echo my own excitement. Her voice was flat. "On bail. Big bail…"

"But…?"

"I'll explain in full later. The highlights are that my lawyer got me off on bail and Clay and Fiona put the B&B up against it. Merline wanted to put up her home and business, but the Fencotts insisted. Rosie, they've been amazing." She said it on a yawn, and I was struck again by how stressful her night must have been. "Anyway, can you come into town and get me?"

"Absolutely. I'll be there before your next yawn."

There was a half laugh and then, "Too late. They're coming hard and fast."

"So, hang up before you fall down. I'm on my way."

I realized that was a futile and erroneous promise as soon as I reached for my keys—which weren't there. I'd traveled back with Jonah yesterday, meaning my car was still in town. Midge had been brought out by Frank and Bobby Don, so ditto for her car. Midge's purse was here—along with her keys. But I was stranded.

For a second I wanted to ring Jonah, but he'd had so much time out of late that I was reluctant to drag him away from his work again.

As I was contemplating, a message pinged through my phone. It was Fiona, telling me that she and Brenda would be out later with my car—right after their Library Lovers meeting and after they dropped in on elderly Widow Weissman to bring her weekly groceries as they always did on Tuesdays.

Knowing they were headed out here to my little farm, I figured it was likely Fiona was already driving my car with Brenda following. Whenever I left my car in town, I always also left the keys with Clay and Fiona in case it ever had to be moved—or was needed. Tracing her route in my head, I realized they'd be backtracking and wasting considerable time if they went back for my car after their trek. My shoulders slumped; they were definitely already driving around in my car. It made pure sense.

Which all meant there was no way I could get that car quickly.

It was rare moments like this when I admitted to the benefits of a city. A cab would have been very handy right now, but of course, a cab driver in Airlie Falls could grow old and die between fares.

My fingers went back to my phone, deciding I'd have to call Jonah after all, when a familiar honking reached my ears. Aileene, aka my temporary mail lady, was pulling into the yard. She was early today, but I was glad. In fact, never had I been so grateful to see a mail carrier. Apart, of course, from the times when they were delivering a swag of new mystery novels I'd ordered.

I raced onto the porch to wave her to stay and then darted back inside. Hoping she wouldn't remember too much about our last encounter and take fright and run, I made haste. And resorted to blackmail. Armed with my purse, a still-warm banana bread, a peach crumble, and a package of cookies, I hurried back outside and pulled on my boots, brushing flour off my aqua tank top and cut-off denim shorts as I went. If Aileene was able to help me, the towns-folk would have to take me as I was this morning. No time for tizzying.

Relief was my first emotion—relief that she hadn't taken off. Hope was my second; we hadn't exactly parted on the best of terms last time. That was obvious by the wary look in her eyes. "Aileene? I don't have a car here, and I need to get into town as quickly as possible."

There was a definite question in my voice if not in my words, and the ball was in her court.

There was no answer for several seconds. "I dunno… You say, you have to get in there, into town, like, urgently?"

She was still frowning.

Time to bring out the big guns. I nodded. "I surely do. And to thank you I'd like to offer these baked gifts—I've just taken them out of the oven this morning—and also as an apology for last time." She was eyeing the packages now, and her nose twitched as the fresh-baked aroma wafted around us.

"Well, I don't know…" Her eyes were still on the treats. "You sure are a good baker—I learned that last time. But you know, I'm trying to watch my waistline; it's only once a girl gets married, you know." I willed more of those delicious smells into the cab of the truck. Eventually, she sighed. "Oh, all righty. Climb on board. But don't think it was those desserts that made up my mind. I'm just bein' neighborly. And the reason I hesitated is that I'm not supposed to take on passengers. Tampering with mail is a federal offense, and I'm not supposed to take chances."

I wasn't giving her a chance to change her mind. Thanking her profusely, I climbed in and set my stash up on my knee. She ground the gears, and we hopped a couple of times until she smoothed out the ride. "No, siree," she continued as though she hadn't almost wrecked an entire gearbox, "I'm just doing this because I can see you're in dire straits. And by the way, is that peanuts I can smell?"

"You surely can," I answered on a smothered grin. "Here, taste one as you drive."

She took the now barely warm cookie, inhaling the sweet

nutty scent before taking a hefty bite. "Oh my, oh my…" she muttered moments later, spraying crumbs as she spoke. "They are good! Real good! Would there be another?"

I happily fed her as we drove. When she took a break she looked across at me. "So, you have an emergency?"

"Not in that sense. I just have to get to town really quickly." When she darted yet another questioning look, I shrugged. It's not like secrets lasted long in this town. "My friend Midge? She was arrested yesterday, but she's been let out on bail."

Her smile was broad. "Oh hey, that's great! You both must be relieved. Does that mean, like, there are questions about her guilt?"

"There is no guilt—she's completely innocent. Well, that's my belief, anyhow… As for bail, most likely they consider her a safe bet to stick around and not leave town. Although, I'm pretty sure the evidence they're basing the case on is circumstantial."

She was nodding, and I was grateful for her support. I was still hopeful we could be friends; Aileene was a happy, bubbly person—a nice person to be around.

"So, how's your head? I heard you took a tumble in that café."

I rubbed the slight bump. "It's fine. Only hurts if I press on it so…"

"…don't press on it!" we said together. Our laughter pushed away any residual tension, and we chatted for a few minutes until we were interrupted by my cell phone.

Midge. Smiling, I answered. "Getting anxious? Almost there. I'm coming to spring you from the Big House, baby! Or should that be spring you from *the Joint*?"

Even as I said the words, the cerise bougainvillea–covered sheriff's department came into sight and I prepared to dive out. "Thank you so much, Aileene. I'm not sure what I would have done without your help. I know it would have taken a whole lot longer, and I might not have got my baking done for the potluck tonight!"

"Oh, that would be bad…"

As I opened the van's door I turned back to her for one last goodbye, and for a moment she just stared at me with a look I couldn't comprehend. Confused, I fumbled with my purse and phone. "Now, you enjoy those treats!"

I wasn't sure what I expected, but her response was, again, quite subdued, and I wondered if every time I said goodbye to Aileene, I'd be left feeling guilty for something.

Still confused, I was staring after the mail van as it drove away, when my phone began its familiar melody.

In my haste I accidentally pushed Speaker, and a voice came down the line immediately. "Rosie, honey? Are you there? Hello? Hello? It's about Midge…"

"Miz Merline?" I flicked the speaker off. "Merline, it's me. I'm here."

"You're there? Oh, I—"

I smiled and hoped she sensed it through the phone. "It's

okay, Miz Merline…"

"It's just that I was worried about our poor young Midge and with her bein' in jail… Oh, Rosie, I'm just heartsick about it. That poor girl! Has that bail been fixed yet? I tried to talk to her at the jail, but they wouldn't let me! I'm tellin' you that Frank Kinnead might be my best friend's husband, but he better watch out or someone's likely to tamper with his taco, if you get what I mean!" She sighed, seeming to have blown away some of her hot air.

I held up a hand to signal her to stop talking, but of course she couldn't see me. "It's okay, Merline. Midge is out on bail and she's fine. Aileene, our temporary mail lady? She just dropped me here in town, and I'm just about to collect her now."

"Oh, that's wonderful news. Midge will be so relieved. Hopefully I'll get to thank Aileene for her kindness tonight. I've invited her to our potluck tonight, and I sure hope she comes. That's tonight. You did remember, didn't you, dear? Church hall?"

"I remembered, Miz Merline." And mentally wanted to smack myself. I'd been so distracted that I was bragging about the potluck and completely forgot to add my invitation to the woman who'd saved our butts today. No wonder she'd been a bit cool with me.

And the disgust with myself didn't ease any when Merline continued with, "You know, that Aileene's been so helpful to folk around here—even Fiona and Clay. She's a sheer wonder—found my little lost doggie wandering the street and brought him home, she did. There'll be plenty of food tonight. Always is. I so hope she comes."

I began to respond, but Merline wasn't finished yet, though thankfully this news didn't add to my guilt. "And oh, did you hear the news about that mysterious body? They found his car, hidden in the old quarry of all places. Janet says they'll have an identification real fast now. Such a relief for his family…"

And maybe for us as well. Because an identification might also tell us what he was doing here—and how he was connected to Clausen or his murder. Frank might not think there was any common ground there, but I wasn't convinced.

Chapter Eleven

I F I'D EXPECTED Midge to be weeping with relief that I'd arrived to rescue her, I would have been sadly disappointed. I'd found her perched on the edge of Janet's desk, and although there was no notebook in her hand, I'd recognized the look on her face. She was working, gathering facts. Whether Janet, the sheriff's sister-cum-receptionist, who'd put aside her crossword for the chat, understood she was being interviewed was something else entirely.

What was apparent was that, despite seeming to have it together, Midge was beat. And so I hurried her away and back out to the farm. Thankfully she'd gotten the paper off to the printer before she'd been arrested, so with luck she'd be free to catch up on some sleep.

Once I'd ensured she'd eaten and was resting, I headed back into town, Midge's car laden with the gifts I'd packed earlier. My meeting with Ally was up first, and then I was determined to track down the mysterious woman from Arcacia Street, especially since I was beginning to have an idea of who she was and maybe even what she looked like.

Ally was a surprise. I don't usually judge people on appearance, however, her perky cheerleader looks did throw me for a moment. Long, perfectly straight golden hair went with her long legs and perfectly straight teeth. She was beautiful, and my experience of women like this in my former job hadn't been great. Mostly, I found all that perfect beauty took a perfect load of time and that usually meant others carried the bulk of the load while they perfected.

But then she smiled and spoke, and my perceptions took a step left. She was warm, smart, and enthusiastic. Her knowledge of food and food construction surprised me, and for someone who looked like she'd break out in a rash if someone even mentioned the *S*-word—*sugar*—in her presence, her passion for sweet baking had such depth I felt I could almost reach out and touch it.

By the time we'd ended our visit, my perceptions were so far left they were in the next state. Ally was going to be an amazing asset, and I suggested we begin right away.

I'd left my loaded basket and a box near the front door. "Your sister said you guys are having it tough now, so I brought these. I know they won't make a load of difference, but they might ease some tension. There's probably more than you need right now, so you could freeze them or share them with your neighbors."

She smiled. "Thanks, Rosie. I know they'll be appreciated. And especially thank you for the opportunity to work with you."

I shook my head at her. "I have a strong feeling I'll be the one thanking you before long. Bye for now, and I'll see you soon. Okay?"

My mood had shifted dramatically since I'd set out on this part of the journey. Sorrow for what these people were suffering was drowning out my determination. Until I remembered the source of their grief.

Clausen.

Frederick Norman Wellington Clausen.

That's all it took. It was good to feel that fire start to roar through my veins again.

I straightened my back and sharpened my step, glad that even in summer, boots were a fashion staple here in Texas. Thankfully, I could get away with wearing them with the short swing skirt and tank top I'd changed into because, though I refused to admit it out loud, there was still a slight twinge from where I'd twisted my ankle the day before.

Arcacia Street was set back from Main Street, away from the town center a bit, although still easy walking to the stores and post office. The plots here in Airlie Falls were way bigger than in the city, but on this street, yards were generally smaller than the town average. I took a moment to take this in—wondering what had been so attractive to Clausen's company. What was the purpose of buying it all up? Clay had told me the land-zoning laws were really strict and tight, so what had Clausen hoped to achieve?

It was getting on for late morning and the sun was high. The cute cowgirl hat Jonah had given me as a kind of joke gift after I'd ribbed him about his was very welcome, and I'd never tease him again about his hat.

That sun and heat was evident in other ways, though. As I walked, counting off houses, it was impossible not to see the ravages of yet another Texan summer. Yards and garden plots that were otherwise well cared for boasted brown patches, and some bushes and shrubs hung limply, as though they'd already given up on fighting through the day. An occasional sprinkler, probably sourced from a well, swayed defiantly, determined to put up a good fight.

The Lipskie house offered the rare impression of cool comfort with its crisp lemon color and bright white trim. It appeared to be freshly painted, as did the porch furniture. Up closer, evidence of the porch flooring having been newly refinished and furniture cushions that hadn't yet been faded by the relentless sun all spoke to money having been recently spent. How had that gone down with the Lipskies? Spending a heap in refurbishment only to have their home sold out from under them for a pittance?

My hand hovered over the heavy, old-fashioned knocker. Was I uncovering even more motives and suspects? My head clouded in protest. How on earth could I find a murderer when there were so many suspects? The net was cast too wide. My neat little lists now seemed ridiculous. Futile and childish. Frank was right to tell me to butt out.

The decision to flee was taken out of my hands, however, as the door was quickly pulled open and middle-aged woman wearing an apron—clean, I noted—and suspicious eyes glared back at me. "Can I help you?"

Given the woman's demeanor, I wasn't sure that proposal was sincerely offered, but taking a deep calming breath, I took it at face value. "Miz Lipskie? My name is Rosie Hart, and…" And what? My brain froze. "I… um… I have the dessert stand at the markets and"—I pulled a wrapped banana bread, the last, from my basket—"I'm offering a free sample!"

Her changing expressions were fascinating to watch. Hostility to confusion to wariness to acceptance. And then excitement. "Really? Oh, you know I've heard so much about your food. I promised myself I'd go over next time and treat myself. And Rudolph—my husband, that is—of course. I'm Irene, by the way."

No mention of the supposed relative. Either Miz Lipskie thought she wasn't deserving—or perhaps they expected her to be gone by the time the next market came around.

She reached for the package. "Are you going door to door?" She glanced behind me as if she'd be able to track my path.

"Ahhh, not exactly. I called in on a few people…" Well, surely one large family constituted a few; it wasn't a complete untruth. Still, I sent a silent apology upstairs just in case. "And I had just one left, and your house just looked so appealing. It really called to me, you know? You've got it looking so pretty."

She beamed, but as that quickly faded, I guessed what she was thinking. I was right. "Thank you, it is pretty. We waited years to get it fixed nice, and now it's all going to be wasted. Along with the money we spent."

I touched her hand. "I heard about the Clausen deal, Miz Lipskie, and I'm so sorry."

She pulled an ironed handkerchief from an invisible pocket and wiped her face. "Well, they say it's not over yet, but I gotta be honest: I'm not holding out much hope. Clausen's corporation is real slick." She paused. "And we were stupid. Got caught up in all the fearmongering. Signed away our properties without any one of us seeking counsel on it."

"Oh dear, I've upset you with this talk. Perhaps you should have some water or maybe some tea?"

That seemed to snap her out of her misery. "Oh, look at me! My mama would be so disappointed. I didn't even offer you any refreshment—and you bein' so kind and all." She glanced at the banana bread that still hung awkwardly between us. "Would you like some cold lemonade? Just freshly made."

"That would be lovely, thank you."

She darted a look around her, glancing at the door and then at the furniture on the porch. I made it easy for her. "Why don't we have it out here? As I said, it's so pretty."

It was like I'd offered the answer to the sixty-four-million-dollar question. Her smile was luminous. "Yes. Let's!

Now, you make yourself comfortable, and I'll go and get that lemonade. And maybe a knife and some plates?" she asked hopefully, again glancing at the banana bread.

"Great idea!"

It took her no time to gather the things and return, during which I spent the entire time fighting my conscience and justifying the fact I was taking advantage of this poor woman.

The lemonade was icy and delicious, and we chatted idly for a few minutes, getting to know each other. The banana bread had just the right amount of spice, or so she said, and apparently the walnuts made it a standout for her.

It was all lovely, but I had a purpose. Rivers of condensation rolled down the side of the etched glass jug, reminding me time was passing. "So, there's just the two of you here now?"

"Our children have moved away…"

I nodded. "Must be 'specially nice, then, when relatives come to stay."

She was focused on her apron and she didn't lift her head, although I saw the frown forming. "Relatives? What makes you say that?"

"Oh, just that it's more company, is all." I put my empty glass down. "Company is always fun! I remember thinking that when I heard at the general store about you having relatives staying over right now." I pretended to ponder that. "Oh dear… Maybe I got that wrong. Now, was that you or someone else I heard that about…?"

Her frown deepened. "Why would folks at the general store be talking about me?"

"Oh, it wasn't you specifically. I've got to remember now. I think the conversation came up about newcomers in town. Kind of came about due to that body being found out on Redrock. It was just idle talk. People mentioning who was here…"

"Oh…" she answered, her face clearing slightly. "Well, yes, I have a cousin here for a short while."

"That's lovely," I gushed. "Where is she from? Is she at home? I'd like to meet her and welcome her to Airlie Falls."

I swear her body stiffened. "Well, as a matter of fact she's out right now."

"Oh! Maybe she'd like to come along to the potluck tonight? Bring her along. At the church hall at seven."

Miz Lipskie stood then, so abruptly I almost dropped the napkin I'd been using to wipe my hands. "Well, it's been real nice, and I thank you for your kind gift, but I have chores to finish. So, I better get back to them, I think."

It was my turn to utter the *oh* response. "Of course. You think about tonight, though. Everyone is welcome."

She didn't reply, unless you counted the tight little smile that made a brief appearance. That wasn't the only hasty move. Irene Lipskie had that tray piled up and in her hands and was headed toward her front door before I could even gather my basket and purse and stand up. She certainly wasn't one for prolonged goodbyes. With me, anyway.

Walking away, I knew one thing for sure. Aileene had been right. There was something fishy about this supposed relative. Actually, I knew two things: Irene Lipskie and her *cousin* would not be attending the potluck tonight.

Back in my car I put the AC up to high and headed back home. The morning's events were rolling around in my head as well as the fact I'd promised Fiona I'd make her contribution to the potluck. And my own, of course. And I'd also hoped to make a trip to Colton about an hour east, to talk to the security firm with Midge.

COLTON WOULD NEVER be a contender for the Prettiest Town award. The overall impression was brown, dry, and tired. Its big draw for the locals, Airlie Falls included, was being the hub for farm equipment. New, old, and repairs. And a half dozen businesses servicing that work lined the dusty main street.

Core Security sat roughly in the middle next to a building with a brand-new, shiny green tractor perched on its roof. I not only marveled at how they got it up there but also how it hadn't fallen through and squashed someone. The whole building looked like it would tumble down if a person sneezed too close.

In contrast, Core Security was housed in a building that,

naturally, looked about as secure as could be—and just as ugly. It was a low, squat structure built of red brick, with a flat roof and bars on the windows. Nothing said welcome to a town like bars on windows.

Inside, air conditioning and electric lights replaced any air or natural light from outside. There was a counter and behind it several desks with men and women manning computer screens, all wearing those headset and mouthpiece phones. I'd assumed *Core* meant basic security, like *core strength*, but I was wrong. A photo on the wall showed a man named Joseph Pennifold Core—founder and owner. Below that was a year date: 1963. Okay, they'd been around for a while now.

And it seemed it was mostly staffed by family members. Even from the counter, I could read name tags, and most of them were Cores.

A girl about my age stepped up from her desk to waddle over to the counter. In fact, she was a girl exactly my age. I hadn't noticed because I'd been so fascinated by her huge pregnant belly that I hadn't looked at her face.

She spoke first—and that was when it finally clicked. "Rosie? Rosie Hart? Oh my goodness! I haven't seen you since college!"

Chapter Twelve

I T WAS TRUE. Bethanne *Core*—as she was now, according to her name tag—and I had been roommates for a while in college, and sadly, we'd drifted apart, as people did. Seeing her now was a double delight. It was truly great to catch up with an old friend you'd been fond of, and secondly, my day suddenly seemed brighter, my task lighter. I'd worried about trying to get someone to talk to us—and now… I crossed my fingers. Bethanne and I had always gotten on really well.

I leaned across to hug her—as best I could with a counter and imminent baby between us. "What a surprise! It's so good to see you. And you're having a baby? That's wonderful. You look like you're ready to pop."

She sighed. "I am. Our first. I'm *soooo* ready. In fact, I'm overdue now." She rubbed that belly affectionately. "This little tyke was supposed to come two days ago, so I guess it's any time now."

"Wow—we'd better be quick, then," I joked before introducing Midge. But my heart wasn't really in the joke. Her presence at work confused me. Lowering my voice, I added, "Why are you still working? This isn't the Dark Ages.

Shouldn't you be home resting?"

She rolled her eyes. "Don't you start, too! I have this whole family"—she waved a hand behind her to encompass the dozen or more people there—"who agree with you. But I'm just so bored at home! The days drag. Jay works long hours—they all do here—and I was going stir-crazy. There's only so many times you can clean a pristine house and only so many times you can adjust things in an empty baby nursery. I'm ready; I'm prepared mentally and physically," she sighed. "Well, I think I am, but when I'm on my own, I start to think too much, get a bit anxious. Give myself the heebie-jeebies. Being here gives me company and helps the days pass. And Jay's folks are great. I'm really only taking up space—I'm not actually working. They set up a camp bed in one of the back rooms, and no one cares if I disappear to nap for a while."

I squeezed her hand, which was much easier than trying for another hug. "Well, I'm thrilled for you. And kinda thrilled for me as well because I've got some awkward things to ask and talk about. At least if you throw me out, it'll be gentle and we could still catch up for coffee later."

She frowned. She'd always been pretty in that wholesome girl-next-door way, and though her eyes told of her general weariness, she also now had this kind of radiant beauty that was both calming and mesmerizing "Awkward questions? Like what?"

"Well, it's about the Clausen murder. Frederick Clausen?

He was one of your clients, and I"—I waved a hand between Midge and myself—"that is *we* are trying to find the identity of the killer."

Her hand went to her mouth and her eyes swiped between Midge and me. "You're investigating? You're with the police now? I thought you were in finance? Somewhere in Arizona?"

"No, yes and no, not now." I sighed. "After that I got a transfer to Dallas. It's a long story, and I'm afraid you'll go into labor and have this baby before I'm through. I'd love to catch up with you after—and meet this little one—and explain fully. But for now, no, I'm not police, but the police have got it all wrong. They're accusing someone who didn't do it."

She had always been astute. Her gaze went straight to Midge. "You?"

Midge nodded, and the way her fingers twitched, I knew she was thinking about ice cream. She'd admitted she intended to make it her complete diet in case she was incarcerated and unable to ever have ice cream again.

Bethanne turned and said something to an older woman, who smiled warmly at us before nodding at my old friend who, in turn, went to a filing cabinet and removed a folder. And as Bethanne came around the counter toward us, the woman offered a small wave before going back to her work. "My mother-in-law. She's a sweetheart. So's my father-in-law. If Jay hadn't wanted to marry me I think I would have begged them to adopt me!"

"Lucky you!" I answered as we followed her down a short hall on the other side of the building and into a fairly large lunchroom.

She headed to a machine and grabbed a diet soda. "What can I get you? We have pretty much everything."

The machine was obviously company-provided because we needed no coins to make our selections. "Come, take a seat," she directed. "I'm intrigued but not surprised. You always loved those mystery stories!"

I simply grinned a reply; I had this urge to get right to the point. It could have been the size of her stomach and the fact she was overdue. Who was I kidding? Of course it was the size of her stomach and the fact she was overdue! I didn't know how she could stand the tension of knowing it could happen any second. I was stressed, and I was only looking on.

I took a deep breath and hurried on. "So, the night Clausen was murdered, Midge had gone to see him—"

"We should explain here that I'm the owner and editor of the *Airlie Falls Gazette*," Midge interjected. "But I'm not here in that capacity today."

Bethanne nodded. "Oh right. We've done a bit of advertising with you. Now that I've met you and know the association with Rosie, I'll make sure we do more."

Midge nodded her thanks and waved me on.

"So, that night, Midge was able to drive right in. The

gates were wide open, no intercom needed. Now, given the other security Midge noted around the place, we thought that was pretty weird."

Bethanne nodded. "It was. In fact," she said, opening the folder and scanning some printouts, "because of that, one of our guys went out there to check. He was an older retired guy we call in from time to time. Poor man found the body—he's still recovering from the shock. Terrible thing… Just terrible."

I pointed to the pages she held. "You can tell if the gates weren't working properly?"

"Absolutely. We have monitors set up that signal if something doesn't perform as it should at the site. It says here we tried calling Mister Clausen several times, and when he didn't pick up, we went out to check."

"I saw your guy arriving just as I was leaving. That's how we knew it was your company," Midge explained.

I so wanted to read those papers Bethanne held, but something told me that would be pushing the friendship too far. "Does that report tell you when the gate opened that evening?"

"Sure!" She scanned again, and Midge pulled out a pen and paper. "Mister Clausen—or someone inside the house—admitted someone at 7:16—"

"Clay," I murmured.

"He reopened the gate at 7:43…"

"So Clay could leave," Midge said quietly.

"Then," Bethanne continued, "it was opened again to admit someone at 8:06." She scanned down farther. "It closed on that person. It was reopened from inside at 8:24. And it didn't close again."

I nodded. "Bethanne, what time did your guy arrive? Do you have that?"

"It says here that Warren radioed in to the main command at 9:22 to say he'd arrived at the house."

"That," Midge said on a sigh, "corresponds with the time I was leaving. I guess I must have been there for six or seven minutes trying to make him hear me. Then I left."

All these times were jiggling in my head. Lining up, trying to make sense. "So, someone definitely closed the gate after admitting someone at 8:06?"

"Uh-huh... Definitely. Within a minute or so. Just long enough, I'd say, for the visitor to clear the gates and start up the drive."

"So, that begs another question that's bothered me from the start. How was the gate reopened when that person left? I mean, I'm assuming it's coded, right? The person would have to know the code to open the gate."

Bethanne nodded. "Jay told me that was why the police originally decided Clausen had been alive and had done it himself. Until we explained that our mechanism had been overridden." She shrugged. "It would have taken someone pretty clever—and someone who knows a lot about electronics—to do it, but the fact remains that they did."

Midge snorted. "That alone should count me out. I can't even work Rosie's DVD player."

"It's true," I agreed on a shrug. "She can't. I thought I was bad, but she's hopeless."

I took a sip of my drink, idly perusing the room as my thoughts clarified. On one sweep back I caught a speculative glint in Bethanne's eyes. She was looking at my ring hand.

"So are you in a relationship? I seem to recall a guy at college?"

I shook my head. "Long gone." Then I felt my face growing warm. "There is someone now, though. Someone very special."

She grinned. "Look at you! I can tell. Anyone I know?"

"Perhaps—I don't know. Jonah Fencott?"

Bethanne squealed. "Jonah Fencott! Those Fencott boys are hot with a capital *H*. Wow! Go you." Still smiling she added, "Jay knows him. They used to play on some team or other. Oh wow. What a small world! Actually," she continued, "I was also thinking something else as I watched you both. You know you could be sisters, right? You are so alike! It's a bit spooky, in a way."

Midge and I looked at each other and shrugged. "Yeah," I answered. "We've noticed and we've had other people mention it, but it's just a fluke. As you say, weird."

Bethanne turned to Midge, then, to ask about her relationship status. "Jay's always on about me finding cute girls for his farm pals. Sometimes these farm guys out here work such long hours they don't get to get out and meet people."

Midge held up both hands in mock horror. "No relationship for me at the moment. Still bearing the scorch marks from the last time I got burned." Before Bethanne could commiserate or even arrange a blind date, she rushed on. "Actually, I'm really happy the way things are right now. I have a lot invested in the paper, and it takes a load of time. I have to give it my focus for the time being. And of course, now there's this murder charge…"

That pulled me right back. "Bethanne, is there anything you can tell us about him? About Clausen?"

"Well, since we were talking about love lives, I guess you know about his girlfriend? Phew… What a piece of work she is. My old granny would say she's the kind of woman who wouldn't do any damage if she fell flat on her face."

Midge frowned. "Meaning she's hard-faced?"

"Hard everything, from what I've seen and experienced. She's a tough lady. Gossip is they'd been together for a while and she ruled the roost."

This threw me. "But he was married. I've just been researching him."

"Estranged," Midge corrected.

"Yes, but from what I read that was a very recent thing. So, what are you saying? That this woman has been his mistress all that time he was married? Before he and his wife separated?"

Midge and Bethanne both shrugged.

"Don't you think that puts a cloud over the fact that his wife is missing?" Even as the words passed my lips, my earlier thoughts were resurfacing. "Although, I have my own suspicions about that. What I don't have are reasons. Motives."

"I'm not sure what you're talking about, but money is always a good motive in my book," Bethanne offered. "For just about anything."

My confusion probably didn't need words, but... "And that means?"

"Money! She has the money. Julia Savage-Clausen has all the money, and he lived off her. And apparently she'd been getting pretty mad with all the money he was losing on deals that went south. Rumor has it she cut him off."

I'd known about her wealth but had assumed he was self-sustaining as well. "Clausen didn't have money of his own? How do you know?"

"The usual way. Our accountant knows her accountant, et cetera, et cetera." Her regret at such a flippant reply was obvious when she dove straight back in with, "I don't mean our accountant is indiscreet, nor hers. It was a legitimate confidence. You see, our invoices to Mister Clausen are paid out of Julia's checking account—and he was a big client. He had—still has, really—a load of security out there, meaning his invoices are substantial. When the separation came about, Mister Clausen got behind and our accountant had to check it out fast before it got out of hand. That's when we were told she'd cut him off. Services were suspended for a while, but then recently, Mister Clausen and Julia must have made up or something because the invoices were being paid again."

"From the same account? From Julia's account?"

"I think so."

"So, his wife is suddenly missing and he has access to her checking accounts. And now he's dead... So, who will pay the invoices now?"

Bethanne shook her head. "I have no idea. His lawyers, I expect. There'll be some kind of authority in place for now, until the estate is sorted."

The conversation slowed, and I was just about to say we should leave when Bethanne suddenly pushed forward and let out a huge groan. I was out of my chair so fast I left a smoke trail. Turning to Midge, I yelled, "Quick, it's happening! Call 911! Get the family. We need to boil water! And towels! Get towels!" I added as an afterthought, trying to desperately to recall the details of every movie I'd ever seen that involved childbirth.

My bluster had alerted the troops, and within seconds the room was filled with anxious people all wearing anxious expressions.

Actually, all except two.

My current housemate, Midge, who wore an expression I'd seen often. Always directed at me. Her *here we go again* expression.

And my former roommate, Bethanne, who was doubled

up, legs crossed awkwardly. And caught between laughter and agony. "Stop! Stop!" she called between heaving gulps of air. "Stop. I'm fine. Or I will be if I can get to the ladies' room without peeing myself! Laughter and a baby sitting on your full bladder is never a good combination."

I froze. "The baby's not coming? You just need to pee?"

With her husband—I'd seen his name tag earlier—holding one arm and an older man, who could have been her father-in-law, holding the other, they awkwardly led her to what I assumed was the ladies' room. They looked like two burly fishermen carting a wounded seal. Over her shoulder, she called, "Wait till you're pregnant. You'll learn. It's never *just* 'need to pee.' Trust me, peeing becomes a whole new experience."

Luckily Jay's family shared a great sense of humor and everybody was laughing, which was better than any alternative I could imagine. They returned to work, and after Bethanne's return, we exchanged details and offered our goodbyes, appreciation—and apologies. Well, the last were just from me.

THE POTLUCK SUPPER was looking like it would be a great success. Food was set up inside, and tables had been scattered outside under shade trees and seating massed around in groups. The permanent white lights that wound through the trees were glowing feebly in the twilight, waiting to take center stage when the sun finally sank in the west. Midge had begged off; the day had been big enough for her, though I was pleased to see Fiona and Clay, looking tired but with their heads held high.

Clay helped me unload the car, and I laid out the food and assisted some of the older ladies, marveling at the selection and aromas. Bobby Don had donated a couple of pots of chili that were sure to go fast.

It had been a big day for me as well, and I was starting to feel the effects of my early start and all that had happened. And yet, too, I was edgy. Nervous energy, I guessed. I still had much to process. Finally I was beginning to see a direction emerging, and I wanted to keep going forward. And dash it all, I wanted to see Jonah. The hours we'd been apart seemed interminable even though the actual number wasn't that big.

I pounced on the sheriff as soon as he and Brenda arrived. Brenda and I chatted about her preserves and how she wouldn't need me next week, as she was pretty sure she had enough stock. She was tut-tutting about poor Fiona and the missing money and how no one at the *commune*, as I was calling it, would open up to Frank or Bobby Don. She was just saying how he was hitting walls when a glare from her husband reminded her she was gossiping about privileged information, and she clammed up.

That glance smashed any hope I'd had of getting news

on anything—the missing money, the murder—or even the identity of the other dead man. As usual, Frank was tight-lipped, although it was interesting to discover he was getting nowhere out at the commune.

"You're not poking your nose in, are you, Rosie?"

I feigned shock. "Whyever would you ask that?"

He did that kissy thing with his lips that he does when he's thinking hard or about to deliver bad news. I hoped it was the first, not the latter. "Well, a little birdie told me you were out delivering goods in Arcacia Street yesterday. Giving out free samples? Just that it seems not everybody was privy to those samples, that you were particular about which houses you went to."

What was the use of prevaricating? "And you don't think it's unusual that we have strange people in town at the same time we have two deaths and stolen money?"

One eyebrow lifted. "That's the difference between me and you, Miss Rosie. I can think what I like, and I don't have to share it with you. In fact, it's my job *not* to share it with you. Whereas it's also my job to encourage you to share *everything* with me."

I sniffed. "Not a very fair arrangement from my side…"

"True," he answered, "but in the words of a very famous fellow American: *That's life.*"

"That's your argument? You're quoting Frank Sinatra at me?"

His cowboy hat sat low, and he stared down his nose. It

was a formidable sight. Then his mouth twitched, and I relaxed and launched into speech again. "Frank... Sheriff. You have to look beyond Midge. She didn't do it! She didn't murder Clausen. And what's more, there's something fishy going on with his money. Or, rather, his wife's money. His wife is missing." I didn't add my own suspicions about that. "They're estranged, and yet she's still writing checks for him. And what about the fact the security code was overridden at Clausen's mansion? Midge is hopeless with anything electronic!" I paused, my mind whirling, hoping to shock him into listening to me. "And what about Simone Grant? What about the fact she—"

He cocked that eyebrow again, waiting. "She...?"

I forced a bright smile and waved at the very woman in question who'd paused in passing behind Frank. Probably at the sound of her name being used—because she was staring at me, and it wasn't a *nice to see you* kind of look. My chest tightened uncomfortably and I felt my face heating up. Which was natural. I'd been caught red-handed and was hoping I could squirm out of it. "Sh-she came to the potluck!" I lifted my voice and waved again. "Hi, Simone! I was just about to ask if anyone had invited you, and I'm glad to see you came along!"

Frank's initial reaction was confusion, but then his eyes gave him away and it was obvious he'd clicked and thought the whole thing—*me being caught in an awkward, embarrassing position*—very funny.

Unable to suppress his grin, he turned. "Miss Simone? Like young Rosie here, I'm sure glad you joined us. There's a mighty fine spread in there," he said, indicating the open double doors. "You won't go hungry!" With that he tipped his hat to us both, leaning in to whisper, "My office. Tomorrow. That's an order."

Simone had simpered under the sheriff's warm welcome, even though he was old enough to be her father. Once he was gone, that syrupy simpering turned to ice blasts. Directed at me. She didn't say a word, but I felt the burn from that freezing stare.

And like the coward I am, I smiled and turned to flee. I'd blindly taken one step when strong, warm arms wrapped themselves around me. And a gravelly voice whispered, "I've missed you."

My night to be whispered to by big strong men. This one not so fatherly. And the one I'd take all day—and night—every day. My lips grazed his cheek. "That's the sweetest thing any one person can say to another. You know that?" I whispered back. "Unless of course they're aiming a gun at you!" I added cheekily.

His rumbling laughter rocked through me, and I pushed closer against him to savor that. "I'm completely unarmed, ma'am. You can pat me down to check, if you like."

I rested my hand against his chest, feeling the crispness of his blue plaid long-sleeved shirt, my fingers creeping up to tip his hat back a bit. Smiling up at him, I said, "You're looking good tonight, cowboy." As his grin grew to a smile, I smacked a quick kiss against his lips before pulling away. "And I sure have I missed you, too."

I'd begun to tell him everything I'd learned that day, when I recognized the sounds behind me. The squeak of an oil-deprived rolling walker, the clump of canes hitting solid earth. The shuffles, the heavy breathing, and the twitters.

"Jonah! Rosie! Hello, dears, we've been looking for you," Lori Sue called.

The remainder of the octogenarian Fab Four, which I'd learned early on had nothing to do with the Beatles, were right behind her with their beaming faces and cotton-candy hair in varying shades of white, blue, and pink.

E.T. paused and leaned heavily on her walker. "We just came to say hello. I hope we're not interrupting something here?"

Betsy leaned forward. "We came over on Riverbend's bus, you know. Plenty of room," she whispered, adding a conspiring wink. "It's free right now. We can act as lookouts for you, if you want to...you know..." She followed that with wagging eyebrows and a hip jiggle.

"Oh my..." Amid the gasps from Betsy's companions, I choked.

More accustomed to Betsy than I was, Jonah just chuckled. "Thanks for the offer, Miz Betsy, but we're good right now." He leaned down to his aunt for a peck. "Howdy, Aunt Lori Sue. It's great to see y'all."

We both greeted them with hugs and kisses all round.

"So, whatchy'all been up to?" If Jonah had asked many other people who spent the majority of their time confined to a retirement home where every day was Groundhog Day, that could have been a cruel question. But for the Fab Four? Not so much.

They proved it with Betsy's excited response. "Well," she said, leaning in close, "you're not gonna believe what Jordy Thomas told his dad, George. He saw a real-life abduction! Right in broad daylight, 'cepting, of course, it was pitch-dark night."

Martha nodded, waving her Chinese fan in an attempt to create a bit of cool air. "He was goin' home late from visiting his lady friend, and he saw these lights. Flashlights. He figured someone had lost an animal, so he headed on over that way."

As usual they told their story in relay fashion. E.T. took up the baton. "Seems they weren't huntin' down no animal; they were huntin' down a woman! Jordy was a ways back so they didn't see him, but he saw them grab her and push her into a vehicle!"

Betsy was fit ready to burst. "Stripped the clothes right off her back! She was buck naked!"

"Betsy!" Lori Sue looked like she was going to have apoplexy right at that point. "You got to stop listenin' to those trashy audio novels! You keep gettin' 'em confused with real life!" Pausing to take a deep breath, she calmed herself before clarifying. "No one was naked. But it did seem like the lady didn't want to go with the people who were with her. At least according to Jordy."

Usually my response to their stories was a mix of shock and hilarity. No one told a story like the Fab Four—even when it was bad news. This evening, though, the story was an eerie echo of what I'd seen myself recently and my overriding response was concern. Jonah was right on my wavelength. "Did Jordy tell the sheriff?" he asked.

"Well, he mentioned it to Bobby Don, who is convinced it was probably the Hestlers' elderly aunt. The one with dementia? He says she's always going out and forgetting who she is and where she is," Lori Sue answered.

E.T. wiped some beads of sweat from her brow with a lace handkerchief, and wisps of lavender perfume drifted my way. "But Jordy swears this was a younger woman. He even thinks he saw her or someone like her at the meeting."

Prickles skittered up my spine. "E.T., did Jordy mention when this happened? A date?"

"Sure!" Martha said, pointing that fan our way. "It was the night of the big meetin' between Clay and that Clausen creep."

"No need to speak ill of the dead, Martha," E.T. chided. "Just because he was a sidewinding, yellow-bellied snake with beans where his brains should be when he was alive is no reason to disrespect him now he's passed over."

I wanted to laugh; these women had no idea how funny

they were, but I was remembering the ghostly image that had caused Jonah to pull off the road that night. And the scrap of material still on my bedroom dresser.

Suddenly everything I'd been thinking started to make sense.

Still, it didn't tell me who murdered Frederick Clausen.

And only one place held the answers. But how would I get them to talk to me?

At that very moment, Merline wandered past, and a tsunami-sized brainwave smoothed out the confused spaces in my head.

Oh wow. Could it be that simple? And yet that complex…

Chapter Thirteen

AFTER A RESTLESS night, I woke to the glorious smell of fresh ground coffee, warm cinnamon, and news that slowed up my plans for that day.

Midge was sitting at the table on the porch, watching the morning, and Jonah had arrived with banana-cinnamon muffins. The expression on his face as he handed me the warm cake was priceless. "I know, I know… Giving you any kind of baked goods is like taking oranges to California. And these are just freezer muffins that I picked up at the store and warmed in the oven—which is probably even worse. But you know what? I thought it would be nice for you, for once, to not be the one making stuff for everybody else."

I took the plate and lifted it to my face and sniffed. "You know what? You're right. This smells delicious. Thank you."

He kissed the top of my head and led me to the porch. Midge had the coffee pot on a warmer and mugs waiting. Once settled and with rejuvenating coffee soaring through my veins, Jonah grinned at us. "I know everybody's got a lot of heavy stuff on their minds, but I thought you gals would like to know one mystery's been solved. Or will be by noon or so today."

That got me sitting straighter. Yesterday's paper sat between Midge and me, and my glance fell to a headline citing that the unidentified body remained unidentified. "Our mystery guy?"

He nodded. "Dad called. The guy's name hasn't been released because his family has to be notified, but I can give you his age and general origin. The car was a rental and the rental period would have been up today anyway, so by tomorrow the police would have been alerted when it wasn't returned."

My mouth full of spicy muffin, I urged him on with a slight jab to his leg.

Grinning again, he said, "Thirty-five years old. From somewhere out in Nevada."

"Nevada again? Didn't Fiona say Simone Grant was from Reno? Did someone leave a gate open out there? Seems like a whole lot of their inmates are escaping." Meanwhile this Texan recent inmate wanted to bang her head against a wall. There was a connection right there. Surely. And yet I couldn't see why, how, or what. "And we don't know what he was doing out there, right? But he rented a car for a week…" I crumbled the last of the muffin crust. "To be here in Airlie Falls? What's our big attraction all of a sudden?"

Jonah shrugged, trying to project innocence, but no one could have missed the cheeky gleam in his eyes. I was ready for whatever was coming. "I dunno—I heard they have a great new market stand selling the most amazing desserts. I believe it's called *From the Hart.* You think that's what's bringing 'em?"

"You're saying my desserts stand is drawing people down here so they can get themselves killed? Remind me not to put you in charge of marketing."

Grinning, he held up both hands in mock surrender. "Okay, okay—levity abandoned!" True to his word, he sobered as he poured more coffee. "We don't know he was going to stay in Airlie Falls. This may have just been one of his stops."

"So, you're thinking," Midge said, holding out her cup, "that he was some kind of salesman?"

"There seems to be a bit of that going around. Isn't that what *Simone* is supposed to be doing?"

Midge's head snapped up. "Rosie! I forgot to tell you. Just before I was arrested, I had some free time so I contacted the head office of Columbus Insurance—and they don't have a representative down here." She paused to shake her head in wonder. "I guess when Frank and Bobby Don picked me up at the office, it just went out of my head."

I reached over to pat her hand. "We'll get there, I promise." As the words hovered between us, I prayed she couldn't sense the doubt I was feeling. Forcing a smile, I thanked her for the information, wondering what in the heck it meant and what we should do with it. "If only I could get her phone... It'd be the one thing that wouldn't hide her secrets—or her lies."

I looked across at Jonah, who repeated his two-handed surrender. "Don't look at me like that, darlin'. Two break-and-enters? Frank's a fair cop, honey, but he's a law-abiding cop. I was hoping to see more of you, not less." His glare had bite. "And bi-monthly visits while you're doin' two-to-five in Gatesville doesn't exactly fulfill the brief."

Leaning my head back against the high plantation-style chair, I stared out over the fields opposite. Thinking. "Doesn't have to be *breaking* and entering. Maybe just *entering*?" I said slowly.

Opposite me, Midge was nodding. All we had to do now was come up with a plan.

Shaking his head, Jonah leaned in to kiss me, grabbed his hat, and stood to leave. He paused behind me, both hands on my shoulders, gently massaging the tense muscles in the most delicious way. "I'm outta here. If I don't know anything they can torture me all they like and I can't tell." He tipped his hat. "Stay outta trouble, ladies. *Please.* I'll see y'all later. I hope."

As soon as he left, I jumped up myself. "You think about a way to get that phone. I've got an early appointment with Merline."

Midge glanced at her phone. "At seven in the morning?"

I nodded. "Seven thirty. She's opening early for me—before any prying eyes and ears arrive. I'm meeting Fiona there, and I'll explain when I get back. I'll possibly be a couple of hours."

"Don't you have a meeting with Frank, too? An *order*?"

My heart sank. "Oops, I forgot about that. I'll make sure I get there later. Or tomorrow."

MERLINE OWNED THE title of genius; she'd well and truly earned it. I surveyed myself in the mirror when I got back home and could hardly believe what I was seeing. Midge was even more amazed. *Speechless* was one word she used. The only word, so in fact she'd spoken the truth.

"Never, ever would I have imagined you as a blonde," she said finally. "But you know, it kinda suits you. It goes with your tanned skin—maybe like those cheerleader types."

I jerked back to the mirror. "Cheerleader! That's not what I'm going for. Whoever saw a cheerleader in a red Coco Chanel power suit? Don't ask how Merline got it. I was told not to," I explained quickly.

"Oh? Oh. Of course you don't look like a cheerleader. I was simply remarking on all that blonde hair and your tan." She touched her own hair, which was not quite as unruly as my real hair. My hair was its own barometer. And needed warning signs. Wavy when dry. Curly when humid or wet.

"I'm just realizing what I'd look like if I went blonde. Interesting. But it's definitely a wig, right? You didn't do anything drastic?"

"Definitely." Long and straight but with loads of body. "What do you think of the makeup?"

"Well, how do I say this politely? Um, Merline does the stage makeup whenever there's a local production, right?" Without pausing for an answer she said, "Let's just say she does a good job with stage makeup."

I continued to survey myself. "Hmm. Clownish?"

She tilted her head one way, then the other. "Not quite. She fell just short of clown, but she *did* park you in the lot right next to the Big Tent." She stepped back, still assessing. "Maybe *overdone* is the word I need."

I nodded. Satisfied. "Good. That's what I wanted. And the eyeglasses?" The heavy, dark plain-glass rims were ugly enough to be fashionable. "We tried contacts, but they were murder—and we've got enough of that. So, Merline and Fiona suggested these glasses. The thing is—do I look like me? Would you recognize me?"

"Not your face. Not at first glance, anyway. But your voice is yours. That would make me look twice. Can you make it higher or deeper? Which could you sustain the longest?" As I experimented, Midge frowned, her thoughts drifting. "So Aunt Merline went along with this plan? She thinks it's okay?"

My smile was gentle. "Apart from the fact Merline is the best sport and has the kindest heart, she knows this is for you. She jumped at the chance. You know she'd do anything for you, don't you? She adores you."

Midge lowered her head. "I know," she said softly. "And she adores you as well. Do you ever stop to think how lucky we are? Two random girls from dysfunctional families adopted by the nicest mom-and-pop town in Texas? Well, at least…"

"Hey, I know, I know. Just don't forget they believe in you; they're all behind you. Behind us. It's shame the pastor and his family are away, but you know, this town proves over and over it beats as one heart."

"So, what's the plan? Are you driving out there?"

"Sort of. Fiona's chauffeuring me. She's got a friend who owns some kind of limousine service. He brought one over during the night so we could borrow it. She'll wait in the car. Oh, Midge! You should see her as a flaming redhead. I actually reckon Clay will go nuts for her. She's always stunning, and when we changed her look she was even more of a knockout."

After that we both fell silent. It was one of those moments when there was so much to say yet so few words to adequately convey it all. Swallowing deeply, I simply nodded and grabbed my bags.

I'd actually turned to go out the door when Midge asked one last question. "Does Jonah know?"

It was the one I knew I'd have the most trouble with. I didn't want to deceive him, so maybe this was the best way. "No, not yet. Fiona will tell him and Clay tonight if needed." I found a weak smile. "I know he won't stay mad with me, but he'll be mad to start with. Only because he'll think it's a foolish plan."

"And it is," Midge answered, her voice heavy with emotion. "But a brave one. And I'm so grateful to you…"

Tears filled her eyes, but I didn't go to her and hug her. I needed to be away from here and not start crying, too. I wasn't sure if this makeup was waterproof.

NOT A COMMUNE—A spa. Of sorts. A "back to basics" rejuvenation clinic. Not that there was anything basic about the office I'd been shown into. I'd had no idea what to expect when I'd begun planning this adventure, although a couple of things had jelled when I replayed the video in my head. As the memories rolled by, I tried to focus on the small things: The air of the women I'd seen from this place. Their manner, posture, speech patterns. The nails on a couple— and the surgeries. I hadn't been close enough to be certain, but I was close enough to be confident. All those things had hovered in my mind, waiting for me to join them together, and—fingers crossed—it looked like I'd been on the right track.

It had taken Fiona and me a while to discover the entrance to the commune, which was separate to Clausen's mansion. The exterior was very discreet, and the reception area I'd been shown into by a maid was dark but still airy and cool, the carpet thick—muffling any sounds. Antique furniture gleamed and formed the backdrop for glass and porcelain pieces that sparkled under a crystal chandelier. A huge bowl of summer roses perfumed the air. A couple of lesser-known artworks by the old masters took pride of place under strategic lighting. They weren't just hung—they were displayed to highlight their value. Their preciousness.

Impressive. If they hadn't been fake. Art had been one of my undergrad subjects. I'd hoped to marry art and finance. I hadn't; however, I could spot fakes. Not because I was an expert but because I recognized both pieces as being ones that were permanently housed in European galleries. Not in teeny Airlie Falls, Texas.

Was everything else fake? I guessed it probably was. I was even tempted to touch the roses. Still, the overall impression was classy.

A tall, elegant woman wearing a lavender suit with a wisp of white lace at her cleavage and lavender satin pumps strode across from an inner door. Not the one marked FREDERICK N. W. CLAUSEN, DIRECTOR. That door was firmly closed.

The woman's hand shot out—her manicure made me want to hide my hands, until I remembered Merline had taken care of that as well. Our fellow fake nails didn't acknowledge each other as they passed, and her palm was as soft as her grip was firm. "How do you do. I'm Glorious Rodriguez. How can I help you?"

Glorious? Everything about her was as she was named.

Her flawless skin, gleaming dark hair tamed into a chic chignon, doe-shaped eyes. Even her soft, deep, well-modulated voice. Was this Frederick's mistress?

Whoever she was, she was a perfect front man. If you were going for cold and intimidating. "Pleased to meet you. I'm Helen Henderson." I'd borrowed Hank's surname. It was common enough so that any investigation of me on their part wouldn't be easy.

She'd been perusing me just as I'd been inspecting her. "We don't have many people turn up at the door," she purred. "Normally we book via the phone or email. We're not a hotel—it's not like we can assure accommodation."

Another woman, just as elegant but slightly warmer, strode into the room via the same door as Glorious. "Jackie Kennedy. No, not that one. Obviously." It was said as one sentence, almost. I held out my hand. "Take a seat, Miz Henderson," Jackie Kennedy said.

Now I was confused. Was *this* one the mistress?

At their direction we all retired to a lounge setup off to the side. They perched on one two-seater. Me, opposite on the other. Alone. It was significant.

I went on to gush and tell them I'd heard about their program in my new higher-toned voice and poor Atlanta accent. Hopefully they'd just think I traveled and my accent was blurring. "I just think it would be a blast!"

"And where did you hear about us?" Jackie asked.

I flapped my newly manicured hands, hoping I didn't

look like a taloned bird on dope. "Oh, you're not gonna believe it. From Angelina and Heather and Reese and Sandra and Nicole." I counted off on my fingers. "They were all talkin' about it on the private jet on the way to Monaco." I leaned forward. "Thankfully we were stayin' on Daddy's yacht. I tell you that place is crazy in summer! You can't bat an eyelash without hittin' someone! Anyway, they're all busy with their stuff, but we all thought it'd be fun if I tried it out and then we can decide whether to come back." As I pulled out my checkbook, I added gaily, "Was it Reese who said it would make a fun movie? Oh, you know, I can't remember now! Silly me."

They were passing glances back and forth. Glances I couldn't decipher. Possibly they were wondering whether to call the medics. The ones with straitjackets. Hopefully they were more focused on the checkbook.

Obviously they were. After telling me they could accommodate me for a few days, I was asked to wait while one disappeared to do the paperwork and another to get my *uniform* for my duration.

Just what I wanted. Uncaring of whether there were cameras watching me, I stood and casually walked toward the artworks, the ones near Clausen's office. I studied them for a second or two and then slid left and tried the door handle. It pushed open and I stepped in.

The décor matched the reception area, and unfortunately for me, the desk was clear of all paperwork. The room was stuffy from being closed up and not helped by the over-whelming odor of stale cigarette smoke that hung like an invisible cloud that surrounded and enveloped me. Cigarettes, not cigars. Interesting. Most smokers of his age in Texas preferred cigars.

Covering my mouth so as to not choke, I quickly darted a glance around the room. A map of Nevada hung proudly along with a state flag. Not Texan, then.

More significant was yet this further reference to the western state. That place was definitely developing sticky edges. It seemed every bit of information I'd come across in the past few days came with that one common denominator.

Individually the references meant nothing. Together they were like peel-back stickers, just waiting to be useful. Together they would create a picture. The only problem was that picture—in my mind—was like a Picasso painting: everything in the wrong place.

A framed copy of an old news item was next. I could only scan, but it was something to do with the founder of a town called Wellington. Frederick Norman Wellington Clausen's name suddenly had some context—he'd been named for a town. That was some kind of proud. Maybe there was Texan blood there somewhere after all. The one area every Texan excelled in was state pride.

The filing cabinet called, and I darted one glance back over my shoulder, my heart pounding as I listened for any footfalls on that carpet. But what would I look for? Was there something more easily found?

On the inner side of the desk I hit gold. The sliding pullout under the main surface. A wide strip of white paper, thicker than a normal page, stood out against the dark hardwood of the desk. With a quick look at the door that I'd left slightly ajar, I sucked in a breath for courage and slid out the panel. It was a blueprint.

A real spy or detective would've been ready and armed with a camera or phone. Mine was sitting in my purse in the reception area. All I could rely on, therefore, was my memory. There was nothing to indicate what it was or where it was to be located, but it seemed like a plan for a tract housing development.

Up in the right-hand corner was a shaded area and the words *ARCACIA ARCADE* printed neatly in black ink. The subtitle *185,000 SQUARE FEET* was listed below the name. A dawning realization tickled my consciousness, but I had no time to react.

I was still trying to absorb as much as I could when I heard a soft click and my heart took flight. Shoving the pullout back into place, I hurried closer to the door. There was no time for an escape, so I turned so I was facing the interior to make it look like I'd just entered—and then held my breath until my eyes were red and watery.

In another heartbeat a voice was beside me. Glorious. An unhappy Glorious. "What are you doing here? This is out of bounds!" The words were hissed.

When I turned her eyes were scrutinizing the room, perhaps wondering what I could see. An elegant tissue box sat on a side table, and I crossed to it and snatched up the soft paper and held it to my face.

Glorious had taken hasty steps to follow and stop me, but she stalled when I turned and she noted my red eyes. "Oh, that poor man!" I sobbed. "He's the one. The one who was m-murdered..." I continued sobbing, continued to maintain my appalling accent. "So cruel! So heartless! I was just sittin' out there and looked up and saw this was his place of work. And I just felt so drawn to pay my respects. Glorious, would you mind if we took a moment to pray for him? To pray for poor Fred..."

"Poor Fred?" she asked weakly. "Oh, of course."

I began a fair appearance of deep weeping into my tissue before turning to her to say, "Would you say the words? I'm just so overcome..."

I figured she was probably thinking about my check while she debated whether to throw me out. The check won as she began speaking softly. Waves of relief rolled over me while I listened to her stutter and blather for a few minutes, offering my own prayer of thanks for being saved. Again.

My loud and hearty *amen* must have landed midsentence because her expression was at first startled, then relief took over.

"Thank you so much, Glorious. I feel so much better now." I turned and marched from the room, with her sedately following. Never would there be a more tragic moment for an air punch to be denied...

Back in reception, I stood tall, hoping to give the impression of a woman who'd regained control of her emotions. As though unsure of what I'd do next, both women hovered close as they explained the rules and handed over the clothes I was to wear—which consisted of the same cheap, floral shifts I'd seen the other women wear.

Moments later, I was grateful for the placement of an easy chair when they at last quoted the fee. *Jumping jaguars!* One night was a month's wages for most people! Had that chair not been there to catch me, Glorious and Jackie might have been scraping me off the floor. And that reaction from a gal whose daddy owned a private jet and a yacht that comfortably accommodated several fictional women, who coincidentally had names similar to current Hollywood actresses, would surely have raised flags.

To cover my sudden drop, I looked up from my now sitting position with what I hoped was cheerful triumph. "Just remembered! My plastic surgeon said standing creates varicose veins!"

Both women looked at me blankly.

Then I just couldn't help myself. "He says the same thing about walking." I leaned forward as though to share a secret. "Crawling. That's the answer to maintaining faaabulous legs. Crawling instead of walking. You should try it!" I glanced at their legs and frowned. "Hopefully, it won't be too late…"

This was proving to be way too much fun, and it was only when it was time to hand over the check that I realized a huge problem. Trying to not exude any indication of panic, I excused myself to go and collect my personal things from the limo before going any farther. Their strained reactions to my behavior had already proven they thought I had a few screws loose—a rich crazy person—so they didn't exhibit much surprise when I changed direction at the last minute.

Out at the limousine, I took my time, aware that the two vultures watched me from inside. "Fiona!" I whispered as she alighted from the car to greet me. "I have a problem. They want a check, and it'll have my own name and address on it!"

She kept her head down. "You're stayin'? Oh, Rosie! Is that wise?"

"Just for one night. They think I have wealthy friends. *Really* wealthy friends. They also think *I'm* really wealthy. I've got an idea of what Clausen was up to in Airlie Falls. Land development. Tract housing and shopping complexes. That's what he meant about bringing us into the twenty-first century—urbanization. But while that opens up motive, it doesn't give us any idea of who might have killed him. I'm also pretty sure his wife is held here, and I want to try to find her."

"Rosie! That sounds really dangerous! Jonah's not going to be happy with either of us. In the words of my boys, I'll be in for a right old butt chewin'! He'll disown his own mother!"

"Tell him I wouldn't listen. He'll know you're telling the truth. But what can I do about this check? Any ideas? I can't stall them…"

"After I get your bags and I get back into the car, come to the driver's window as if to give me instructions, and I'll slip ours to you. It's in our company name and the address is of our accountant in Dallas. I'll warn him in case they investigate you. But please, once more, won't you reconsider?"

I saved my answer for several silent moments until I moved to the driver's window. "I have to do this, Fiona. Frank's getting nowhere out here. I already know a heap more than he does. And just quickly? I just got the lowdown on this place. Not a commune. It's a fad. They describe it in different terms, but basically it's a game for bored, rich women. They come here to get 'back to basics' for a couple of weeks so they can go home and boast that they know how the poor people do it. And it's a bargain at an average month's wages per night." At her gasp, my nerves started to kick in. "Look, I have to go; they're watching me. Be back here at ten thirty in the morning. Okay? That's checkout time."

As expected, once I was back inside, the check was carefully scrutinized, and I knew they'd be contacting that accountant. I hoped Fiona got to him quickly.

THE ACCOMMODATION WASN'T too bad. I'd expected hard boards and paper-thin mattresses, but the modern décor was very comfortable. Luxurious, even. "Back to basics" obviously had a different connotation for the mega rich: private rooms with full bathroom facilities, heavenly beds, a common room with all kinds of distractions—except a television. That was their one nod to hardship? Unbelievable.

There was a small kitchenette for creating snacks and tea or coffee—right next to the room-service phone. And all meals were provided. So far, apart from television, which I didn't necessarily think was a great loss, and wearing a *uniform*, I was struggling to find the back-to-basics part.

I changed into my shift, feeling strangely comfortable. It was soft and easy to wear. Just as I returned to the common area, a young woman with fair hair, about my age, and a face as red as a beet hurried through the door, stopping dead when she saw me. "Oh, I thought everyone was in the garden."

I didn't let on, but I recognized her from that night at my market stand. Unless I was mistaken, she was the one who'd lost her cool and purchased that boatload of desserts.

"Is that a problem?" I answered. "I just arrived, and I'm not sure where I'm supposed to be working."

"Working?" Her sarcasm intrigued me. "Oh, you *are* new…" She sighed. "Sorry, that was rude. My name is

CeeCee Jerome, and I'm not one of you, so sometimes I say inappropriate things."

I shook my head. "Not one of who? I'm confused. By the way, I'm Ro—Helen, Helen Henderson. That's the Montgomery Hendersons," I added for effect. "But you were saying?"

Her color had begun to subside. "Look, maybe we should just let it go. I have a habit of getting riled up about things and running off at the mouth. I keep forgetting I need to check that here."

I smiled, laying a sugar path of southern charm. "Hey, you're Australian!" At her nod, I continued. "Gosh, you poor sweet thang… You look so overheated! And so am I." And my wig was itching like crazy, but I couldn't say that. "Is there some cold water or a Coke around here? Or do we have to go pump a well?"

She laughed and the tension in her face started to ease. "You might be the only one I've met that I can stand to be with for more than a few minutes. Please tell me you worked for your money and that you didn't marry it or grow up with it?" Just as quickly she held up a hand. "No. Don't answer. Again, that was rude. And the Cokes are over here, by the way."

An integrated fridge freezer was hidden behind a cupboard door and filled with all kinds of soft drinks and bottled water. I chose water; she chose Coke.

Sitting on comfortable lounge chairs she explained. "I

apologize. I've developed an unflattering opinion about people with money since I've been here. And again, I apologize if I'm insulting you as well; it's just that these women are so stereotypical! It's all about who they know and what they buy and where they eat and who does their hair and…and…and it never ends. They drop so many names it's a wonder they can take a single step without tripping over them!" She sighed. "They each have enough money to make a difference and they don't and don't think they should even try!"

I sat back, surprised. "So, how did you get in here if you're not one of *them*?" Too late I realized I'd dropped my fake accent. I saw her frown, but she didn't say anything.

"I'm a journalist, here to do a feature article. My editor thought it would be amusing for me to come and experience what they experience. The owners here thought it would be great publicity. Unfortunately they don't know me or my editor." Her head dropped back. "And now I've said too much. Not that I'm hiding my identity, just that I mightn't be as enthusiastic as I should be."

I smiled again. "Secret's safe with me."

She nodded, frowning again. "So, you happen to have a cigarette on you?"

"Sorry, not and never been a smoker."

"Right, right… Partner a smoker, is he? Family?"

It was my turn to frown. "I'm not following, I'm sorry. No one around me smokes cigarettes. Why the questions?"

She sniffed the air. "The smell. It's all over you."

My eyes widened. I'd changed clothes, but this darned wig would have absorbed that heavy aroma. "Oh, I guess I picked it up—" I waved idly toward the reception area, which was in a complete other building.

She nodded again, a small smile hovering. "So, pretty shocking news about old Clausen, yeah?"

"Absolutely. Must have been terrible for his wife and family. Do you know any of them?"

"No kiddies and the wife's AWOL, I believe."

I gasped, feigning shock. "And what about you? Were you nervous once you knew what had happened?"

"Nah," she answered with a shrug. "I'd just arrived that day. And all the excitement was up in the house, not down here. To be honest, I half expected them to ask me to leave, but they said they'd need the positive publicity now more than ever. I'm checking out tomorrow, though. I can't take any more. I'll go crazy if I have to stay here another day."

"You don't like the work? The simplicity?"

At that she burst out laughing. "Oh, you really aren't one of them. So, my question is...who are you?"

Chapter Fourteen

M Y HEART WAS banging so hard it felt like it was trying to escape. Praying I was a better actor than I believed I was, I feigned innocence.

Her eyes were huge. "You really don't know what goes on here?" Exasperation dripped from every syllable. "Helen, there *is* no work. No 'back to basics.' They lark about and pretend to dig a few things, and they're keen for me to take photos so they can prove how tough it was—but it's a crock. The whole thing. These lazy girls simply do what they do at home. Nothing. They just do it without the glitz. Most of the time they sit about gossiping about how tough their lives are." She assumed a false voice: "Can you imagine having two children and just *two* nannies? It's just too, too terrible. I ask you, what if one nanny gets sick? What are they to do, then? Pitch in and look after their own offspring? Unheard of!"

"Oh no…" Tragic or not, it was impossible not to laugh with her.

On a roll, she continued. "The gardens are just for show, as is the razor-wire security—as are these terrible outfits. The whole thing is an excuse to get away from their *terrible* lives, and afterward they can go home and get brownie points from their husbands who are *sooooo* proud of them—and envy from their friends because it costs a fortune! Some of them even get sponsored for charity. Sponsored to sit around and be a lazy cow while pretending to do it tough! That's bordering on misrepresentation."

"But good for Clausen's business," I added quietly.

She didn't answer.

"So, does everybody stay here, in this building? The glorious Glorious and the whacky Jackie Kennedy who's 'not that one'?"

CeeCee had a nice smile, even if there was something feline about it. "Just the 'inmates,' as I call them. The other two stay at the house. They've just hired a new employee. Another the same as they are; they're 'training' her." She put the word in finger quotes. "You'll probably meet her soon. She floats in on a cloud of red hair and expensive perfume each afternoon, oohing and aahing with the ladies. Making sure they're comfortable."

I nodded. "Have you ever seen anybody else there, besides those three?" Was I being too obvious? She was sharp, as indicated by the quick shift of her eyes, and panicked; I waggled my eyebrows and attempted to add a salacious, gossipy tone to my query. "I heard he has a mistress."

She appeared to think about that. "Glorious looks the part, but my money would be on Jackie K. She's the pants in this operation. Don't be fooled by her softer façade. She's as hard as nails."

Bethanne's description came back to me. If Jackie was Clausen's love, then she certainly didn't seem too cut up by his death. Perhaps because she was responsible?

CeeCee was still speculating. "The other woman is too new." Her eyes narrowed. "Who else did you expect to be there?"

I tried to act nonchalant, but my airy "I don't know. No one, really. Maybe I was wondering who else lives in that enormous mansion" may not have worked as well as I'd hoped.

Thankfully, the clatter of returning feet and voices distracted CeeCee, and I caught a break.

Up close, the other guests of this place supported everything my new acquaintance had said about them—and validated my impression from that night at the market. Signs of buff and polish under their minimal makeup—even though the rules suggested no makeup at all—were only outnumbered by signs of outright tampering: overblown lips; extraordinarily high, taut, bulging cheekbones; and brows that didn't move, no matter what emotion their owner was expressing. Up close and face-to-face with them was almost an entertainment in itself, a party game—Guess What I'm Feeling?

They'd arrived for lunch, which was set up in another room I hadn't yet seen. As we gathered there, I was introduced and naturally the questions began. I dodged most of the tricky ones, like which celebrity beauty parlor I attended and if I'd smuggled in my private cosmetologist, by pretending to live elsewhere. That way I could avoid any faux pas.

I quickly gathered that their hobbies, passion, and work all revolved around one thing: maintaining their beauty and halting the aging process. I should have guessed, therefore, that when I was asked about my own hobbies, my answers would be a showstopper. I'd been caught up in their conversation and momentarily forgot who I was supposed to be…

"Baking, reading, and gardening. Mostly I grow vegetables and some fruit, although I'm still learning."

The only thing that broke the stunned silence was the sound of CeeCee spewing Coke across the crisp, pristine tablecloth.

Following that, the others seemed to not know how to address me; I had aligned myself with that demeaning alien notion: domesticity. In their world, that made me a freak, and so they talked around me rather than to me. That, at least, gave me an opportunity to study each one, searching for that one face.

In one lull, I ventured back into the conversation. "Is this all of us? No one still to come?"

CeeCee's glance was again curious, but the others responded without interest and hurried back to the safety of their world and the weighty topic of dermabrasion. Still, I did glean that they knew of no one else staying here. So, who had I seen that night outside the church hall? The ladies could check out whenever they wanted, so perhaps she'd already gone? I asked, and that question was answered with the same lack of interest and the beginnings of impatience: No, no one had departed the premises in the past few days. Or week.

Blocking me out completely, the conversation went back to flowing around me rather than including me, and when I feared there would be blood drawn as the argument over the best Botox clinic escalated, I knew I had to escape. If all those implants exploded at once it would be ugly. And messy. Very messy.

THE GROUNDS WERE well cared for, if not what I'd expected. I'd been led to believe there were vast produce gardens to be tended by these women. I'd even imagined some kind of livestock, but one garden patch near the road and open to view via wire fencing was their token. CeeCee was right. This was a game. Their conversations swirled in my head as I walked. No one here was serious about making a difference or changing their perspective.

My stride lengthened, and traveling east, I found myself in a walled garden of the kind you'd find in a posh hotel. Far, far away from prying public eyes. Lush gardens, palms, and shade trees. No pool, but a hot tub and sun loungers and ornate, metal tables with matching lace chairs shaded by colorful umbrellas. A woman in a white smock was placing robes near the hot tub, and another was setting up jugs of icy lemonade.

So much for hardship and basic living.

Apart from that, this place was fairly new, so establishing a garden with trees of this maturity would have cost an absolute fortune. No wonder the fees were so high.

I found a corner and surveyed the whole area. It seemed the house—mansion—was to the front, but the back was accessed through this garden. Interesting. There were no other outbuildings save for a small gardener's shed in one corner. I'd take a stroll there in a moment, although I doubted anyone could be hidden in there. They wouldn't last a day in this heat.

I made my way to the jugs of lemonade; I'd only picked at lunch—as had everybody else. For me, however, it was nerves, not fear of calories. Watching them *almost* eat explained their reactions to my desserts stand. They weren't unable to buy them; they were terrified of the sugar and calories. And probably fearful of losing those rich husbands if they dared to gain an ounce. Or maybe now I was just being catty...

Still, it was a tragic scenario on so many levels, but one memory from that night made me smile. CeeCee's comment about "testing" them when she'd made all those purchases. My imagination had run riot with that comment, but now I saw the simplicity. Having watched them all in action, it was an easy conclusion to draw: I'd bet CeeCee had led them around to see how much self-control they really possessed. That girl was hilarious. And very naughty.

I should have been pleased to have another little mystery cleared away so innocently; however, the answers hadn't helped me one iota.

The lemonade was delicious, and with it, discreet refrigerated glass-fronted units offered a selection of fruit and cheese so I picked at some for a minute, taking my glass with me as I walked on.

I was right—the shed wasn't even locked and it was empty of anything except garden requirements. Finding a secluded spot, I stood and looked back over the grounds. They were extensive but not as big as we'd been led to believe. From this end, too, I had a good view of the layout of the property. From what I could see, if that woman was hidden here she had to be either in one of the guest rooms or in the main house.

A sick feeling curled in my stomach. What was I doing? I'd convinced myself this missing woman had something to do with Clausen's death, but what if she didn't? What if I was just letting my mystery-loving imagination get in the way of finding Clausen's killer? What if I was just wasting precious time?

And now that I was here, I was beginning to doubt my decision to stay. What did I hope to achieve? To discover?

Did I expect a confession?

I'd been sure the answers were here, but were they?

With no real plan in mind, I made my way toward the entrance to the mansion gardens. It was beyond the end wall of this garden and through a vine-shrouded gateway. Like everything else it was electronic and operated on a code. Today, however, a green light signaled it wasn't locked. *Dare I enter?*

Of course I did.

The same opulence existed here as in the walled garden. It was cozier, though, and had the required pool complete with spa and fountain to bring it to mansion standards. A flagstone patio led to a wall of glass doors that opened into the house. They were closed, probably in deference to air conditioning. I crept closer, keeping myself protected by the jungle of lush tropical plants. The interior was dim, but I could make out furniture. From what I could see, nothing moved. Did that mean no one was in there? Where did Glorious and Jackie K. spend their days? In the office or in the mansion?

It was so quiet here...

So deep were my contemplations that I barely registered the first nudge to my arm. I swiped at it idly. The second pulled me to complete consciousness, and I spun in fright, pulse thundering and unable to control a little squeal.

Someone else did. A hand rapidly covered my mouth, and a voice whispered to me to hush.

I blinked. CeeCee?

When she lowered her hand, I gulped in air. Not that I'd been deprived, just that I needed it. Every cell in my body was shuddering, my head and heart pounding as one.

"Sorry," she whispered, "I tried to warn you I was here."

Pushing her away from me, I shuffled back into the bushes, feeling the scrape of a date palm thorn tear the flesh on my shoulder. "What are you doing here?"

Her eyes widened. "What am *I* doing here? Isn't that my question? After all, I'm the one who found you snooping."

"I'm not snooping, I'm just…just…"

"Snooping," she repeated. "Hey, it's okay. I snoop for a living. I'm all for snoopers—as long as they're doing it for the greater good." She paused, eyeing me speculatively. "Are you?"

I sighed. What was the use? I'd played my one great role in the office earlier. I sucked at this acting stuff and had no more to give. Nodding, I said, "The greatest. I'm trying to find out who murdered Clausen. My friend, a journalist like you, has been tentatively charged with his murder. And obviously she didn't do it."

"Oh, wow. Bad stuff." I knew she meant it, so the grin that followed seemed out of place until she said, "I knew you were a snoop when I first met you. Knew you weren't one of them. It's why I followed you."

"How did you know?"

"Clausen's office. It stinks. I know because I've snooped

in there, too. That cloying cigarette smell was all over you. Besides, you seemed too normal to be one of them. So," she continued, rapidly changing direction, "what are you trying to find here?"

"If only I knew." My head dropped back, and I searched the trees above me. "I'm so confused now. I thought his missing wife had something to do with his death. I'm also sure she's being held here against her will. And I'd really like to help her, but the more important thing is to clear Midge."

"Sounds fair enough. And you need to get in and see for yourself, right? Otherwise you'll always be wondering. So," she continued again, "the best time to break in is about five. The house staff take a break before they serve dinner, and the executives—Glorious and company—have a very liquid meeting in the office. It never changes."

My eyes were wide. "And you know this because?"

"I've already been in there twice. Found nothing, by the way. But?" She shrugged. "Maybe I wasn't looking for the right thing. Anyway, my advice right now is for us to get back before we're missed. Besides, you have blood trickling down your arm, and if we don't get it wiped away it could be the catalyst for mass hysteria. I doubt these ladies have ever seen real blood. Or real baby poop, for that matter. Or real house dust. Or a broom. Or have ever emptied kitty litter. Or..."

I didn't argue. I just followed her, my stifled giggles finally drowning out her words.

CeeCee knew her way around, and she'd administered all the necessary first aid with no fuss and no one any the wiser. Now that my secret was out and the barriers down I invited her to my room to share information. Maybe she knew something that could help.

"So, do you have suspects and all?"

"Yes," I answered. "The only problem being that I have too many suspects. Like, there are a whole heap of people Frederick Clausen cheated out of the true value of their homes."

She whistled. "That there is motive, all righty."

"I know, and then there's his wife. Apparently he was going through her money like it's water."

"Okaayy… And?"

I counted off on my fingers. "Then there are two women who are sketchy because I don't have motives for them, but something's niggling at me. Both are acting suspiciously, and both arrived the same time Clausen did."

She made herself more comfortable, tucking her legs up under her on the two-seater couch. "I know this is going to come out all wrong," she said, holding up both hands, "because this is serious stuff, but it's kinda fun!"

My heart was heavy. "I get what you're saying, I really do. But this is deadly serious."

"So, I'll get serious. My issue with the last two you mentioned is motive. You don't know much about them?"

"Hardly anything." I explained about Simone's multiple

identities and secretive behavior and the questions surrounding the real identity of the Arcacia Street woman.

"Pretty weak, you gotta admit."

She wasn't telling me anything I didn't know. As our conversation moved on, the subject of the mysterious body came up. Suddenly CeeCee sat forward, asking loads of quick-fire questions.

"That guy? He's dead? How?" she repeated, mystified.

"Accidental, apparently. He was allergic to something and had an anaphylactic attack. Why the interest?"

She sat forward. "Helen—"

"Rosie," I corrected. "If we're going to be completely honest I have to fess up. My name is Rosie, Rosie Hart."

She shrugged, then her gaze suddenly sharpened. "Rosie Hart? As in *From the Hart*?" When I nodded, she raised her eyebrows and grinned. "Oh man—did I have some fun with your cakes! They're good, by the way—very good."

I started to thank her, but she was moving on; back to business, and her tone this time was steeped in regret. "The thing is, Rosie, he came here to this place. Your mystery guy. I caught him sniffing around—just like you were. I knew right away he was a fellow journalist, so I invited him in. He was on a completely different story, and he chatted for a while. He even shared my lunch."

"What?" I couldn't believe my ears. "The mystery man was here at Clausen's? He was investigating Clausen?"

"No," she said shaking her head. "Not Clausen. This guy

was asking questions about some woman. I can't remember her name. She was wanted in Nevada on a string of serious crimes, and he'd been following the story for a couple of years."

"Well, we're definitely talking about the same guy. The mystery guy was from Nevada…"

"And?"

I didn't respond right away. So many fractured thoughts shuffled around in my head, and I let them roam, hoping they could find their place in the puzzle. "Nevada," I repeated slowly. "That's kind of a common theme lately."

"Fred Clausen had a map of Nevada on his wall."

"I know." I'd been thinking that exact same thing. "CeeCee, do you think it's odd that a man from Nevada, who turns up dead, is asking questions at the residence of another man from Nevada, who also turns up dead, yet they're supposedly not connected?"

Both brows lifted. "Well, when you put it like that…"

I was still rocking over this revelation. "And no one from the police came asking any questions here, right?"

"I have no idea what happened up at the house or in the office, but certainly no one asked us down here what we saw. To keep up the illusion of hardship, we don't have television here and they don't deliver the newspaper to us," she explained. "Strictly speaking we're supposed to hand over our phones, but…" Her mouth pulled into an expression that suggested this was another rule that might not always be followed.

"So, what did he tell you about his story?"

"Could we get some Cokes first? All I seem to want to do in this place is drink. This is even hotter than Sydney, and that place can get pretty hot in summer."

Nodding we darted out and returned with a selection and some packs of chips from a stash in a nearby bowl. Nonfat variety, of course.

Settled, she said, "So, I don't know a heap. Just the outline. Apparently this woman is operating under a false identity. I got the impression she was flying under the radar, staying low, but that could just be my perception." She raised one eyebrow. "He was pretty sure she was working or living in this general vicinity. She's got money—stolen money. So he thought he'd better check out this place in case she was hiding here. But..." She slowed, grinning absently as her thoughts clarified.

"Go on..."

"Well, after seeing a few of these women—even from afar—he felt this wasn't her kind of place. Maybe"—she tilted her head to indicate the common area—"she was too smart for them? Or maybe she wouldn't have had enough patience with them to stick it out?"

Both Simone Grant and the other well-dressed stranger in town—whom I was more sure every day was the Arcacia Street woman—sprang to mind. From the little I'd seen I had an idea that both might fit that description. "He didn't elaborate on her identity?"

"Mostly he was saying that she was bad news. She's already done time for a couple crimes, but currently she's wanted on charges of kidnapping, armed robbery, and assault. And two murder charges. Two victims died," CeeCee explained. "The guard died of wounds after the event. But the kidnap victim was found dead—execution style."

"Oh my…" My words stalled; for that moment I couldn't bring them forward. "We had an evil person like that right here in Airlie Falls? Right under our noses? Who gets to hide that kind of personality without us having a clue?"

CeeCee had no answer to that either. Who would?

Again the Arcacia Street woman came to mind. An almost perfect fit. Perhaps she was blackmailing the Lipskies or paying them hush money. They certainly needed the money, and it could explain the argument I'd heard about. If anyone was flying under the radar, it was this woman. But again, wouldn't it be easier to get *lost* in a big impersonal city? A tiny town like Airlie Falls was hardly a place to live a life unnoticed.

Somehow all this had to be connected to Clausen's death—but how? I was suddenly missing my people very much. Jonah's quiet wisdom and support; Midge's quick pickup of obscure facts; Fiona, Clay, and Hank for their generosity in listening and letting me ramble my way through ideas… Even Frank, whose belief in absolute proof made me work that much harder to prove my point.

And I was missing my whiteboard.

"This is really important, CeeCee. Too important for me to sit on. We're going to have to talk to the sheriff."

She agreed, and we were just about to hurry over to the office when a new voice reached us, and CeeCee groaned. When I turned to her she was rolling her eyes. "It's Norine— the new one. She's here to do her oohing and aahing."

A grin began, but as I glanced behind CeeCee, that grin froze before it was even half formed. CeeCee had described her well. *So* well, I was amazed it hadn't occurred to me. But there she was, definitely oohing and aahing, and heading toward me with her hand outstretched. "Howdy there, Helen! Welcome to New Beginnings. I'm Norine Westerling."

Except that I knew her as Simone Grant.

Chapter Fifteen

I T WAS AWKWARD. At the very least. Even if there was no recognition on her part, surely she would have wondered why my own hand was shaking as our palms met. Thankfully I'd remembered to put the glasses on, and as she was greeting me I was pushing them farther into place, hoping to shield as much of my face as I could.

It was my voice that alerted CeeCee. For the sake of everyone there I'd assumed my higher-pitched tone and appalling accent, but even to my own ears, this time, it sounded embarrassingly clumsy. And I felt, rather than saw, her interest pique. CeeCee shuffled slightly closer. "Helen has a headache," she said quickly. "I've just found her some painkillers, and we're on our way to sit in the shade outside."

Simone tutted soothingly, but I noted her eyes had narrowed and her gaze on me was fixed and steady. And when CeeCee pressed her hand against my back, I didn't linger. Nor did I look back to see if Simone was watching me, although I knew she was. I could feel her eyes burning into my back.

"Thanks," I managed when we were back in the walled

garden. It was still hot outside but the sun was being hijacked by some low cloud cover, and though it looked cooler than it felt, it was still a relief to be out of there.

"Want to tell me what that was about? You know her?"

I nodded and explained the situation as briefly as I could.

"So, your instincts were correct. She is connected to Clausen. But what's she doing here now?"

"I don't know, but those instincts are screaming at me to get out of here and find the sheriff."

There was no reason for our next move, except for perhaps blind panic or nerves. We both heard a noise, a soft padded noise like someone was creeping along the path. Afterward, I realized it could have been anyone, but the way our heads were working, that noise represented the newly discovered enemy. "Quick!" CeeCee hissed. She pushed me farther, and we slipped through the gate into Clausen's private garden. There we hid behind some vine-draped trees, alternatively watching the gate and the wall of glass doors leading into the house.

I lost track of the time we'd spent, but I was still unable to relax, especially as, though no one appeared, I was sure I could detect the drift of Simone's perfume floating my way. When CeeCee nudged me I thought she was going to suggest we return; instead she was pointing to the interior of the house. Household staff seemed to appear from various directions, stopping for a momentary chat or joke before disappearing down an invisible corridor.

"Five P.M.," she whispered. "Staff break. The others will be in the main office now. The coast is clear—you want to do this? This is our chance, Rosie."

To be honest, I was undecided. It seemed to me that we had a lot of information to take back to the sheriff already, maybe enough for him to come out and investigate some more—maybe enough to take some of the heat off Midge.

But what if it wasn't?

Dragging in a breath to try to ease my shaking limbs and thundering heart, I nodded, and we crept forward. Amazingly, the doors opened without alarms or bells warning of our arrival. For a place with supposedly so much security, I didn't understand this. As though reading my mind CeeCee said, "What I've gathered from talking to the house staff is that they've all slackened off since Clausen died. He was a tyrant, but now there are only a few areas that they're particular about."

Speaking of bells, that rang one with me. "Do you know which areas? Wouldn't it make sense that Julia Clausen is imprisoned in one of those rooms they're still keeping locked up?"

She put a finger to her lips and led the way. There was no need for lighting yet, and I was grateful for the shadows of late afternoon. The stairs were wide, modern slabs of granite that appeared to be unsupported—the kind you could slide through if you were small enough.

Ugly brown leather sandals were part of the outfit provided, and as they clattered on the first step, I pulled mine off, slipping up the remaining stairs in bare feet. Less clumsy than I, CeeCee managed to keep hers on and not make a noise.

At the top I hesitated. Low lights were burning as there was hardly any natural light up here. The gloomy open space separated into several halls. "Clausen's study," CeeCee mouthed and pointed the way. "The other one was his office—this is his private room."

Inside, a strange feeling came over me and I faltered, and not just because it was quite dark. This was the place a man had died. Died a violent death. He wasn't a nice man, but did that make it right? Reading my thoughts, CeeCee pointed to a spot on the carpet where someone—one of these poor household staff, probably—had tried valiantly but failed to eradicate a stain.

A nudge from behind snapped me back to my purpose, and I moved farther in, hoping to see something that would help—and trying not to inhale all that stifling stale cigarette smoke.

Again this room was an homage to the state he loved. Maps, flags, furry animal heads on the wall that snarled back at me. Football memorabilia. Admittedly it was all tastefully done; he'd obviously had professional help to create a space that could have been bullish and crass and yet was reminiscent of a gentleman's club. As I stared I realized the room was a metaphor for the man. Polished on the outside, twisted on the inside. I glanced around once more, and glassy eyes that had seemed to follow me stared salaciously down at me. Yep, the room said it all. Clausen: a real wolf in sheep's clothing.

"You're wasting time!"

Jumping, I started shuffling around the room. The filing cabinets had been emptied, and from CeeCee's expression, emptied since she was last here. That didn't bode well for us to find anything else. And as expected after that, the drawers in the desk and low bureau were free of all except basic office staples.

Focusing on the décor because that was all that was left, I examined the desktop. Two gold balls, each the size of large grapefruit, glimmered in the light filtering in from the hall. It was a funny décor item, and there was something odd about their placement, but then again, I wasn't exactly an interior design expert.

Still, in a low drawer I found something that intrigued me. It was a frame, fashioned out of the same gold. I pulled it out. Turning it one way and another, an idea occurred and on a hunch I placed the frame over the balls. Unless I was wrong, it was a modern, stylized version of a pawnbroker's symbol. That made sense—his grandfather had been a pawnbroker—I remembered reading that in Midge's files.

Of course, a pawnbroker's symbol featured three balls— three connected balls—whereas these were loose. Loose. Stylized. And heavy. And only two… Eerily Frank's words came back to me. *"Banged on the head with something mighty heavy."* I wondered. Something like this? I hefted the globe in my hand, feeling the weight push down on my wrist. The thought of something similar to this smashing into the side of someone's skull sickened me, and just momentarily my vision blurred.

I tried to shake away the fuzziness, but it seemed everything, not just my own befuddlement, was against me. The scant light in the room was fading fast. That cloud cover was gaining control and bringing night shadows in earlier. The afternoon had been heavy and broody; maybe a storm was fixing for a visit.

As though I'd willed it to happen a booming crash shook the house; my yelp of surprise drowned in the echoing reverberations and the tinkle of crystal decanters and glasses lined up on the bureau. There was no recovery time before the room was sheathed in the piercing purity of white lightning. It was gone almost before it arrived. Fast. Furious. And left us in a black so deep I could barely see my hand before my face. It had taken out the power.

That didn't frighten me. But the face I'd seen in that moment of brilliant light did.

It wasn't CeeCee's.

Simone Grant was in the room with me.

And CeeCee wasn't.

My heart jerked and picked up speed. Another thunderous peal echoed around us—this one not so close. The answering lightning was slightly slower to catch up and gave me a moment to move. I crashed my foot against the desk as I went.

Swallowing the pain, I kept my eyes fixed on that one place I'd seen the face. Waiting for the glow that would reveal her again. But when it came, the spot was empty.

Had I imagined it? Should I call to CeeCee? The lump blocking my throat made sound impossible. My thundering heart was a rival for the storm outside, and surely she could hear it? Of course no one could hear it except me, and it was masking all other noises.

I jumped. Had that been something? Someone?

My hands clutched the desk, trying to navigate the room I'd been in for mere moments before being plunged into this black abyss. My foot hit something. A chair? I reached out but immediately pulled back, trying to retrace my steps. Not a chair.

A person.

And she had fast hands.

Her grip was firm and her long, talon-like nails dug into my flesh. "Get out of this place now. I'm giving you one chance. Fiona Fencott has been called. Guess what?" Her voice morphed into singsong mode, but there was nothing sweet in the tone. "Apparently you're a bit unwell and need to be collected and returned home. Immediately. Do you understand me?"

There was nothing to gain by refusing her order. I nodded, wondering if she could sense that in the dark. "My things?"

"Packed. Near the bushes at the entrance to the main gates. I've opened the gates. Take the front exit." In the nearby flash of yet another lightning strike, I saw her free hand directed toward the front of the house.

When she released my arm, I almost fell and had to hold tight to the desk to regain my balance. And start to breathe properly. Anger was beginning to slowly replace fear and I straightened my back, but when the lights in the hall flickered back to life, I still instinctively shielded my face. Perhaps expecting, what? A blow? But she was gone. I was alone. No CeeCee, no Simone...

The light was dim, though good enough to see by. The hall leading back to the main area was long and shadowy and closed doors lined each side. I made a path down the middle, my ears on alert for any sound that might indicate someone was there. Waiting to grab me. Or waiting for me to rescue them.

It was the former, and without warning I was pulled into a door alcove. "Don't scream," a voice whispered. "It's just me, CeeCee. I saw her—what did you call her? Simone? Anyway, I saw her coming and slipped out behind her when she checked a couple of rooms on her way to the office. Sorry, I had no time or way to warn you, but I was listening and watching out for you."

"We have to leave," I whispered back.

She smiled. "No, *you* have to leave. I have a job to do, a story to write—and it's not going to be some fluff piece about a rich lady's playground. A fellow journalist is dead and another, your friend Midge, is up on a phony murder charge. I owe it to them. Besides, it might not hurt my own career," she added on a cheeky grin.

She held out her hand. "Been nice to meet you, Rosie Hart."

I pushed away the hand and hugged her. "Likewise, CeeCee Jerome. Take care."

She nodded. "You'd better go now. She's gone downstairs, but she'll be watching from somewhere to make sure you leave."

THE BUSHES OUT front provided good cover from prying eyes, although not such a comforting place to be in a storm. Thankfully it had moved on somewhat, back toward town and beyond, I suspected—but in such close proximity to the looming trees surrounding the property, I was still a bit nervous. There was no rain, which was both good and bad. Good that I wasn't getting soaked, but even so, that would have been a small price to pay for the desperately needed rain.

A shudder bullied its way through me, shaking away the nerves and bringing everything into focus. What was I doing? Where was my head? A woman had just threatened me with—what? What had she threatened me with? My life? Trouble? Violence? That I had no answer confused me. But the issue remained that I had definitely been threatened, and yet my mind was considering the weather.

That same mind was struggling with all I'd learned in the past several hours. As the darkness took further hold and I tried to put that information into some kind of order, all I got out of it was a headache. I'd hoped ditching the wig might have helped, but this was a different kind of headache. When headlights broke though the gloom and a truck slid to a stop beside me, I dove in, only realizing how much tension I'd been holding when every bone and muscle in my body sighed with relief.

Then immediately tightened up again when strong arms reached out and dragged me up close. Just as his lips were about to reach mine I whispered, "Jonah?"

His answer was a growl. "You better not have been expecting anybody else to do this."

I was smiling into the kiss that held as much frustration as passion. And I knew I'd have a lot of explaining to do. And I got it. Being in a relationship came with certain responsibilities. He didn't own me and I didn't own him. However, I owed him the respect of not deliberately throwing unnecessary worry his way—at least without warning him first.

Being Jonah, he didn't yell or berate or take his frustra-

KAZ DELANEY

tions out on me, he just waited. But *why*s and *if*s could wait. There was too much else to get out of my head. A few fat raindrops fell as we made our way back toward the storm, and I tried to review the facts in as much order and with as much clarity as I could.

"The woman that dead journalist was hunting down has to be that woman from Arcacia Street, Jonah! Everything fits. But who killed Clausen? Her? And if she did, why is she still here?"

The half dozen spots faded away, even though lightning still speared the sky ahead of us. Sharp, jagged bolts of electricity that lit up the night in rapid succession. Someone was getting hit hard, and Jonah's frown spoke as much to the issues at hand as to the possible danger ahead. We were driving into that. "If it is her, darlin', maybe runnin' right now would highlight her guilt. Maybe she's just waiting it out. If Midge gets convicted, then she can move on, and no one is any the wiser."

"Ooooh—that's so cold-blooded."

"And murder isn't?" He turned, taking his eyes off the road for a mere second. "She hardly sounds like a saint, honey. She's not gonna care who takes the rap. But you're gettin' way ahead of yourself. We don't know she's the woman yet."

I wanted to argue my case again, but his phone beeped a particular tone we both knew well. With a resigned glance, he tossed it to me, and I answered, listening intently to the

256

curt voice on the other end. "Fire," I told him unnecessarily after I'd ended the call. "Lightning struck an old barn out at the Dawsons'. We've got to meet them there immediately."

Hauling in a deep breath, Jonah's focus intensified as he continued way out to the other side of town. I'd joined the volunteer fire service months ago—as soon as my name was cleared of murder and it was evident I could stay and live in Airlie Falls. They'd saved my own property once, and I knew how vital the service was to the community. As did everybody. Most people were members, including Clay and Fiona, but it was a fact of life that not every person could attend every time, so as many members as possible were needed. There was no one else close enough to call. We were it.

Everybody carried their own gear; Jonah's and mine were stowed in the back of his truck. No one left home without it.

"They're out there moving livestock to safety. There's no hope for the dry feed Mike Dawson has stored in the barn— which is going to hit him real hard in this drought. That feed's going up like tissue paper, and Dan wants you to come in the main entrance. Apparently he's got people coming in from all sides to try to form a barrier." I looked up the sky. "Come on! Stop showing off and rain!"

Dan Casey was the fire chief—and also our local pharmacist. His wife Vicki ran the general store. She'd be there, too—along with any teenagers old enough to help and people in their seventies and eighties, who were still driving and had been doing this for their neighbors all their lives.

Another bevy of helpers, young moms and those too old or otherwise to be of use at the fire, would be at the church hall now—organizing shelter for the family if it was needed and refreshments to be taken out to the firefighters. No one argued. No one questioned.

Pride surged in my chest. And we had a job to do, so now wasn't the time to continue our conversation, but it would be as soon as this was over. Right now, I knew Jonah, as the deputy fire chief, was going through various scenarios in his head. Preparing himself.

We would have known we were close even if we'd lost our way. Flames shot high in the air, jumping and winding through towering trees. Through the open truck cab window, the crackle of dry leaves and snap of limbs falling competed with the oppressive smoke.

Jonah whistled as he screeched the truck to a halt well out of the way of the fire and raced to the back. I was on his heels. He tossed me a jacket, boots and helmet, grabbing his own simultaneously and then hopping one-legged to get suited up while moving forward and yelling at me to stay to the back and use the tools to stomp out the ground embers.

I wasn't offended. I'd done my training with the others, but I had the least experience and I'd heard all the stories about newbies causing more chaos than the fire by putting themselves in danger when attempting things they didn't have the experience to handle. "Experience comes with time," I was told.

The heat was intense—even toward the back of the main fighter rank. Jonah jogged back to me with a bandana soaked in water that he tied around the lower part of my face. Without a word he returned to the front and repeated the action for himself. In moments I saw him relieve a smaller man of the hose and watched the stream of water soaring high, swaying back and forth trying to cover as much area as possible. And I prayed the well was a healthy one with a good strong feed.

Our one and only water truck rumbled in, and bodies ran to meet it, attaching hoses and running back to the fire front. Lightning still speared all around us, lighting the night and offering fractured images of familiar faces—old and young. And thunder tried hard to outdo the clunk of farm and garden implements as they continued the staccato *thunk* of metal against damp earth and axes felling burning trees.

Smoke burned my face and eyes, and sweat joined soot in running down every bare surface as I chased down those low-shooting flames trying to escape to create more havoc. I whacked and dug and buried alongside the others back with me. My back felt like a flood under the heavy jacket as sweat rolled in rivers, but I dared not remove it. Feeling as I did, I couldn't even imagine how hard and hot it was for those right at the front and in the thick of it. Like Jonah. And Fiona, Vicki, and young Ally. And the older ones like Hank and Clay.

It must have been an hour or more before we felt the

inklings of relief. Fat drops that teased us at first with their paltry offerings—and then the skies opened up and down it came. Heavy, determined—and wet. Thank goodness. Very, very wet.

The cheer that went up brought more tears to my eyes. It was a joyous cry that sounded as one and brought energy back to the group who worked harder and faster, not wasting a drop of that precious gift from above.

I caught the profile of one blackened face in a quick flash of light, and it gave me pause. Miz Lipskie. Recognition is never easy when everyone is wearing similar garb and faces are blackened with soot and grime, yet I somehow knew it was the woman from Arcacia Street, the one with the mysterious cousin I'd had such trouble tracking. Perhaps it was the quick, darted glance she shot back over her shoulder, but instinctively I turned my gaze over the group beside her. And then following that inexplicable instinct, heart racing, I kept turning back toward the cars and trucks haphazardly parked way back from the fire front.

Without the reflection of the flames and heaven's spectacular electric show, it was dark. Very dark. Flashlights were being utilized, throwing scattered light, with the only other help coming from the occasional jag of retreating lightning.

It was in one of those jags that I saw her.

The elusive cousin. I recognized her from that day in the café—the day I'd begun to suspect her identity. Now I was sure.

She stood in the partial shelter of an open car door, enjoying the cool relief the rain was providing—her normally carefully coiffed, dark blonde hair flattened against her head. I stepped forward, faltering when everything went dark again. Moments later when another feeble jag offered a defiant farewell gesture, she was gone. But this time I could see the reflective glisten of her eyes. She was back in the car. And this time she wasn't getting away.

Dropping my garden hoe, I slunk farther into the shadows, darting way back behind the scattered cars, and worked my way back to my mystery woman. The semi-circular route brought me to her from the rear. Even from behind, I could see the tension in her shoulders as she hunched forward, peering—I suspected—into the night. Looking for someone? Or hiding from someone?

The door wasn't locked, and I read the regret in her eyes as soon as she saw me. Despite her grappling to wrench it from my hands and pull it closed again, I held firm. "I know who you are!"

Her grip slackened, and I sensed a strange calm come over her. "You do?" It was asked conversationally, not in surprise, not in accusation.

And that was chilling.

Very chilling.

It rippled down my spine, bringing everything further into focus. Stupidly, I looked toward the figures in the distance, outlined only by random flashlights. All with their backs to me; none facing in this direction. Rain still fell, forming a curtain between me and them, effectively creating a noise barrier. Momentarily, I closed my eyes. I'd cut myself off from everybody else, in the dark—with a possible murderess.

After last time, I'd vowed not to be so foolhardy—and yet there I was doing it all over again.

Opening my eyes I flicked a glance back at the woman before me. Again those eyes glittered in the night like those of a cat. She broke eye contact with me to also flick a glance forward—and then return her gaze to me.

And smile—a white flash in the darkened interior of the car.

Just like she'd read my mind.

My heart rate built to a deafening thud. Flee or fight?

The decision was ultimately made by her. "If you know so much, you know I'm the Lipskies' cousin, visiting from out of town."

Her voice was calm, cultured, educated. Just as I'd expect of an associate of Clausen's. And somehow that made her all the more frightening. Her confidence bore the air of someone who was used to getting what they want, ruthlessness just below the surface. Or maybe not even that deep. Midge was sharp, but in a courtroom this woman would be sharper. And that made me mad.

Rain pattered noisily on the roof of the car, competing with the din of my heartbeat. The storm trapped the smoke, keeping it low, but the acrid taste in my mouth came from my own anger.

"I think you're lying. You've been heard arguing—hardly the behavior of loving family."

Even as the words left my mouth I regretted them. They were weak and pointless. And she proved it by laughing. A cold, cynical laugh. "Oh, dear, you don't know much about families, do you? Arguing with family is almost mandatory. And in case you missed it, this is their car. See? I'm only here because we were out driving together when the fire call came in." I assumed the shadowy movement was a shrug. "I doubt I'd be doing that if they weren't family."

My face flamed in the darkness. "There's more." I sucked in air, heedless of the smoke I took on board. "I know about Nevada…"

The words were a shot in the dark—in more ways than one. Miraculously, they hit their target. It was the silence that alerted me, but still I was unprepared for what happened next. The back door of the car opened abruptly, so abruptly it almost knocked me off balance. And she came charging out. Instinctively I stepped back, but I suddenly realized I wasn't her target.

Ripping open the driver's door, she threw herself inside and gunned the engine. "You know nothing!" she hissed. "Tell my *cousins* I've taken the car."

They were her last words as she scooted the car backward, spinning it on the damp earth before speeding back out onto the road. Helplessly I watched her leave, catching one last glimpse of her face in a distant lightning jab.

And again I was swamped by the sensation that she reminded me of someone.

I wasn't sure how long I stood there; it was long after her retreating taillights had disappeared. With the adrenaline spent, my body suddenly felt heavy, and as I finally made to return to the others, a sense of failure overcame me. I couldn't have handled that any worse.

Over and over the scene replayed in my head, and I longed for quiet time to just sit and work everything out. However, despite the rain, there was still much to do; everybody was busy, and it was at least another hour before Dan and Jonah declared it safe enough to start to pack up. The barn was long gone, along with the feed, but the rest of the property, the livestock, and family home were safe. The rain had eased, but we hoped it hadn't left completely. There were a lot of tanks and reservoirs that needed refilling around here.

I so badly wanted to tell Jonah what had happened, but after all that analyzing there was little to tell. The Lipskie *cousin* had admitted nothing, and while her actions and demeanor had fueled my belief I was on the right track, they weren't proof of anything. And the sense of failure plaguing me was joined by frustration almost strong enough to wipe it out completely.

A figure appeared beside me in the dark. Fiona. Her arms

pulled me into a quick tight hug. "Oh, darlin'! I'm so glad you're safe! I've been worried sick all day. Just knowing I shouldn't have let you go to that place! And when that woman called… Whoeee… I thought my heart was gonna burst!"

"That woman was Simone Grant. You knew that, right?" I said, pulling back from the embrace.

Even in the scant light I saw her frown. "Simone? But she said…"

"She's working out there under an assumed name, which is chancy in my opinion, but I guess none of those people out there come into town, so the risk of catching her out is slim." I took a sip of the tea someone had provided, which wasn't as good at cutting through the smoke as beer but was still working fine. "The thing is I don't know why she didn't throw me to the wolves. Why did she cut me loose? She's involved somehow, and I just wish I could tie all these ends together."

She patted my back. "You're doing good, sweetheart. You're a good, loyal friend, but I think this is getting a bit too dangerous now, so maybe we should back off and leave it to Frank and Bobby Don."

It was hard not to argue with her, still I was pretty sure both of those allies were looking in the wrong direction. It was possible Bobby Don wasn't even on the same map page.

Fixated on the damage before her now, Fiona sighed. "It just breaks my heart to see this family suffering." Helmet in her hands, her face streaked with sweat and soot, she closed her eyes and laid a hand on me for support. I turned to help, her but she shook her head. "It's okay, darlin'; I'm just sad. Those funds that were stolen would have gone a long ways to rebuilding the barn and replenishing it with feed." She sighed. "We'll organize a charity drive, but people will be wary. And I can't say I blame them…"

Frank had been walking toward us and had obviously overheard. My heart jumped at the sound of his voice. My latest encounter aside, I had much to share with him. His words, though, pushed all that onto the backburner. It would have been unfair to Fiona to do anything else. "Well now, we might be starting to catch a break on that little issue."

Fiona's face lifted to his, hope etched so clearly it was almost heartbreaking. "The missing funds? How so?"

"Well, I was on my way to tell you when the call for this fire came in. Those federal guys have arrested a guy they've been watching for a while. Seems he boasted on that Twister or Twitter thang that he was the one who'd hacked into a big account that had made the news. Couldn't help himself— had to tell someone. The thing is he thought he'd scrambled his accounts so well that no one would be able to trace him—but he overlooked a little bitty thing somewhere along the line, and they were able to swoop in."

That shocked me, really. "He boasted about Fiona's account? Was that a big enough deal to cheer about like that?"

Frank scratched his forehead leaving two grimy pale tracks above eyes that were drawn, weary and bloodshot. "No, I'm sorry there. Got a bit ahead of myself. You see, the account he hacked was a very big deal—some government body or other. When the boys seized his computers, they found the lunkhead hadn't deleted any of his old emails, and he hadn't covered his tracks on other hacks he'd performed in the past year or so." His yawn punctuated his words, and it took a moment for him to continue. "Long story short, they called me. They're sure their guy hacked your accounts, and they're now just backtracking to see who he was working for. I can't guarantee you'll get the money back, but we should be able to prove Fiona here didn't embezzle that money and wasn't careless with it."

Her squeal was almost as wonderful as the glow in her eyes and the smile that lit the night. Careless of how filthy they all were, she launched herself at her old friend, hugging him and thanking him. Then she turned on me, all the while squealing for Clay—right in my ear. And I didn't care. In the midst of all this horrid stuff, it was so nice to hear something positive.

As Clay came running, I left them to their celebration while I ran to find Jonah. We'd always known his mom was innocent, but it would be such a huge relief for him to hear it officially. Arms around each other, we trudged back, and of course, by now a crowd of well-wishers had gathered and there was much shouting and laughing. Jonah pushed through to hug both his folks, and a warm syrupy feeling rolled through me when Clay reached out to drag me into their family hug.

When we broke away again, I searched for Frank, but I couldn't find him. I'd heard him mention to Clay that he still had some things to do. All that meant was I'd have to try and catch him somewhere else tonight. Or at the very least, tomorrow. My whole body itched at the thought of waiting, and I tried to clamp down the feeling that we were somehow running out of time. Rationalizing it, I had to admit I was tired and overwrought, that tomorrow would still be okay—all the while praying that tomorrow came quickly.

To ease those nerves, I threw myself into the remaining work. The cleanup—the bit that could be done before morning—took on such a festive air after the fire had been doused by the rain that I wished Midge was here to enjoy it, maybe take some of that hope and hold it close. It was weird that as hot and tired and wet as they all were, when it was all done there was an air of reluctance to leave. It was like one cloud had been lifted and they wanted to enjoy it.

For me, that cloud darkened again when we made our way back to the truck. I was so thrilled and relieved for Fiona and thrilled even more to have one worry off my plate, but now I had to go back to all this sordid other stuff.

I had to drag all this information out of my head and hope I remembered it all.

And that it made sense and helped prove Midge's innocence.

No pressure, really.

Chapter Sixteen

D ESPITE BEING NEAR midnight, everybody headed out to the church hall, the Dawsons included, where welcome refreshments waited. Fruit punch, soda, tea, and even coffee—despite the hour—were laid out either in ice buckets or large commercial thermoses.

Platters of sandwiches, cold chicken, and cookies sat on laden tables alongside steaming casseroles. As people tucked into the food, I realized most of them, like myself, hadn't had time for dinner or had walked out of their homes part way through eating, and as usual the community was working together. We were all damp and smoky and grimy, which helped disguise my *uniform* from Clausen's, but if anyone recognized it, they didn't say.

News had spread fast and Fiona was reinstated as the leading lady of Airlie Falls, but as thrilled as she was, there was a reticence about her. Some of the sparkle had left, and I could only pray time allowed it to return. The residents might not have known it, but Airlie Falls might not continue to thrive without her at the helm.

Clay reflected much the same response, yet still his happiness didn't seem as whole as it had been before all this had happened. Tonight he hadn't left Fiona's side except to fetch something for her. Healing was going to take a little time.

Holding no hope, I searched the faces for my mystery woman, but of course, she wasn't there. It was becoming habit to search for her now. Neither the Lipskies nor their cousin were there. I managed to track down the man who'd given the Lipskies a ride back to town, but he—Evan, from the local garage—simply said they'd been quiet the entire trip and had asked to be taken straight home.

My search for Sheriff Kinnead was just as fruitless. "He and Bobby Don have been called to help out an RV that overturned out at the Gray Hollow intersection, darlin'," Merline told me after showering me with a barrage of questions about what I'd discovered out at Clausen's and how it related to Midge. "The owners were probably gawking at the fire and forgot to watch the road properly. It can get tricky out there, especially if they hit those soft sides. Anyways," she concluded, "I don't think any of us'll be seein' him before tomorrow."

More and more, I was feeling as though I was peddling uphill on a unicycle. Frustration at hitting brick walls was fighting with exhaustion, especially as it turned out we were the last to leave. Dan and Jonah had stayed on to ensure the hall was locked up, chatting for a while about the fire and what they'd have to do the next day. This day actually. The other today was now yesterday.

In the truck, we were both quiet at first. The past twenty-four hours had given each of us a lot to absorb—together and individually. My ordeals, the fire, his mother's news—and all the stuff I'd tried to share with him earlier. A lot had happened...

And a lot more had to happen to clear up this mess.

I was having trouble keeping my eyes open despite all the things going on in my head. The rain had begun again, falling steadily, drumming against the roof of the truck. It had been falling on and off, enough to make the dirt backroads slippery and the sides soft.

It was hypnotic, not that I needed much prompting to close my eyes. I yawned. Bed was calling. For a few hours at least, then I'd get up and attack this problem armed with all my new information and a fresh, clear mind.

"Go with it, darlin'," Jonah whispered across the darkened cab. "I can carry you up if you're still asleep."

I leaned across sleepily to squeeze his arm at the very same time he leaned forward, his face close up against the rain-smeared windshield. "What...?"

His tone roused me, and I sat up, peering out and trying to see what he could see. With no street lighting or moon, the night was black save for the twin strips of light that allowed vision for just a few feet ahead. The rain was heavier now and the images were watery and blurred. Shrubs and trees lined the edge of the road, and I thought I could make out a larger shape. I squinted, my eyes tired and sore... "Is that something moving out there?"

"I think it's a flashlight… I'll stop back here and go and have a look. You stay in the truck."

I didn't argue. It was pretty wet out there. He'd left the headlights on, and I watched him make his way up to what was another vehicle. I was able to make out another person coming around the truck with the flashlight Jonah thought he'd seen.

In a moment he turned and jogged back to me. Whipping open the driver's door he said. "It's Aileene, the mail lady. She says she knows you. Her tire's blown out, and her truck's gone down the ditch a bit—slid down the soft side. I'm going to have to try and get her out. You want to go on home? I can get her to drop me at your place when I'm done—but it could take a while."

He'd had a much tougher day than I'd had. There was no way I was leaving him here. My answer was to open my door and jump out. "I'm getting my fire jacket. You should, too," I called over the rain.

Coated up he hurried back, and I moved his truck up closer so as to make the most of the light from our headlights. There, I dove out to see how I could help.

"You poor thing," I said, giving her a quick hug.

She had water dripping off her regulation rain jacket and hat, but they'd done a good job of keeping her dry. I hadn't recognized her from afar because the outfit made her look even shorter and more chunky than normal.

She kept expressing her gratitude, but it was getting tougher to hear over the rain that was really getting crazy. I waved her away and went to Jonah who'd tried to get some traction under the blown-out tire. "I need to get it up first," he yelled pointing to the truck. "If I take the wheel off, the whole thing will sink farther. Can you get Aileene to try to drive out while I keep trying to get traction?"

I went back with instructions, and handing me her flashlight, she happily jumped up and gunned the engine. "Take it steady," I warned.

Running back to Jonah, I found him straining. "Have a look in the back of her truck, will you?" His words were little more than grunts. "I've used everything we've got. I need more to build up under this wheel."

The truck wasn't moving, so despite Aileene still gunning the engine, I flung open the back door and rummaged in the van for anything I could find, pushing aside things that were obviously important to the mail service. My hand landed against sturdy material, and I roved the flashlight over the area, confused when a strange memory tickled the edges of my brain.

As intriguing as that was, there was no time to pry the memory free. I had to find something quickly and get back to Jonah. The stuff in the back of the mail van was proving to be frustrating. Not only was there little to choose from, the bags seemed to be rolling away from me, too. It was probably the angle of the leaning truck, but panic was building as minutes slipped by.

"Come on, come on…" I muttered.

It was only when I sensed someone beside me that I realized the motor was running; however, Aileene was no longer revving. Turning, I deliberately kept the flashlight off her face, but only until her hands grabbed my arm. The grip tightened, and in frustration as much as anything else, I lifted the light so I could read her expression. "Aileene, you're hurting me! What is it?"

Her eyes were wide, and fear fizzled through me like a bolt of electricity. But she just stood there, saying nothing.

Now it was my turn to grab *her* arm. "Aileene! What is it? Talk to me!" I'd had to raise my voice above the drum of the rain, but my next words were barely a whisper. "Oh my God… Is it Jonah?"

Her eyes said it all, and I didn't wait for any words. I flew back to where he'd been working to keep the mail van upright, and despite it being mere steps, my mind conjured a dozen horrific possibilities. My heart was in my mouth, which was so dry I choked even on each breath. "Please, please…"

She was behind me. I heard her ragged breathing. "I came round, and there he was! I think he's been hit with something!"

"What?"

He was slumped forward, and I dropped to my knees to lay him back and cradle him. Warm, sticky blood oozed over my hands, disappearing in a pink river where it mingled with the rain. "Oh my God! He's unconscious! What happened?" My fear now was literally like a thousand spears jabbing every part of my body. I couldn't think. My phone…I had to get to my phone. It was back in Jonah's truck—but I couldn't leave him. "Jonah! Jonah, honey? Please answer me…"

Frantic, I turned to Aileene, but she'd stepped back out of sight. Something was wrong. *Something else…* Spinning as best I could, I saw her—the other woman—standing there in the rain, staring down at the scene. And my heart sank.

The woman from Arcacia Street. Aka the Lipskies' cousin. And my mystery woman. The two were one and the same.

My mind was jumping trying to make sense of what I was seeing, and as some puzzle pieces fell into place, rage replaced fear. "Aileene? Have you got your phone?" I said quietly, hoping she heard me over the rain. "We need to call 911." Aileene moved in close to my back. "Ambulance and sheriff. That woman murdered Frederick Clausen."

I sensed Aileene's hesitation. *No, no no!* I screamed in my head. *This is not the time to fall apart on me!*

The woman on the periphery of light moved in closer, and I tensed anew. She'd had one go at the man I loved; she wasn't getting another. I shuffled off my knees into a crouch position ready to launch at her. I kept my eyes glued on her, and in the process, I lost my sense of Aileene's position. I didn't care if she'd crawled to safety leaving Jonah and me here, as long as she made that call.

The heavy boots I'd dragged on were sinking in the mud, and the sodden shift I'd been wearing since my visit to Clausen's place dragged beneath me, so I shuffled again, needing to be able to move quickly when the time came. But I also needed something—anything, and quickly—to press against Jonah's wound. The ankle-length dress was the obvious choice, but I dared not take my eyes off the woman. Instead I pressed my hand there, hoping it was enough.

Closer now, I saw her frown as her eyes brushed over Jonah. "Is he okay?"

"If you're asking if you killed him, the answer is no." I barely recognized my own voice, such was the fury burbling inside me. "And if you're thinking of finishing him off, you're going to have to kill me first—and I'm not going to make that easy."

Her eyes narrowed. "Why would I want to kill you?" She was still using that faux reasonable, calm voice she'd used out at the Dawsons' fire. The same reasonable calm that psychopaths employed to entice their victims and then claim their innocence. It was terrifying, but thankfully, anger was still my driving emotion, and I was determined to keep it that way.

"Why? Because you're a cold-blooded killer. Because all you care about is not being caught." Heart racing, I stared her down. "I told you I know who you are."

One eyebrow came up in disdain. "You know nothing—and you just proved it."

The rain suddenly eased, and I shrugged, careful not to release any pressure from Jonah's wound, wishing I could drag him farther into the safety of the truck. "I may not know your name, but I know the authorities are looking for you! Can you deny that?" I spat.

Her answer came with the merest shrug. "That's probably the only thing you've got right. Not that it's of any consequence."

I couldn't believe her arrogance. That and her calm demeanor were starting to get to me. Where in the heck was Aileene? Had she gotten through to the sheriff? Why wasn't I hearing distant sirens? I glanced down at Jonah, hoping to rekindle my anger; it was all I had on my side—all I had to use to save Jonah and myself.

But all I could make out was his pale face, and now that the rain had eased, I felt perspiration along his upper lip and forehead. How much blood had he lost? And fear crept in to overtake anger. Fear, not for myself but for him…

Sensing movement, I jerked my head up to see her advancing on us. "Don't come near us! I'll…I'll…" Frantic, I felt around the wet ground with my free hand, relief swelling through me when I landed on something long, hard and cold. A tool of some kind. Maybe a tire iron. Lifting it, I swung it in her direction.

But she didn't stop.

She kept coming.

Madly I swung again and kept swinging, hindered by my reluctance to release the pressure on Jonah's head but determined to keep her at bay for as long as I could. Nothing seemed to faze her. The same arrogance evident in her words was there in her actions. Arrogance, determination, and a sense of power.

Her hand slipped into her pocket, and I swung with even more fervor. Wide, wild strokes. If I connected I'd do damage, and I didn't care. Below me, Jonah moaned and began to move, to thrash, regaining consciousness. I had to keep him still, and yet I had to keep this madwoman away.

Aileene! Where was she? "Aileene? Help!" I dared not take my eyes off the advancing woman. "I wouldn't come any farther," I warned her. "The sheriff's on his way. Aileene's called them!"

The woman ignored me. If she got to me what would I do? I'd be easy to overcome because I was only able to defend us with one arm! Could I keep her at bay with just one arm and a tool? There was something in her hand, something small. *What? Where are the police?*

I had to keep trying. "If something happens to us, they'll know it was you!" To my left, I thought I sensed movement. "Aileene? Is that you? Did you get them? Are they still on the line? Tell them their fugitive from Nevada is here. Tell them she's dangerous. And hurry!" To the woman, I said, "They'll check the notes of that dead journalist. Check his computer at his office. It'll all be there."

However determined I was, the woman was more. Her face showed no other emotion.

Aileene suddenly and finally appeared from the shadows. And relief washed through me. Before me, however, the other woman gasped and then faltered, muttering something incoherent. I ignored her and focused on Aileene. "Thank goodness! Where have you been? Did you get them?"

"Yeah," she said. "They're on their way."

For the first time, I saw the woman hesitate and hope flared. Her eyes flicked to the side, and I could tell she wanted to check behind her. Desperately I wanted to jump up and grab her, but there was no way I was leaving Jonah.

Somehow, I knew she was going to run before she made her first move, and I yelled at Aileene to stop her. Surprisingly Aileene was fast, and despite the vast difference in height, she hung on to the other woman, dragging her back to the side of the van.

"Should I tie her up?" Without waiting for me she answered herself, "Yes, I should tie her up." When the woman heard those words, she struggled more, and I was amazed at Aileene's strength. Amazed wasn't the feeling I had moments later when Aileene managed to secure the woman's arms behind her back. Scarily, it was almost like she'd done it before, and while I was glad she was on my team, I also didn't like how rough she was being with the woman.

"All we have to do is secure her, Aileene," I said quietly.

"She's a murderer! You said so! So I'm not taking any chances."

Yes, she was. So…?

Aileene roughhoused her into a sitting position near Jonah's feet. The other woman initially made no eye contact with either of us; once she'd been bested, she'd stared stoically ahead into the night. Now, though, as I stared across at her she turned, deliberately connecting with me. And what I saw there chilled me.

And gave me pause.

Behind me, Aileene was chattering, but my head was a sudden jumble of questions and half-formed answers. So intense were my thoughts that her words were intrusive; I didn't want to hear them—wanted to block them out, but still a few slipped through. Something about people being safe now and pretty white bedrooms.

Aileene disappeared around the back of the van again. And for the first time since she'd stood beside me with that worried look on her face, for the first time since I'd discovered Jonah lying here in the rain—unconscious and injured—I forced my mind stop panicking, to slow—to step back and take it all in from a different angle.

What had happened just immediately prior to Aileene's appearance that prompted my memory to stir, to bring forward something? Something, *what*? Something unpleasant? What had I touched? The canvas mailbags? And then there was more… Something else.

My foot. The café. Why was I thinking of that day?

It all came rushing back like floodwaters bursting through a dam wall. Aileene had been there that day. At the table beside me when Liz had told me about her concerns regarding Midge. It had to have been Aileene because it was a heavy mailbag, just like the one I'd touched earlier. A mailbag that had blocked the chair and inadvertently caused my fall. I remembered, now, touching it as I hit the floor. Seeing it for just a second, and then it was whipped away.

How had I forgotten that? People had come running, Confusion, chaos. Faces, hands, noise. Being carried home. The spectacle we'd made. The day had gotten worse then. First Fiona's new heartbreak and then Midge's arrest. Bigger issues had taken precedence.

My heart was fluttering too fast, and I pulled Jonah closer to me. I hadn't seen her at the café that day. I'd been so engrossed in our conversation, so worried for Midge—and when I stood to leave, Aileene must have already moved away from the table for a moment. To pay her bill? To visit the ladies' room?

In the chaos that followed she'd slipped out, unseen, with her bag. And then later seeing her—that jangle of bracelets and bangles waving at me as she drove past.

Aileene had been there and heard our conversation. Had seen me on the floor. And yet she'd pretended she hadn't...

She'd said she'd *heard* I'd had a fall.

Why lie?

There was only one reason to lie.

And that revelation brought me to the next. The other thing I'd subconsciously noticed in the back of the van.

I shuddered, and it had little to do with the cold water running down under my collar. *Oh my Lord. Aileene is the murderer?* It didn't make sense, and yet it did...

The storm was returning. A rumble of thunder quickly followed by a bright flash, but I was so lost in my thoughts I only registered it on a distant plane. The flashes kept coming, as did answers. In one brilliant burst of light, my head whipped up, and for a second my mysterious friend and I were spotlighted—like we were on a stage. Had she been watching me all this time? Of course she had. Watching, waiting.

"You didn't do it, did you?" I said quietly.

"Took you long enough," she muttered. "I am not who you think I am. I am not a murderess. You are in no danger from me."

"It's her?" I asked, cocking my head toward the back of the van.

She nodded.

"Don't try to tell me you knew it was her all along!" I hissed. Then, in a moment of indecision, I added, "Did you?"

She shook her head, and the weariness I'd seen before momentarily returned. Noises were coming from behind the van. I wasn't sure what Aileene was doing, but hopefully she was out of earshot. "Not at first," she admitted, keeping her voice low. "I knew I hadn't hit your boyfriend, so I figured it was prudent to keep quiet and try to make sense of what was going on. Whether there was a fourth party lurking or one of you was the culprit made no difference. It all amounted to the same thing: One of you was obviously in trouble. But when Aileene appeared, I knew we were all in trouble."

"You know her?"

I heard the frown in her voice. "Not really… We've never met. At first I was totally flummoxed—until I remembered the sister… Maybe I should have clicked earlier, but it's not like there was only one Aileene in the world."

I darted a cautious look back over my shoulder. The latter part of her comment made no sense to me so I pounced on the former. "Sister? Whose sister?"

The pause before her words made me think she, too, was being cautious. "A friend of Fred's. Fred Clausen's. He was very fond of her." She flicked her head in the direction of the van. "That's her twin sister. The real Aileene is dead."

My gasp was involuntary and way too loud—and deserved my new friend's scowl. I held my breath hoping Aileene hadn't been alerted. The clattering continued, and I dared a whisper. "She's taken her dead sister's identity? How can you be sure?"

"It wouldn't have been hard—they're identical twins. Apart from that, the real Aileene contacted Fred just before she died, to say goodbye."

"But why would this woman pretend to be her sister?" As soon as the words hit the air, I held up a silencing hand. I knew why. Aileene was the woman the dead journalist had been chasing down. The one wanted on a slew of charges—including murder.

And even as that answer clarified, other associations fell into place. Clues had been there the entire time—I just hadn't expected to see them. I'd dismissed them, not taken the time to interpret them. "Her tattoos—that star is the same star I saw on the flag of Nevada." I wanted to smack myself. And the dog. Not a beloved pet—or something spiritual as I'd first assumed, but a wolf. "Football…" I whispered again, this time more for myself.

That clue had almost been in neon lights—replicated right there on Clausen's wall. I consoled myself by hoping that if I'd gotten the opportunity earlier to lay out all I'd discovered in the past twenty-four hours, I'd have put things together—certain things would have clicked. Hopefully…

Jonah moaned again, and a new shot of desperation coursed through me. *Oh, honey, what have we walked into?* The more pressing question was: *Would we get the opportunity to walk away?*

Not that we'd had a choice in choosing to stop. Someone had been in need, and so we'd helped. No question. No hesitation. That was the way of the South—and the way of the folk of Airlie Falls.

However, that didn't explain why, way after midnight, a

lone woman, a stranger, had stopped on a dark, rain-soaked, lonely road. For her, stopping was a brave and potentially hazardous decision. Or was I missing something? Had I been too quick to jump to my conclusions? Was I forcing pieces to fit?

I cast the doubt aside. There were too many pieces that fit just right. The last provided by the murderess herself. Her chatter, the words I'd wanted to block out. They'd hung there, waiting for me to register their relevance.

Pretty, white bedrooms.

That was no fluke. Aileene could only talk about me being safe in my pretty white bedroom if she'd been there in the pretty white bedrooms in my house. My head, heart, and gut all told me that had been no random comment. All the bedrooms were decorated very similarly, which at this moment was immaterial. The fact remained she'd been in those bedrooms.

And with just one purpose: to plant evidence to implicate Midge.

The conversation she'd overheard in the café that day had been a gift. A witness who could testify she'd heard Midge's threat, giving her motivation. All Aileene had to do was add a bit of pepper to the pie by providing evidence.

And in that moment, I knew I'd just aligned myself with the mysterious woman I'd been trying to track down since I'd learned of her existence. A woman who'd successfully avoided me; a woman who had an association with another woman who had several false identities. A woman who was very familiar with a murdered man. The name Fred had tripped off her tongue with the ease of close acquaintance.

"You know a lot. You want to tell me who you really are? And please don't tell me you're the Lipskies' cousin."

Thunder rolled overhead. The storm was returning— validated by the lightning flash that again suddenly lit up our little tableau. And I not only saw the small smile playing at her mouth but something else that glittered at her throat as well. One thing of cold, hard beauty highlighted by another. Diamonds spotlighted by lightning. Diamonds forming a simple letter...

"Oh my God. You can't be. I saw your photo! It can't be you!"

My words had been hissed in deference to our situation, but I'd wanted to shout them. To her credit, she maintained complete control; there was no reproach in her answer. No defiance or outrage, just a simple, whispered response. "Oh, but I am indeed *me*." She bobbed her head in lieu of extending a hand. "Julia Savage-Clausen. I paid the Lipskies—very well—to pretend I was a relative. They don't know my real identity, but any arguments you heard of were me trying to persuade them not to take his offer. And I am truly sorry to be formally meeting you under such circumstances."

"You're his wife!"

"Estranged wife. Widow now, I suppose."

"But...but...I've been searching for you! I thought

Clausen had kidnapped you. You're listed as missing!" More thunder and lightning rolled over us, and in the fractured light play I saw something else. "You're also the woman I saw on the night of the meeting! I thought you were begging for my help."

She shrugged. "Well, thank you, I suppose, and yes, people are searching for me. But I needed to stay low. That night of the meeting was when I tried to join the group—it backfired. They caught me, but I escaped. No one out at Fred's compound had ever seen me—except Fred, of course, and he was easy to avoid—so I tried to get in. I'd hoped I could sneak in and—"

"See how he was wasting your money?"

Her answer was underpinned by pain, and I didn't imagine the little catch in her voice. It was the first time I'd seen her not in complete control. "No. I was trying to find my sister-in-law. Fred's younger sister. She's...she's intellectually challenged, and he had her. He knew how much I care for her, and he was using that to ensure I kept paying the bills."

"Blackmailing you?"

I sensed her nod. "I can't say I was sorry to have him turn up dead, and in honesty, I wasn't surprised it was murder. He was a very unscrupulous man."

There was such bleakness in her words, and the slowly building rain added to the poignancy.

That rain started to fall harder, and I shuffled back into the scant shelter from the side of the van, trying to drag

Jonah with me. Julia used her feet to push as I pulled. When I'd gone back as far as I could go, she maneuvered herself sideways, bottom shuffling so she was closer to me. "Look in my pocket. If it's not drenched there's a sizable handkerchief there. I was trying to give it to you before. His wound is serious, and this weather can't be helping him."

I dug it out of her pocket and pressed it against Jonah's head. His eyes flicked open and he groaned again. "Why didn't you run when you had the chance?" I whispered.

"Because by the time the cavalry arrived, she'd be long gone and you'd be dead. This way we at least outnumber her. Two against one."

"Three." The voice was weak, but an angel's choir couldn't have been sweeter. I tried to tell him, but my voice caught, jammed on the lump that had suddenly appeared in my throat. Tears rolled down my face, and I squeezed him tight, unable to control the little sobs that had finally escaped. Raising his hand, he patted my face in acknowledgment. His own face was in deep shadow, but I felt his muscles clench under my arm, bunching as he made an effort to sit up. Soothing him, I pressed him back.

"Easy," I whispered.

The effort obviously took more than he'd expected because after a couple of futile attempts, he fell back against me.

"We need a plan," Julia said close to my ear.

The words reached me as I soothed Jonah, but they

weren't what caused me to pause. It was the silence. The rustling and clinking noises had ceased. When had that happened? Or was the heavier rain muffling the noise? We'd talked for mere minutes, and I forced my mind back, straining both to remember every detail and to listen. When had that noise stopped?

Where was Aileene? Had she heard us talking?

"Ssshhh…" I warned. Using hand signals, I motioned for Julia to turn so I could release her wrists. Why hadn't I done that immediately? Once done, I signaled to her to pretend she was still bound.

Heart racing, I turned to the opposite direction, unable to keep my eyes off the rear side of the van, waiting forAileene's return—wondering what in the heck we were going to do.

Julia was right—we needed a plan. And we didn't have one.

As I watched, my head was spinning in time with my pounding heart. *What am I doing?* Sitting and waiting passively for Aileene to return was crazy. What if she'd overheard us talking? What if she knew we'd guessed her true identity?

I spun back to Julia. "Help me."

To Jonah I said, "Honey?" His eyes fluttered open. "We have to move. All of us, and you have to help. Okay?"

There was a brief nod, and he tried to pull forward. "Wait! Let us get hold of you first. We'll do most of the lifting. You just come with us."

With us each under an arm and Jonah's determination it was easier than I expected.

"Where to?" Julia whispered.

I nodded toward the other end of the van. From the noises I'd heard, Aileene was at the back of the van. We'd head around the front and try to circle back to one of the other vehicles. The lightning had faded, and the world was black away from the vehicles' headlights. That was our one advantage.

Two advantages—the rain was the other.

It was falling harder, torrential rain hammering against the vehicles, pounding into the earth. It was possible she was in the back of her van, sheltering. I hoped so. I prayed so.

We were a good team. Julia's car was the obvious choice: less risk. Instinctively she understood my thoughts, and without words, we steered Jonah in that direction. My legs were shaking, and my hands kept slipping against his slick coat as I held him, but his arm tightened over my shoulder, pulling me in closer, and we pushed on.

Thank the Lord Julia had left the car unlocked, and as quietly as we could we piled Jonah onto the back seat. "What now?" she asked as we huddled together in the front. "She took my keys."

"I left our keys in Jonah's truck, but it's right behind her. She's using the light from his headlights to do whatever she's doing."

PRESERVING THE EVIDENCE

Julia's eyes darted in that direction. "What do you think that is?"

I shrugged. Who knew, but it couldn't be good. "We can't leave so we'll have to try and overpower her. She doesn't know we're a team yet... Doesn't know the bluff is over."

"But she will as soon as she comes out of that van."

"I know, but I can't see how we can take her while she's in there. I doubt a polite request would work. And we don't have any kind of weapon."

"Rifle." The word came from the back. Bless him, he was trying so hard. "Under seat."

I whispered my thanks and tried to pour all my love into those few words.

Amazingly Julia started to giggle, and I caught the shake of her head. "Ya gotta love Texas."

"Yeah, I guess you do," I said on a frown, "but that seat is only about six feet from Aileene. And that's counting the truck's hood. If she's in the back of her van looking out, it's right in her line of vision."

"But she's probably not armed. What could she do?"

"I don't think we can count on that." My mind had gone back to the unusual box the police had discovered behind my dresser. A box to hold the components of a weapon? Could it have been? And if it was in pieces and she was inexperienced... That could account for the clatter and the time. "In fact, I think we have to assume she is. And she's not going to

291

take any chances."

"Then we smoke her out," Julia said. "I'll go back to the side of the van and bang on the panel. When she comes out, you dive into the truck."

"Too dangerous. She'll kill you straight off if she's got a gun. If she thinks I'm still on her side, she could claim it was self-defense and hope to put the blame on you until she can get away." I paused, thinking. "It'll have to be me. I'll cause the diversion, and you get the rifle and come up behind her."

From the back I could hear Jonah trying to get up, his protests weak yet vehement. "Rosie...no..."

Tears pricked my eyes, but I had to ignore him. What I hadn't said was that I was the only one with a smidgeon of a chance. Aileene would definitely kill Jonah—she'd find a way for it to be accidental. After all, he knew she was the one who'd hit him.

So instead, Julia and I went over the timing and details. "Okay, on three, let's go."

She darted one way, me the other. Heart in my mouth, I hunkered down beside the van where we'd been sitting and assumed a position of capture—hands behind my back. And waited. Within moments a rock came sailing over the van. It hadn't been our signal, but I knew what it was—Julia was ready. Closing my eyes, I said a quick prayer and then thumped that van for all I was worth.

It was dark, but true to our plan, Aileene flashed out of the van and spun around toward me. The waning, watery light from the headlights backlit her, and as per my fears, she was pointing a small-barreled rifle at me. Maybe a sawed-off shotgun—I couldn't tell. I had to act fast.

"Thank God! Where have you been! She tricked me! Tied me up. She's taken Jonah hostage, and she's gone!"

Her voice was tight. "Jonah's conscious?"

I had to be careful. "Just barely. She got him to his feet, but he's still not saying anything! Quick, we have to help him!"

For a second she didn't move. Had this worked? Where was Julia? Why wasn't she coming up behind Aileene?

Oh heck no. Had I made yet another mistake? Only the tension curling through me prevented me from losing the contents of my stomach. If Aileene found Jonah...

Then I saw movement behind Aileene.

And finally I heard Juliet's voice. "Hold it right there, Aileene. And put down your weapon."

Aileene spun, and I sprang to my feet and dove on Aileene. "Duck!" I yelled. "She's got a gun!"

I expected Aileene to fall to the ground, but she hung on; she was a couple of inches shorter than me, but the twenty or thirty pounds she outweighed me by held her steady. Her rifle swung wildly, and I clung on to her back, using every bit of my strength to force her down. She got off a shot, and I heard a scream. Fear drove me. I kicked her, clawed her— tried to get my hands up to her throat. Still she swung madly, like a crazed animal trying to shake off a weaker predator. She was strong, way stronger than me, and she used it. Her guttural growls and roars filled the night. With each swing of her body, I lost more grip. My hands were slipping! The rain was on her side!

Then there was more movement. Fractured images, a blackened figure danced in the light. And suddenly we were both going down. Her face first. Me on top of her.

She didn't move, and out of breath, I lay there, too. When I finally lifted my head, Julia was crawling across to me, nursing one arm, and Jonah lay unconscious at my side, the rifle in his outstretched hand. And more tears filled my eyes as I rolled to him, cradling him.

Julia said nothing, just reached into Aileene's side pocket and found her phone. Nodding, I took it and tearfully called 911.

It was the first call they'd received that evening.

Aileene had had no intention of any of us leaving that night. Unless it was in body bags.

When they arrived, I told them I was also pretty sure they'd find the murder weapon that had killed Frederick Clausen in the back of the van in an otherwise empty mailbag. *The missing third gold ball from his office.* I'd known it seemed like there were supposed to be three, and if I'd had a couple more minutes earlier, I'd have known the truth a lot sooner.

One of the bags had rolled away. It, and the canvas bags, had pricked a memory—a thought—but the shock of finding Jonah had chased it away. For a while, anyway.

Chapter Seventeen

JONAH WAS KEPT in the hospital for a couple of days and then released into Fiona's care. She was nervous about stepping on my toes, even though I assured her that being at his folks' house in town was the right decision. "You're closer to the doctor and that's the most important thing—not who he's with. Besides, I'm staying, too!"

She'd been delighted, even when I arrived with not just a bag but Tiny in tow as well.

Now, this morning, walking into the living room with a loaded tray, I smiled at the big dog who'd barely left Jonah's side since he'd arrived home. The perceptiveness of dogs was something I was still learning, and Tiny was the best teacher.

My eyes moved to her master. His head wasn't fully bandaged, although a huge dressing covered a shaved patch of his head. Hair would grow back, but even if it didn't, it was a small price to pay.

The wound was deep, but it was the concussion—the shake to his brain—that the doctors had been so concerned about. He'd been unconscious twice, and even though the second was from exertion, it still counted.

After our ordeal, I was happy for him to rest safely in hospital for a couple of days—and I'd have gratefully climbed in beside him. Fighting bad guys takes its toll.

Up till now, we'd obeyed the doctor's orders that we not press Jonah for answers for a few days, but now seemed like the right time. Sitting here in Clay and Fiona's living room, me holding his hand—with his parents, the sheriff, and Midge—we hoped to clear up any loose ends so everybody could get back to living their lives properly without all this hanging over them.

With permission, Frank had asked Julia Savage-Clausen—her left arm dressed and in a sling after having her bullet wound tended to—and Simone Grant to join us. *Simone* declined to reveal her real name, adding that she was obliged to give it to Sheriff Frank Kinnead and no one else.

Her work as a deep undercover private detective, she explained, was worth more to her than friendships. Suited me just fine. And answered a slew of questions. The only missing factor—who'd employed her—was now fairly obvious.

She and Julia had been working to recover Julia's *kidnapped* sister-in-law. "Fred held guardianship, so I had no right to demand he turn her over to me. He never really cared for her. He was happier to dump her in an institution, even though all she needs is someone with her. There are no outward physical signs of impairment. She's beautiful—and she can do most things for herself." Julia faltered. "And she's the sweetest girl with the best sense of humor. I love her."

Her voice broke on the last words. "In fact," she added on a sigh, "I've come to understand it was probably my care and concern for Candice that blinded me into thinking I loved Fred."

My heart went out to her. "It was her photo I saw on the Net, and I thought it was you."

Julia nodded at me. "She's occasionally been mistakenly identified as me. I'm very particular about avoiding photos. Even private ones."

I didn't say anything, but my mind went back to the kidnap attempt when she was a baby. How awful it must have been for them all to live under that cloud of fear.

As she'd answered me, Julia had been simultaneously patting the hand Fiona placed on her shoulder. "It's a good thing you have her back, then, honey," Fiona said. "Now you get that paperwork fixed up real fast."

"What I want to know is what got you conked on the head, son," Clay asked, adding a slice of raspberry swirl cake to a caramel pastry already on his plate.

Jonah grinned ruefully. "My big mouth and good old southern manners. Basically, I was just making conversation and she panicked. She went to hold something for me, and I saw her tattoo. I mentioned the Wolf Pack and made an innocent comment about Nevada being a common topic of conversation lately, and she obviously freaked."

"'Freaked' is an understatement. She lost it completely!" I turned to Julia. "You saved my life. Just as you turned up, she'd come to lure me around to Jonah. She was either going to knock me out, too, or kill us both right then. When she'd hit Jonah, she panicked and left herself no choice. But then you turned up, and she had to rethink her plans. Why did you even stop? It was dark and wet…"

She sighed. "Believe it or not, I'm not all bad. I'd acted poorly earlier, and I somehow wanted to make amends. I saw you there—I thought I could help, make it up to you for acting so foolishly."

"And you did."

Her voice had a faraway tone. "Maybe I did. Maybe it was to make up for…" She stopped suddenly, confusing us somewhat with the sudden change of direction. "I—ah, I mean I can only assume Fred recognized her—Aileene, that is—and that's why she killed him. He would have been shocked to see her, but I can see why he invited her into his home."

"Do you think he threatened to expose her?"

"Probably, Rosie," she answered. "He was a difficult man and, as I later learned, immoral and unethical. He could have threatened her, especially if he was really mad that she'd taken over her sister's life. You see, Frederick wasn't a man partial to love and affection—that was another thing I learned too late—but for some reason he felt a strong connection to the real Aileene. They'd known each other as kids—and he'd always had a soft, protective spot for her." Still thoughtful, she continued, "If she'd had money, he would have been with her and not me. I only learned of her when she died. I'd never seen him so devastated over anything. She was a good girl, he told me. Unlike..."

"Coralene—her sister," Frank supplied. "Coralene's been in and out of prison since her teens. She's claiming it was Aileene's idea for her to take her place and bury herself—the real Aileene—as Coralene."

"It sounds like what I know of Aileene," Julia continued. "How funny life is. The twins' plan would have worked but for the local postman winning a prize holiday at the same time Frederick Clausen was in town making a name for himself. A chance meeting put all this into play."

"And the journalist?" I asked Frank.

He looked pained. "Unfortunately it *was* my wife's preserves that were responsible for his death. He was severely allergic to the fireweed she'd added. It's not grown around here, but she's cultivated a pot of it to use in some preserves. It was clearly listed right there in the ingredients, though the most likely scenario is that he didn't even know he was allergic. The other possibility put to me was that it was a combination of two random elements that caused the attack. So, maybe not the fireweed on its own but ingested with something else. The full conclusive report probably won't be ready for months." His hand rasped across his face, and his voice hardened, "Still, if those gals out at Clausen's place had acted quicker instead of worrying about themselves, forensics say he could possibly have been saved."

"But how did that young man consume the preserves in the first place?" Midge asked.

I put up my hand. "I can answer that. My new friend CeeCee shared her lunch with him, which included the preserves Clausen's people had picked up at the market. My guess aligns with yours Frank," I said, looking up at him. "I'm sure he didn't know he was allergic because he didn't check the ingredients and took a sandwich with him when he left."

Fiona shook her head. "All these pieces fitting together…"

"Well, while we're on that subject, I might as well add a few more pieces to fill out that picture puzzle. I'd be a fool to think I could keep any police secrets in this town," Frank continued, a note of sarcasm tingeing his words. "Those two girls who worked for Clausen, Jackie and—"

"The glorious Glorious," I inserted.

Frank paused, his narrowed eyes focused solely on me. "Thank you, Miss Rosie. You know, though," he continued in his easy drawl, "a man could start to think you're after his job…"

I was getting used to him by now. In earlier times, I might have been embarrassed. Now I waited. While others began to chuckle, my wait was finally rewarded. The lips quivered. And then came the wink.

As laughter grew around me, the sheriff leading the way, I nodded and joined in. "Well played, Sheriff. Well played."

As the amusement of my so-called friends subsided I added, "So, have I killed the moment, or are you still willing to share?"

He replied by diving straight back in. "Well, those two gals are squealing at the moment. Blaming each other. I have my suspicions, but we're still working out which one calls the shots and which follows. Not that it matters one iota where their guilt is concerned. They're both equal there." He paused to draw breath. "Once we learned from Rosie that the journalist fella had been there at Clausen's place we put the heat on. According to them, it seems he had that attack right on their premises—and when they found him, they panicked. They didn't know who he was or why he was there, so instead of taking any chances, they moved him and disposed of his vehicle." He shook his head. "Didn't want the bad publicity."

Gasps filled the room. How could human beings be so heartless! "I don't really understand, though—wasn't this Clausen's business? Why were they so loyal—especially after he'd been murdered? It doesn't make sense…"

Julia Clausen lifted her head. "Fred made them partners in the business. It was their idea to milk the rich, but they lacked the resources to set it up. On the other hand, Fred needed a legitimate reason to be here and gain the mayoral position so he could sway Council and the community to support his development plans—so they joined forces. With my money, of course," she added bitterly. "When Fred died, they owned the business outright, and they weren't going to let anything ruin that for them."

"I just can't believe they'd be willing to keep a young woman prisoner just to get use of his—sorry, Julia, *your*—money," Midge muttered.

Frank shook his head. "Well it seems you were completely off base with that assumption, Rosie, as were you, Miz Julia."

"I know that now," she agreed.

"What?" My eyes darted around at every face gathered there. "You mean his sister wasn't out at the commune?"

Julia's eyes filled. "When all my inquiries produced nothing, I assumed, like you, Rosie, that Candice was with Fred—however, I should have known better. He'd already placed her in an institution, but under another name so I couldn't find her. In fairness to Jackie and Glorious, I don't think they even knew about Candice."

Apart from some muttered curses rightfully aimed at Frederick Clausen, there was relative silence for a short while as everybody processed.

Fiona was shaking her head. "I'm just still so surprised that this nice girl was a cold-blooded murderer. A woman who would have murdered my own beloved family!" She sighed. "She was so helpful in other ways. She was finding dogs and fixing things for people. You know she even fixed a problem we had with that derned new television we have upstairs. They sell you these new-fangled things, and they forget to tell you that you need to have a degree in electronics to operate them!"

The words hit me like a bomb exploding in my head. "Aileene was good with electronics? And you knew this?"

I darted an incredulous look toward Midge, and Fiona suddenly looked uncertain. "Well, yes, honey. But…"

I swirled on the sheriff. "Did you know that?"

He shook his head, his mouth in a straight hard line.

"But you knew that whoever murdered Clausen had overridden the electronics to get out without setting off the alarms?"

This time he nodded.

I shook my head. "Of all the things that get shared in this town, I can't believe that no one mentioned this one thing. This one thing that would have made a world of difference." Then I stilled as Merline's words filtered back. "Merline told me how helpful Aileene had been—she even mentioned you and Clay, Fiona, but somehow we all missed what it was she'd done to help."

"Are you saying if I'd told you…?" Fiona asked, her voice shaky.

I rushed to reassure her. "You had so much on your mind, and really it was such a trivial thing." I turned back to Frank. "Way back when this all began, do you remember Brenda mentioning something about your television remote being repaired? It was as you were leaving. She said something like, *You'd be surprised to know who'd fixed it.* Did you ever ask her about that?"

Frank's brow creased in concern. "Well, you know—I didn't ever do that. What with the meeting, the missing money, and then Clausen's death and that mysterious body—it went straight outta my head." He groaned. "You're gonna tell me it was Aileene, aren't you?"

I shrugged because it was a guess, but Fiona jumped in with a reply. "It was! After Aileene fixed our television, I told Brenda, and she asked her about your remote!"

A loud, general discussion broke out—everyone adding their opinion. But honestly, except that it was so serious, I wanted to laugh. In a town where everybody knew everything about everyone else—the one piece of information that might have shed a light on this murder investigation had, for some unexplained reason, remained unaired. Private. And for no good reason other than the fact that with so much else going on, it had been overlooked. Incredible.

"What about her fiancé? Did anyone notify him?" Jonah asked when the hullaballoo settled down.

Frank shook his head. "Well now, y'all, I gotta a feelin' that she mighta fabricated that little tale. A lot of what she said didn't make sense, but I'm figurin' that at first, she thought she'd be able to win over Clausen. Could have even been why she went to see him that night. He'd loved her sister—why not love her? I think she'd convinced herself and couldn't let that fantasy go—even after she'd murdered him." He paused. "Miz Julia has identified that ring Aileene was flashing as a gift Clausen had tried to give her—"

"To try to soften me up to get more money out of me," Julia put in, cutting Frank off mid-speech. "Sorry, Sheriff, that was rude of me." When Frank merely shrugged, she sighed. "I'd refused to take the ring, and I assume it must have been in his office. Probably to give to a more grateful recipient."

"And Aileene took it..." I said softly. "That was brazen, flashing it like that, but I guess no one even knew there was a ring missing, let alone recognized it. She certainly fooled us."

Frank's voice hardened somewhat. "She is a very disturbed woman, Rosie. I'm guessing that when Clausen threatened to expose her, she snapped. She'd completely deluded herself into believing she really was Aileene, and when he told her she wasn't and that he wasn't interested in her and then made the mistake of threatening to expose her, her brain imploded." With a sigh, he continued. "She'll be placed somewhere that will get her some help—but we'll be asking for her never to be released, and I think the courts will comply."

It was a lot to absorb... And again the silence that followed indicated I wasn't the only one thinking that.

Finally, Midge, who'd been uncharacteristically quiet, said, "I have a question: So, the box Aileene had planted to supposedly implicate me—it was for the gun—or rifle—she used on y'all? Is that right?"

I nodded. "Yep. Remember, we knew it was for something that held pieces of a whole? Like maybe a fancy fishing rig? The gun—in its box—was the only other thing she'd taken from Clausen's study, and she knew it would have his prints on it—therefore proving you'd been in his study, right?"

"Right…"

"Well, it had held the pieces of a very exclusive weapon that had to be assembled before use. The thing was she'd thrown all the parts of that weapon into a bag so she could use the box to frame you. Remember, she didn't have a lot of time to think anything through; she had to act quickly." Midge nodded her understanding, and I continued, "But when she needed the weapon, she had to try to make sense of those pieces in the dark, and she struggled—which was what took her so much time. Thank goodness," I added quietly.

"I remember him buying that weapon," Julia said. "I hated it. Put it completely out of my mind…" She cleared her throat. "There are other things that I can't put out of my mind, though, and I won't. My former husband has caused unforgivable heartbreak, and these concerns need to be addressed." She took a sip of her cooling coffee. "Of course, by now, we know that, as usual, Fred's intentions were anything but honorable with regard to this town. His bid for mayor was to gain control and feather his own nest. I want it known that no one will lose their home, there'll be no big shopping complex, and restitution will be made for everyone's hardship and suffering."

There were lots of mumbled approvals and words of gratitude.

"Frank," I asked, "what about Fiona's situation? Have you got any proof yet that Fred was behind that, too?"

The old policeman kept his eyes lowered, and his mouth went into that kissy mode I knew so well. The one that was about to deliver unpleasant news—and my heart gave a little kick. No! Surely we had to find a way to absolutely clear Fiona! It was the last thing we had to clarify. All eyes were upon him. "Well…"

"Sheriff Kinnead? Allow me. They deserve honesty." Julia paused and inhaled deeply. "The horrors suffered by Miz Fencott were not the sins of my former husband. They were mine." Shock settled over the group, over the room. It came bundled in a silence so pure and so tangible I could almost touch it. "I did it," she continued brokenly, "because I wanted him discredited in a way that wouldn't directly involve me. I knew he was asking for the market paperwork—but only to make himself look interested and involved. I took it further—I'd hoped it would put him under suspicion, but it backfired." She closed her eyes, but her unease was still evident for all to see. "And I regretted it the moment I saw what pain it had caused. I had—and have—every intention of repairing that damage, but I was selfish."

For the first time, Simone spoke up. "To do so at the time would have put our own task at risk, and we decided finding Julia's sister-in-law and getting her to safety were more important for the moment. Julia has every intention of returning all the money and then some." She turned to Clay. "I'm sure this fair town will be happy to reinstate you as mayor."

Julia hung her head. Clay's mouth was set in a straight line, but Fiona nodded and simply patted Julia's hand. There was a lot still to work through there.

However, it was Clay who broke the ensuing silence. "Rosie, I have nothing stronger to toast you with but my and Fiona's undying gratitude."

"And mine!" Midge chirped.

Clay nodded and continued. "And Midge's as well. Your determination to help your friends and clear them of these horrendous charges is something we'll all be grateful for." He raised an imaginary glass. "To our own Jessica Fletcher—who's a lot younger and a heck of a lot prettier!"

The cheer that followed was heartwarming, but honesty was more important. "Thank you. There's so much I could say about you precious people and this amazing town—and what you've done for both Midge and me. I know you've heard it all before from us. But I must say this: I don't know that I really solved any crime here. It's true I'm determined, but I think all I've done is make the guilty people jumpy enough to reveal themselves." I shrugged. "I just annoy them so much they want to get rid of me to keep me quiet."

Frank shook his head. "I can relate to that," he mumbled.

Everyone laughed, myself included—he'd sounded so forlorn it was impossible not to—and I was rewarded with a good-natured grin in return.

AFTER EVERYBODY ELSE left to allow Jonah some rest, I helped get him settled in his old room.

"You saved my life," he said quietly.

I smiled. "Actually, I think you saved mine. I still can't believe you got yourself out of that car and conked her on the head with that rifle butt!"

"And I can't believe you put yourself in the line of fire! I had to do something to help you."

We sat there then, grinning at each other stupidly.

"I'm just glad it's over," he finally said. "But could I put in a request? If you have plans for any further adventures, could you give me a heads-up so I can get myself ready?"

I laughed. "Well, I do have a plan as a matter of fact. And it involves you and hopefully not any murders—but you never know, right?"

As jokes went, it sank like a lead balloon. Murders and murderers were not on his future agenda, but in fairness they hadn't exactly been on mine, either, so I knew better than to predict the future in that regard. I'd already failed at that once when I said the last one was the last one.

"Don't panic, this is right up your alley." I held up my hands in a sign of surrender. "It's a building proposition only, okay?"

He grinned. "My turf? Okay, I'm listening."

Bubbles of joy I'd only felt in Jonah's presence rippled through me. "The old house. The other one—Alice's house?"

"Hmmmn?"

"I know your mom thinks it could be a B&B, but I'd like to use it in another way. To help others."

Jonah offered no surprise or judgment. As usual he let me say my piece before diving in. "Okay, go on."

"I've been thinking about families who need emergency accommodation. A place where people can come and stay until they're on their feet. There are so many people who need help from time to time. Breathing space. And I've got a whole house with seven empty bedrooms!" Excitement had me falling over my words. "The place, the house, it needs an upgrade. I mean a huge upgrade. But, Jonah! All that space. Room for chickens and maybe a goat, a cow. Maybe ponies—"

Jonah held up a hand, his face wreathed in confusion. "Wait—so, will the goats have their own room or will they share with the chickens? 'Cause I gotta say I'm predicting trouble there. The goats might like to sleep in, and everyone knows chickens are up early. Recipe for disaster."

What? I stared at him, my brain frantically struggling to comprehend his response—and failing spectacularly. Had the extent of his head injury just taken a nosedive? Was that even possible? "Wha—"

His sudden grin pulled me up. There was something about it; it was a look I'd seen before. Usually when I'd said something...

I closed my eyes.

Crazy.

When I'd said something totally, idiotically crazy.

Sighing, I sank back in the easy chair that sat next to the bed, silently replaying our conversation. Or at least my part in it, finally raising my eyes to meet his when I reached the relevant part. "Really, Jonah? Really? You really think I'm that clueless?" I sighed. Long and drama-filled. "Of course I wouldn't pair the goats and chickens! Each animal group will have its own room. Although," I added, pretending to think it through, "for milking purposes maybe the cows and goats could end up being compatible roommates?"

After what we'd been through a few nights back, when I feared I'd lose him, his laughter was even more precious. It filled the room—and my heart. That didn't mean he was completely off the hook, though. I eyed a cushion, but given his condition, I thought better of it. "Wise guy," I said none too politely.

He'd noted my glance and guessed my intention. "Remember I'm a poor defenseless invalid." Unfortunately his continued laughter stripped those words of any validity, and when I rolled my eyes he added, "Hey, I wasn't the one who categorically stated she envisioned all the farm animals having their own rooms in Miss Alice's old house!"

When I stubbornly didn't respond, he reached to take my hand. "No one makes me laugh like you do, Rosie Hart," he said softly.

My heart flip-flopped, and I shuffled a bit closer. "Ditto," I whispered back. "And my idea for the house?"

At first he said nothing, his eyes seeming to drink in every aspect of my face. And I waited. I waited for words. But what came was way more meaningful. Bringing my hand up to his lips, he held it there for so long. Tears filled his eyes. My big, tough, brave—gentle—cowboy.

And finally came the words. "I'm so proud of you, and it's things like this that make me love you so much. I'm in, sweetheart. Let's do it."

A gentle knock brought Fiona back into the room. "You two okay? Need anything?"

Assured we were okay, she lowered herself wearily onto the other chair. "We really are grateful to you, Rosie. I'm not sure what's going to happen in the future, but thanks to you, Clay and I can make our own choices about it now."

I leaned over to squeeze her hand.

"Oh, and by the way," she said, her face suddenly animated and more like the old Fiona, "I was just talking to Julia out front as she was leaving. I was asking about that compound Clausen was using. She's already had a company approach her to buy or lease the mansion and surrounds.

They're an event company—they host and organize seminars and social events. The fact the place has so much space plus accommodation for attendees makes it perfect. And guess what?"

Clueless, we both shook our heads.

"If it goes ahead, the first event they want to run is a murder mystery weekend!"

What! My eyes flicked from Fiona to Jonah. I thought I saw him turn even more pale under his tan.

And I got it.

We'd seen too much of murder up close and personal for a game about murder to hold any interest for us.

No, trying to puzzle out the identity of a murderer in the safety of a game was not appealing. Well, not very much…

Or maybe just a bit, but I certainly couldn't do it.

I thought about my piles of cozy mysteries back at the farm. Thought about all the nights I'd curled up, pitting my wits against the wits of the amateur detective in the story.

No, I could never play that game.

Could I?

My silent response felt like a mental shrug.

Never say never, right?

The End

Don't miss Rosie's next adventure in
Candy-Coated Conspiracy!

Join Tule Publishing's newsletter for more great reads and
weekly deals!

Recipes

Like Rosie, I am a home baker. I love to bake simple foods for my family. Over the years I've collected thousands of recipes, mostly passed down from my mother and grandmothers and aunts—and shared by friends and neighbors. I have lots of scraps of paper and several well-thumbed, handwritten books where I've kept records of the recipes I've been given, tasted, or come across over an adult lifetime. Many have been adjusted over the years to suit new products and family preferences, but certainly while many of these recipes have been tweaked by me or my family members, in no way do I profess them to be unique nor solely my creations. These are simply much-loved, much-shared family favorites. Just as I guess your own recipes to be. They're the best, aren't they? Tried and true!

However, if ever I do share a recipe that can be accredited—I assure you that baker or creator will receive full accreditation.

Port-and-Blackberry Sauce

This recipe is a departure as we usually feature Rosie's baking; however, not only is this recipe delicious but it is also a tribute to Sheriff Frank Kinnead's wife, Miz Brenda, and her preserves.

There are many recipes for this sauce, but most insist in fresh berries. Rosie and I love this one from myrecipes.com. It can be successfully used with frozen berries.

- 1 1/2 cups blackberries
- 1/4 cup finely chopped shallots
- 1 tablespoon chopped fresh thyme
- 1/2 cup port or other sweet red wine
- 3/4 cup unsalted chicken stock
- 1 teaspoon red wine vinegar

INSTRUCTIONS

1. If applicable, sauté meat until cooked to preference. (Chicken, pork e.g.)
2. Add blackberries, shallots, and thyme to pan; sauté in meat juices 2 minutes or until slightly softened. *Butter or substitute can be used to sauté if not using juices.*
3. Add port; cook 1 minute or until syrupy.
4. Add stock and any juices from the berries; cook 5 minutes or until thickened and reduced to about 1/2 cup. Stir in remaining 1/4 teaspoon salt, remaining 1/4 teaspoon pepper, and vinegar.

Delicious served over turkey, duck, chicken, and ham.

Raspberry-Chocolate Meringue Cake

This was the first cake recipe shared by a neighbor when I married over forty years ago! I shared it with Rosie.

Cake

Heat oven 350F (175 C).

Prepare 7 in x 11 in (approx.18 cm x 28 cm) sheet pan.

- 4 oz (113 g) butter
- 3/4 cup granulated sugar
- 2 egg yolks
- 2 tablespoons shredded coconut
- 2 cups self-rising flour
- 3 teaspoons (dessertspoons) cocoa
- 1 cup milk
- pinch salt
- raspberry jam

Method

1. Cream butter and sugar.
2. Add egg yolks and coconut; beat well.
3. Add flour and cocoa, alternating with milk.
4. Pour into prepared pan.
5. Carefully top mixture with raspberry jam.

Coconut Meringue Topping

- 2 egg whites

- 1/2 cup granulated sugar
- 1/2 cup shredded (desiccated) coconut
- pinch salt

Instructions

1. Beat egg whites with salt until stiff and peaks form and hold.
2. Gradually add sugar. Beat well until sugar begins to dissolve.
3. Gently fold in coconut.
4. Spoon over cake mixture.
5. Bake 30-35 minutes.

Orange-Chocolate Ripple Cake

A very old family favorite.

Preheat oven to 325F–350F (depending on oven) 165C–175C.

Prepare, line, and grease, an 8-inch round cake pan.

- 4 oz (113 g) dark or milk chocolate (preferred taste)
- 4 oz (113 g) room-temperature butter or substitute
- 8 oz (226 g) sugar
- 3 eggs
- grated rind of 1 orange
- 1/2 cup orange juice
- 1/4 cup milk
- 2 cups self-rising flour

Instructions

1. Grate chocolate; set aside.
2. Cream butter and sugar till light and fluffy.
3. Add eggs, one at a time.
4. Mix in orange rind and juice.
5. Add sifted flour, alternating with milk.
6. Spread a third of the batter into prepared pan.
7. Sprinkle grated chocolate.
8. Repeat.

9. Add last third of batter (essentially 3 layers cake batter; 2 of chocolate).

10. Bake 1 hour or until cake springs back when lightly pressed in center.

11. Allow cake to cool, frost, as below, and decorate.

Orange Butter Frosting

- 1 tablespoon soft butter
- 1 1/2 cups sifted confectioner's (icing) sugar
- 2–3 tablespoons orange juice

Instructions

1. Beat butter.

2. Add confectioner's sugar (icing sugar).

3. Add orange juice until frosting is a good spreading consistency.

4. Decorate with candied, chocolate-dipped orange rind or grated chocolate.

Miz Brenda's Blackberry Nip

- 2 lbs (1 kg) blackberries
- 8 oz or 1/2 lb (250 g) sugar
- 3 cups quality brandy
- sterilized jars or bottles with good seals

* Note, the brandy is a natural preservative

Instructions

1. Carefully wash blackberries, ensuring you discard any

bruised or damaged fruit.

2. Mash berries, retaining all juice.

3. Fill sterilized jars or bottles to 2/3 mark with washed fruit including any juice.

4. Very gently (low heat) and very quickly, dissolve the sugar in the brandy.

5. Move quickly so as not to flame the brandy.

6. Pour just warm brandy sugar mixture over fruit and fill to top.

7. Seal.

8. Twice daily for following ten days invert the jars or bottles and shake.

9. Store in dark cool place.

10. Six months later, drain the blackberries, being mindful to remember it's the liquid that's being saved, not the fruit. It's easier to forget than you'd think!

11. Discard fruit and enjoy!

Refreshing served over ice and topped with carbonated lemonade, such as Sprite.

If you enjoyed *Preserving the Evidence*,
you'll love the next books in…

The Hart of Texas Murder Mystery series

About the Author

Award winning YA & children's author, **Kaz Delaney**, and her alter ego, have currently sold 73 titles between them over a 26 year career.

Her books have won many awards, among them the prestigious **Aurealis Award** for best paranormal **and ARRA** (Australian Romance Readers Association) **awards.** Her novel '*Dead, Actually'* **(Allen & Unwin)** was nominated for a Davitt Award, (*Best crime novel, Sisters In Crime*) in the YA section. Dividing her time between teaching and writing, Kaz formerly tutored Creative Writing for CSU's Enrichment Program as well as teaching and creating courses for the Australian College of Journalism.

Having always had a love of cozy mysteries, Kaz is having so much fun writing her **Hart of Texas Murder Mystery Series** for **TULE Publishing**, that she worries it's not legal!

With their family grown and gone, Kaz lives with her wonderful husband at beautiful Lake Macquarie, Australia, a place she describes as a strip of land between the ocean and lake. Like Rosie, Kaz loves to bake and grow vegetables and unlike Rosie, manages to make a mess of every crochet task she undertakes.

Thank you for reading

Preserving the Evidence

If you enjoyed this book, you can find more from all our great authors at TulePublishing.com, or from your favorite online retailer.

TULE
PUBLISHING